THE POST-WAR DREAM

ALSO BY MITCH CULLIN

Whompyjawed

Branches

Tideland

The Cosmology of Bing

From the Place in the Valley Deep in the Forest

UnderSurface

A Slight Trick of the Mind

NAN A. TALESE

Doubleday

New York   London   Toronto

Sydney   Auckland

MITCH CULLIN

THE POST-WAR DREAM

A Novel

PUBLISHED BY NAN A. TALESE
AN IMPRINT OF DOUBLEDAY

Copyright © 2008 by Mitch Cullin

Published in the United States by Nan A. Talese, an imprint of The Doubleday Broadway
Publishing Group, a division of Random House, Inc., New York.
www.nanatalese.com

DOUBLEDAY is a registered trademark of Random House, Inc.

Book design by Caroline Cunningham

Library of Congress Cataloging-in-Publication Data
Cullin, Mitch, 1968–
The post-war dream : a novel / Mitch Cullin. — 1st ed.
p. cm.
1. Older men—Fiction. 2. Korean War, 1950–1953—Veterans—Fiction.
3. Psychological fiction. I. Title.
PS3553.U319P67 2008
813'.54—dc22   2007007905

ISBN 978-0-385-51329-6

PRINTED IN THE UNITED STATES OF AMERICA

1 3 5 7 9 10 8 6 4 2

First Edition

For my sister Charise Christian,

who taught me how to write my name and kept me reading

and for Howe Gelb,

surrogate big brother and my troubadour of choice

As when a man dreams, he reflects not that his body sleeps,
Else he would wake; so seem'd he entering his shadow.

—William Blake, *Milton*

ACKNOWLEDGMENTS

Portions of *The Post-War Dream* were first published under various titles in the following literary reviews: *The Texas Review* (Fall/Winter 2001) and *Iron Horse Literary Review* (First Frost 2002).

With gratitude to those who offered support, research, advice, friendship, and inspiration: Coates Bateman, Howard Bloom, James Brady, Jeff Bridges, Joey Burns, Neko Case, the Christian family, John Convertino, my father Charles Cullin, Marianne Dissard, Nicole Dewey, Jane Dibblin, Luke Epplin, Norio Fukada, the entire Gelb clan, Terry and Amy Gilliam, Jemma Gomez, Tony Grisoni, Amon Haruta, Junko Kai, Patti Keating, Erika and Kainoa King, Steve and Jesiah King, M.A.G.O., Gabriella Martinelli, Tsutomu Nakayama, Frances Omori, the Parras, Joe Regal, my mother Charlotte Richardson, Charlotte Roybal, the God Hisao Shinagawa, Rennie and Brett Sparks, Special Agent Peter Steinberg, Nan Talese, Theodore Taylor, Brad Thompson, Carol Todd, Jeremy Thomas, Jonathan M. Weisgall, Sakae Yoshimoto—and, of course, my comrade in every single thing under the sun: the most humble and kind Peter I. Chang.

Lastly, two works of nonfiction proved invaluable to me during the writing of this novel, and I highly recommend both exhaustively researched and informative books: *The Bridge at No Gun Ri*, by Charles J. Hanley, Sang-Hun Choe, and Martha Mendoza (Owl Books); and *Ovarian Cancer: Your Guide to Taking Control*, by Kristine Conner and Lauren Langford (O'Reilly Patient-Centered Guides), a book which provided needed information during my late mother's struggle with ovarian cancer.

I

THE CACTUS GARDEN

1

Throughout the years Hollis has observed them among his dreams, watching from a distance as they foraged under a blackened sky. After a time he understood that they, like him, had sensed the flux of earth, yet were undaunted: having journeyed perhaps twenty miles in almost fifty days, a procession of cows—nomadic Herefords and Jerseys—grazed onward, wobbling over a moonlit prairie, bulky heads lowered; their hooves crunched sandstone and pumice, and their excreta, hardening behind them, marked the slender trail in uneven circles—testaments to how far they had come, symbols of presence, like the burned-out and rusting wheelless cars they encountered within unkempt pastures of bluebonnets and high brittle grass, or the gutted houses abandoned on good soil (porches collapsing, doors gone, the wind sneaking through busted panes into dim interiors), or any number of fading signposts passed along the way, those many things fashioned by man-made design and then left again and again as the herd proceeded, weaving blindly ahead for no other reason than it must.

And there, too, he has infrequently witnessed the approach of other languid creatures: half-naked human figures emerging whenever the recurring cows failed to manifest, hundreds of pale bodies cutting through the

landscape, angling across the same nighttime terrain but traveling in the opposite direction. That serpentine formation of listless souls wound back into
the darkness—the shapes of children, men and women, mothers cradling
infants, the elderly—coming from where the cows had been headed, drawing nearer while never quite reaching him. But it was the gas mask each one
wore which disturbed him the most—such cumbersome equipment obscur-
ing their faces, too large for the heads of small children and practically consuming the entire bodies of the infants, giving the group a uniform,
superficial appearance not unlike that of cattle. Even so, he perceived their
determined movements as a kind of miserable retreat, a retrogression
toward the past and, indeed, toward the living—where, upon arriving at
their destination, he imagined the masks would be cast aside and all of them
would inhale freely once more.

Yet every step of their bare feet was now preceded by labored breath, a
collective exhalation delivered in unison and released as a muted, staccato
gasp through chemical air filters—while their paper-thin skin contracted
around pronounced rib cages, and many of their arms hung like broken
branches at their sides. As the ragged column advanced steadily in the
moonlight, he realized the physical condition of the people had deteriorated
badly since he'd first seen them decades ago. Their clothing was either reduced to shreds or had fallen away, their ankles and feet were covered with
sores, their hair was so long that it ran the length of their backsides, and the
men's thick beards jutted from beneath their masks. In that stream of pale,
dirty bodies only their protruding bones shone clearly as they marched one
after the other.

"Where are you going?" he had once asked them without speaking.
"What is it you're looking for? What do you want?"

Later on, after having grown accustomed to their rare visitations, he offered the men cigarettes, the women Dixie cups filled with apple juice, the
children Halloween candy from an orange plastic pumpkin ("Please, you
must be hungry—here, have something to drink—have some juice—
please, help yourself—please—"), but his gestures went unacknowledged,
his voice remained unheard. They, as usual, strayed well beyond his grasp,
moving resolutely on the trail, somehow receding even while approaching.

However fast he walked, Hollis was never able to catch up with them. For years he tried without any success, his life evolving from youth to retirement while the processions continued to elude him. But as was always the case, those irregular dreams dissolved with his sudden waking, and he opened his eyes in bedrooms steeped by shadows—his body shuddering as if it had retained something unwholesome from the land of his visions and carried it then into the imperturbable, calm world he has made for himself.

2

Now in the waning months of the twentieth century, snow fell last evening without warning, drifting from above as if the heavens had been wrung in the hands of God, spilling down upon an unsuspecting desert, covering all which lay exposed below the dark-gray clouds. Waking well after midnight—an open hardback of Tom Clancy's *Rainbow Six* resting against his chin, a coffee cup half filled with Glenfiddich sitting nearby on the floor—Hollis was comfortable inside his house, stretched across the living-room couch and kept snug by a beige terry-cloth bathrobe. Lifting the novel, he began reading where he had left off, although his attention wasn't really held by the writing; his eyes scanned paragraphs, failing to absorb sentences, until, at last, he set the book aside, turning his gaze elsewhere as the Glenfiddich was absently retrieved, the liquor seeping warmly past his lips.

On the other side of the living room the front curtains were drawn, revealing the picture window and what existed just beyond it: a torrent of snowflakes wavering to the earth, some pattering at the glass like moths before dissolving into clear drops of moisture. Presently, he was standing there in his bathrobe, resting a palm against the window, sensing the cold while buffered by efficient central heating. There, also, he caught a glimpse of himself as an obscure, diaphanous man reflected on the glass; his transposed image was cast amongst the wide residential street—the adjacent and similarly designed homes, the xeriscaped lawns—backlit by a table lamp but also illumed in that frozen vapor which brightened the night, that curious downpouring which smothered the gravel-laden property and changed his Suburban Half-Ton LS from sandalwood metallic to an almost solid white. He realized, then, that the outside cold had somehow managed to bypass the insulated flesh and blood of his left leg—needling into the marrow of his once torn-apart thigh, reviving the ancient injury caused by a North Korean's bullet that had ripped into his leg, striking him while his M1 returned fire; the throbbing, indefinite pain had been felt by him since, but only in the bleakest of winter months, sometimes giving him a slight limp as if to summon his previous incarnation: a young private in the U.S. Army, a rifleman at the outset of a half-forgotten war.

By daybreak, however, the blizzard had reached its end, and soon sunlight vanquished those low-hanging, thick clouds. When a hard blue sky proclaimed the storm's departure, the neighborhood became a glaring sight to behold; the morning's rays were made radiant in the glossy ice patches embracing asphalt and in the immaculate snowfall blanketing yards. Then Hollis was at the window once again, standing there as if he hadn't ever left the living room. The Glenfiddich had been replaced with decaf, the coffee cup steaming while he squinted to perceive the ghostly reflection in front of him; cast discernibly now on the glass of the window, his chest's silver, coarse hairs looked golden, his forehead's rugged creases appeared less defined. He had slept less than four hours, having fallen asleep at about the time he would normally be waking up. Even so, his body felt rested, his thoughts lucid, the previous night's swift accumulation having enlivened him somehow; he was—as his wife, Debra, remained in their bed—fully awake and eager to venture into that bleak, muted scenery. But beforehand, Hollis decided, he would spend a few minutes at the computer—coffee cup on a coaster, an index finger pushing the keyboard buttons—typing a short addendum to the prologue section of his fledgling autobiography, lest he forget later on.

"Whenever something strikes you," Debra had reminded him, "be sure you take note of it. Anything at all. You'll see, little details help create the best picture of someone."

But he worried that the little details of his life weren't at all interesting.

"Nonsense," she'd responded. "Everyone is interesting, and everyone has a story to tell. If you think on it long enough, you'll see how amazing your life has been up to this point. Look, you've gone from Tokyo to Tucson, and a bunch of places in between. Now that's something to write about."

"I'm not sure everyone is interesting, Deb. I mean, what if I discover how incredibly dull I am, or how meaningless?"

"You won't, dear. Trust me."

It had been Debra's idea that he should chronicle his life, an exercise which she believed could preoccupy the downtime of retirement and, she hoped, would foster some much-needed reflection on his part. Toward that end, she purchased a refurbished Mac and checked out several books from the library that she thought might motivate him (Fulton J. Sheen's *Life of Christ*, *Sam Walton: Made in America*, and Chuck Yeager's autobiography). As a young man, Hollis had considered becoming a writer (having immersed himself early on in the writings of Hemingway, Faulkner, and Steinbeck), but following his military duty, he found serious literary fiction less and less appealing for some reason—perhaps because of the subject matter's growing ambiguity and the unheroic nature of the characters, the increasing emphasis on the human condition's darker extremes. These days, however, his tastes were allied with the works of writers like Clive Cussler and John Grisham, heavily plotted but entertaining novels which more often than not didn't get finished before they were due back at the library; so while he appreciated Debra's gesture, the nonfiction books she stacked near the Mac received the slightest of considerations—the chapters flipped through, a paragraph or two perused at random, a bookmark stuck indiscriminately in the pages to give the false impression of a reading well under way.

But when beginning the process of addressing his own history, Hollis found the breadth of his life almost impossible to envision; it was, for him, like those casually regarded library books Debra had left for him—

observed as fragments, equivocal in its significance, lacking a sustained co-
herence. Naturally there was childhood, teenage years, the war, marriage,
work, and now retirement; yet it seemed so fleeting and generally unspe-
cific, as if none of it added up correctly to the number of years he had actually spent alive. An apple born without a core, he concluded. A tree thriving
without roots. And, as such, he didn't know how his story should com-
mence, or what words he should choose in order to accurately describe it.

"You're making this too hard on yourself," Debra had told him one
night, upon learning almost nothing had been written during the two or
three evenings he had spent sequestered in the home office. "Just keep it
simple, and keep it honest." She encouraged him to write for her, to describe the Hollis she didn't truly know, the Hollis who existed before they
met: the small-town boy, the soldier engaged in frontline combat, the local
hero. He should write about the war, write about Korea, write about that period of his life which continued to remain somewhat of a mystery to her—
simply because he never liked discussing what he had once jokingly called
the pre-Debrazoic era, shrugging his military service off as something he'd
rather not revisit in a million years. "Who knows, it might become the first
of your many books to come. Could even end up a major bestseller, you
never know. Now wouldn't that be something?"

When she said this, Hollis recoiled his head and stared at her with dis-
belief.

"Hollywood might want to turn it into a movie," she said, her voice as
sincere as her expression. "Stuff like that happens more than you think."

Hollis seemed unconvinced, but he nodded in agreement nonetheless.
"That's all good and fine," he said, "except I'm way out of my league here,
Deb. I don't know how to get the ball rolling."

She suggested he begin with lists, abbreviated outlines describing people or events which initially popped into his mind, various moments from
the past and the present: "Like case studies, I guess, and you're the scientist.
I don't think it has to be too complicated, though. One or two things, a couple of lines here and there about what someone does, their jobs, hobbies,
things of that nature. Or if they're dead, something essential you remember
about them. That'd at least be a start, right?"

"That's true."

So he had returned to the office, resuming his place in front of the computer, and let his index finger hover a moment over the keyboard before finally tapping the letter *S*, though it would take almost an entire week to fill half a page with the most minuscule of beginnings.

Subject number:	01
Name:	Hollis Adams
Sex:	Male
Race:	Caucasian
Age:	68
Height:	6 feet, 1 inch
Weight:	212 pounds, give or take

Overweight but not fat, muscular where it counts. Long face. Thinning gray hair still manages to cover entire scalp. Wore bifocals for over twenty years until having corrective laser surgery a while back. Scar on left inner thigh, result of wound while serving in Korea with the 2nd Battalion of the 7th Cavalry Regiment. Likes a drink on any occasion, doesn't smoke. Good at a lot of things but not great at anything. No notable talents. Coupled with wife Debra (65) for almost fifty years now. No children. Spent majority of life living and working in Arcadia, California. Born in Minnesota. Currently retired at Nine Springs, Arizona. Former director of production and sales for Dusenbury-Soper Lumber Company. Hobbies include gardening, fishing, flea markets, and golfing. Sometimes sits in on the Friday afternoon painting class at the Funtivities Center. Needs to get in better shape. Played basketball and six-man football in high school. In tenth grade, won a Civics Award. Lifelong Democrat until voting for Ronald Reagan's reelection. Voted against Bill Clinton in favor of George Bush. Voted for Clinton's reelection. Doesn't really follow politics anymore. Tries to enjoy life. Likes that the house continues to feel new. Enjoys working in the garden. Still hasn't gotten used to the Arizona summers yet. Has to watch blood pressure. Has considered medical hair restoration at some point.

And this morning, after having steered clear of his autobiography for nearly a year, he fired up the Mac long enough to revise that opening description of himself, adding a single line at the end: Looks fifteen years younger when seen on the living room window at sunup with fresh snow on the ground.

Hollis now dressed beside the bed he shared with Debra, quietly putting on thermal underwear, woolen socks, jeans, and a green flannel shirt. Wrapped in a comforter that she had gathered around herself, her head partly concealed beneath an orthopedic pillow, Debra was motionless—tufts of short, gray-blond hair sticking out from one end of the pillow, a lax arm jutting beyond the comforter to his barren side of the mattress—and wasn't disturbed when he sat at the bed's edge to slip his leather winter boots on, keeping still below her cave of sponge rubber. Of late he had been getting up several hours before she stirred, and with all their years of living together, she no longer had to be awake for him to hear her. She could speak to him even now, as he dressed himself, without saying a word, without being aware of herself; for they had had such conversations many times in the past.

"Hollis?" she would ask, and he would answer her, half whispering for no reason, while vaguely aware of the pungent, somewhat sickly aroma permeating the bedroom—the smell of morning breath, of hours spent resting behind closed doors and windows.

"What are you doing?"

Her voice would be flat, raspy, sounding as if she inhabited that murky realm which barely separated consciousness and sleep.

"Think I'll take a drive," he said, pulling the right boot on.

She would ask the time.

"It's almost seven," he said, pulling the left boot on.

She would ask if it was still snowing.

"No, it's finished. We've got sun."

"That's good," she would say, apparently relieved; and then she would ask: "Aren't you cold?"

He told her he was fine. "Go back to sleep," he said. "You need the rest."

He reached for the hand of her exposed arm, wriggling the fingers tenderly but so as not to bother her, then he curled her fingers into a half fist and slid the arm back underneath the comforter.

"Maybe for a little longer," she would say, her voice growing fainter. "It feels so warm here—"

He rose unsteadily, plodded across the room, and entered the large walk-in closet, seeking an article of outerwear he'd had no use for since retiring to southern Arizona: his old duvet jacket. Located on a top shelf, discovered inside a plastic storage box which also contained sweaters and a quilt, the jacket was in much better condition than he'd remembered it being (the innumerable camping trips having done little to depress its down lining or tarnish its waterproof urethane-laminate fabric). When he finally exited the closet—appearing as a heavily padded version of his already stocky self, the cobalt-colored jacket fitting tightly and reeking of mothballs—he could have sworn he heard Debra say something below the pillow, perhaps encouraging him to be careful, to be mindful of ice.

"Don't worry," he whispered, zipping up the jacket. "I'll be home in a bit."

At that moment, Hollis remembered when Debra had once injured herself while skiing at Big Bear, spraining an ankle and bruising the left cheek of her buttocks. As she had said herself, gravity was increasingly unkind to her. The hurt ankle had doubled, the skin expanding in hues of purple, red, blue, and black—and for more than a week she couldn't walk without severe pain. During her recuperation, she had lounged about in sweatpants, sometimes hopping from room to room of their old California home with the wounded leg dangling above the carpet (her arms swinging as she went, grinning all the while as if glimpsing herself objectively and enjoying the absurdity of her precarious, bouncing body); yet she never really complained or sought any sympathy. And now Hollis paused to stare at her shrouded form in their bed, feeling pleased that she had stayed by his side for so long. I'm lucky to have gotten this far with you, he thought. Such an even-tempered and reliable woman, accommodating but also her own person. Still, she had had her moments of ennui, although she had not been prone to prolonged depressions, or unrealistic in her expectations of him, or someone who harbored regrets. She was, he knew, exactly the sort of woman he had wanted to marry—a friend as much as a wife, a lover who could regard his mundanity not as a drawback but as a reassuring, steadfast influence.

With both of them bundled in their respective duvets, Hollis turned himself, promptly leaving her, passing through the preset warmth of their home and toward the sobering chill which awaited him. That was how, on this crisp morning, he found himself brushing snow from the Suburban's hood, roof, and windows, using a flattened disposable coffee cup to scrape frost off the windshield while the vehicle idled in the driveway (its internal heat billowing from the exhaust pipe and thawing a portion of concrete, just as visible gusts of breath floated from his mouth); but not before he almost lost his footing twice on the front porch, or tugged with bare hands to free the stuck driver's-side door—the ice cracking loose, reminding him of wood splintering when the door swung open.

Minutes later, the Suburban eased backward onto the street; proceeding with the speed of a geriatric jogger, he steered it down inactive thoroughfares which were, at places, ivory and sleek—Sagebrush Avenue, Yucca Street, Piñon Way—gliding between medians of evenly spaced saguaros (the stately cacti snowcapped and humbled by the storm, soon to be humiliated further by large Santa Claus hats and Christmas lights) and narrow side lanes reserved for golf carts instead of bicycles. Ultimately, he navigated the perimeter of the expansive golf courses which were designed to encompass many of the newer homes—golf courses which, on this day, summoned the frozen lakes of his Minnesota childhood (lean and agile at fourteen, hunting Big Portage Lake's banks, center-fire bolt-action Winchester ready for ruffed grouse or deer). Then how unoccupied Nine Springs felt, how forsaken this isolated desert community looked: not another resident, it seemed, had yet braved the pristine winterland—no early-morning golfers, or power walkers, or pickup trucks delivering the *Arizona Daily Star*. No one else was compelled to navigate the perilous streets, or to risk the dangers of traversing slick sidewalks—no one else, that is, except Hollis and, as he came to realize, one other foolhardy soul.

3

It wasn't difficult for Hollis to relish the lifelessness of Nine Springs, savoring the illusion of having the entire city to himself. Without snow and ice present, he would have gladly increased the Suburban's speed, disregarding stop signs, blaring the horn for the pleasure of it. He would, if the city had actually been his and his alone, have swerved from the street, violating the curb and sidewalk, aiming his wheels directly for the greens. As it was, though, the stop signs were heeded, the brake pedal getting tapped lightly while he rolled the vehicle to a standstill—where, absent of anyone else in front of or behind him, he paused long enough to survey the nearby golf course grounds. Still, if he hadn't noticed a red-clad figure writhing out there on the ninth hole green (a solitary form striving to gain footing in the snow, like an upturned turtle within a scarlet hooded parka, galoshes kicking, arms flailing beneath the blue sky), he could have easily believed himself to be the last person here.

But Hollis wasn't sure if it was, in fact, another person he was seeing, or, as had been the case after coming home from Korea, he was once more being visited by an apparition of himself: that disquieting doppelgänger appearing when least expected, presenting itself in the strangest of places—

seated at a dinner table, stretched out on the gravel shoulder of a desolate county road, crouched silently among the harvested rows of a cotton field—as if to show Hollis what his outcome might have been had he made different choices in his life. Those unusual, fleeting encounters with himself had occurred regularly for quite a while—from late '50 through the winter of '51—yet he had never dared mention them to anyone else, largely because he feared his sanity might get called into question.

At some point following his military discharge, Hollis had begun hearing about the troubles of ex-cavalrymen, various accounts regarding fellow soldiers whose behavior had turned erratic. DECORATED HERO JUMPS IN FRONT OF TRAIN, one newspaper article stated; other articles related stories of veterans who had thrown bedroom furniture from apartment windows, wandered naked around a busy town square while weeping aloud, attacked their own family members for reasons as minor as letting the teapot whistle for too long or forgetting to set out a butter knife when breakfast was served. His own mental state, however, hadn't really concerned him at first. His nerves, he had convinced himself, weren't shot, nor was he wracked by sleeplessness or plagued with flashbacks of the things he had experienced during battle. In truth, he had to drink just to fall asleep—and drink he did, the rounds commencing by the afternoon and continuing well past midnight, where he soon became a familiar face in all but two of the seven beer taverns which catered to his hometown of Critchfield, Minnesota.

For more than a month Hollis had stayed drunk, doing so once he had been officially welcomed back, paraded down Ripley Avenue in a chariot-red convertible led by the town's sole fire engine, smiling at those lining the sidewalks to greet him with enthusiastic waves (people who had given him little attention just months earlier, faces he had seen throughout his childhood but who had never really spoken to him). "Local hero Hollis," he was called for a while, and with such an honorific title attached to his name, the twenty-year-old had an endless quantity of free liquor placed before him. Even a local tavern owner had told him, "Any fella that's done the tough job for this country won't be paying for his drinks here, at least until the war is finished with. It's on us, son. Drink up, you've earned it."

And so Hollis had begun swallowing his fill—starting off the days with four or five Schell beers, concluding the nights with a combination of gin and a pinch of DDT commonly known as a Mickey Slim—until his legs could barely guide him a few blocks to the two-story Craftsman-style house he shared with his mother, Eden, and stepfather, Rich. Sometimes he passed out on the lawn or across the steps of the front porch, only to be helped inside by his increasingly wary mother. But usually he managed on his own, limping past the doorway, dragging himself up the stairs and into the musty-smelling bedroom which had always been his sanctuary; collapsing upon the twin mattress while still dressed (facedown, a shoe touching the floor in order to keep the room from spinning), he fell asleep beside a wall decorated with the triangular banners of his high-school football team, snoring as sunshine brightened the curtains and the smoky aroma of bacon frying wafted upstairs.

This debilitating ritual might have continued much longer had there not been the singular visitation of his immovable counterpart; for one morning after a particularly reckless night of breakneck drinking, Hollis had raised his throbbing head from the pillow and, blinking awake amid the subdued natural light of his room, beheld his duplicate standing at the foot of the bed. With eyes bloodshot and difficult to focus, it took a moment for him to comprehend what he was seeing, and seconds passed in a befuddled silence. Then like someone surfacing from the coldest of waters, his lips parted with an inaudible gasp just as his pupils dilated. He inhaled, breathing a sharp, pervasive scent resembling sulfur. As if the odor acted as a kind of smelling salt, he shuddered and, rising up on his elbows, began to fully grasp the uncanniness of the situation.

"What is this?" Hollis had uttered, except no reply was forthcoming. But hearing his mother talking downstairs—her high-pitched voice resonating while she spoke on the telephone—was enough to convince him that he wasn't dreaming. "This a joke?" he mumbled, addressing his double with trepidation. As his confusion transformed into fear, there was an increasingly quavering aura to the apparition: while seemingly stock-still, it began conveying a sort of elusive but persistent motion, not unlike the spinning blades of a fan. Nevertheless, it had a manufactured, artificial bearing, like a mannequin posed within a window display. The arms hung rigidly at its sides, and, mirroring Hollis in almost every way, it wore the same faded blue jeans, tan leisure shoes with rubber soles, bright blue Windbreaker, white T-shirt; the two exceptions being that, for whatever reasons, no silver-plated wristwatch was worn and its facial hair was thicker than the day's worth of stubble on Hollis's boyish face.

Before the shock had completely sunk in, the doppelgänger went away, vanishing at the moment Hollis blinked his eyes. Still, the unpleasant smell lingered for a while, and sitting breathless on his bed, glancing from one end of the room to the other with his heart racing, he worried that his screws were coming loose. The nonstop carousing, he was sure, had finally taken its toll. Presuming such errant behavior was the main cause for the hallucination, he vowed to himself to cut back on his drinking (no more Mickey Slims, just the occasional beer), to spend more evenings at home (helping clear the dinner table and doing dishes, enjoying programs on the Zenith tube radio upon finishing the nightly chores), and, most important, to seek at least a modicum of guidance from the Lord (Wednesday and Sunday services would be heeded, the Holy Bible would be kept by his bedside but rarely, if ever, studied); and he promptly set about doing these things without any great struggle, easing the mind of his worried mother and pleasing her with how effortlessly he had righted himself.

But what had once been considered an illusory by-product of too much alcohol soon became a recurring enigma, troubling Hollis during his comparatively sober periods. In the months after his return from Korea, not a week passed when he didn't briefly spot his double—facing him at the opposite end of a grocery-store aisle, on a street corner, at the foot of his bed again—always accompanied by that acidic, distinctive odor. Each evanescent meeting brought lessening degrees of surprise, even as Hollis had repeatedly asserted underneath his breath, "Leave me alone. You get the heck out of here."

"I'm sorry, what was that, dear?" Eden sometimes asked him. "What'd you say?"

"Nothing," he replied, glaring toward a doorway, or down the hallway, or across the living room. "Nothing," he said, while also thinking: Go on, you don't scare me anymore.

From December of one year to February of the next, the same apparition plagued him, the same face and stance—although his twin's hair had
grown progressively bushy and wild, its bearded face ruddy and unwashed,
the clothing wrinkled and soiled in places; with Hollis's fastidious attention
to personal hygiene and general tidiness, the similarities were becoming less
obvious. Max was what he finally christened the thing; Max, he called it,
because the name sounded benign to him—because he had stopped recognizing the mirror image of himself whenever encountering it. As the physical condition of Max declined further, so, too, did the regularity of its
unwelcome appearances. By the spring of '51, once he started working on a
farm in West Texas, the visitations were few and far between (about every
other month, observed from greater distances); and later on, during the
decades he had spent living in Southern California, it was recognized only
a handful of times—usually as Hollis drove San Gabriel Valley boulevards,
perceived momentarily along sidewalks as a run-down, hunched form—
leaving him with the distinct impression of having glimpsed a childhood
acquaintance who no longer had any significant role in his life.

Yet Max's proximity returned two years ago, startling Hollis twice
within the week he and Debra had moved into their Nine Springs home
(materializing in the garage, waiting in the kitchen). Thereafter, it limited
itself to the golf course greens, emerging every so often among the group
of men Hollis joined for organized tournaments or informal competitions.
Regarding Max from a short distance, he remained calm, refusing to let
it affect his game, never addressing it outright or feeling haunted anymore
by its grim presence. Whereas before Max had remained unflinching, he
had since noticed some faint movements—possibly a twitch of the hands,
maybe a slight turn of the head. Moreover, his formerly perfect double had
transformed into a mass of wrinkles, a haggard and pitiable creature, like a
wax effigy of an elderly vagrant. Perhaps for that reason, he fostered a certain amount of empathy toward his old likeness; it looked as if it had traveled through hell just to stand near him again. Harboring a begrudging
tenderness for his own body, he felt sad about what had ultimately become
of Max.

. . .

Now parking the Suburban in a golf cart lane, the hazard lights blinking, Hollis went from the vehicle and started trudging forward. Between him and the ninth hole, a large black crow flitted about, shooting its beak into the snow with pistonlike speed, working its way slowly toward the fallen figure, but when Hollis approached—his boots breaching the frigid layer, his tracks fashioning a curving trail—it screamed once at him and promptly took flight; the bird circled high overhead, following as Hollis veered through a sodden sand trap and angled for the ninth hole. The dull ache in his left thigh sharpened, further hindering his progress. Up ahead, the struggling figure had become listless—legs, arms, and body inert—and by the time Hollis reached him, the individual seemed resigned to his plight.

"Hey, you all right? You okay there?"

Leaning over him, rubbing his bare hands together, Hollis recognized familiar green eyes darting inside the red hood, gazing first at the firmament above—scanning the heavens, giving a sidelong look at the sun—before fixing on Hollis while, at the same instant, a sigh of frustration was expressed.

"Goddamnit," his buddy Lon said, both annoyed and heartened that someone had chanced upon his predicament. "Goddamn—" Puffing with exasperation, Lon arched his big head back, closing his eyes for a few seconds. Digging his heels into the snow, he began rocking his massive chest back and forth, evidently trying to gain enough momentum to flip himself. "Son of a bitch—" Lon's chubby, flushed face grimaced. His galoshes pounded the ground, throwing a spattering of slush into the air. "Oh, fuck—"

"Just hold on," Hollis said, the rotund sight of his friend bringing to mind some toppled snowman or, perhaps, a distressed Santa Claus. "Here—"

Poor Lon, Hollis thought. Poor guy: cursing, sighing, bitching, but forcing a grin once Hollis proffered his hands and—fingers clutching Lon's black mitts, legs braced to keep himself from also falling (the ache in his left thigh contracted to a dime-size circle of pain and, all at once, briefly abated)—helped him sit up, then kneel, then stand on the spot where he had apparently slipped backward.

Not yet sure of his balance, Lon remained standing there for a while, his arms hanging straight at his sides. "Thanks," he muttered, without sounding grateful. He glanced at Hollis with a bemused expression—his face was rosy and damp, thin strands of silver hair were plastered on his forehead.

"Could've sworn I was the last man on earth," Hollis said, swatting clumps of snow off Lon's wet backside. "Guess I was wrong."

"Yep," Lon said, "you were wrong." Then brushing the hair away from his forehead with a mitt, he asked, "So how's Debra holding up today?"

"Well, she's never liked snow, but she's doing okay, I guess."

"That's good to hear."

For a while they loitered there, the two of them staring at a ridge of cumulus which canvassed the Catalina Mountains' summit, until Hollis said, "You know, I should've figured you'd wander into this mess."

"Really?"

"Seems like you'd want to see it before it melts away."

But unlike Hollis, Lon hadn't come to observe the transformed golf courses, the greens gone white. No, he insisted, doctor's orders had him walking at dawn, doing his usual route—from hole one to hole eighteen, hole eighteen to hole one, and home by the time his wife, Jane, finished cooking breakfast: "I couldn't care less about the snow. Doesn't mean a thing. It's just snow, you know."

"Mm," Hollis said, cupping his hands at his mouth and exhaling into them.

But Hollis knew the snow meant something more to Lon; he knew as much last evening when Lon had phoned, gleefully saying, "Hey, you and Debra go to your window and look. It's hell freezing over, it's the beginning of the end." And soon Hollis was peering through parted kitchen curtains as he made chocolate pudding for Debra, surprised to discover the backyard had already become an otherworldly place; his cactus garden had grown fluffy, the swimming pool was a snowy lair.

"My goodness," Debra had called from the living room, sounding tired and miserable, "have you seen what's going on outside?"

"Yes," Hollis had replied, transfixed by what was raining into the backyard, altering the view which he had grown accustomed to enjoying. Even at night the cacti were apparent, the beds showcased in the broad beams of two floodlights, and he had always liked that his garden was visible from the kitchen and dining-room windows. For some reason, he found its nearness comforting. Often he would sit at the dining table for prolonged periods, drinking coffee while staring at the various things he had cultivated. Time evaporated during those meditative breaks, as it did last night when he had first glimpsed the snowfall. After a while he glanced at the stove clock, then he pivoted and walked from the kitchen, leaving the pudding to chill in the refrigerator, going to where Debra lingered wearily in front of the television (the *TV Guide* near her face, an index finger scanning a page, her body emitting a faint odor which hinted at sickness). Without acknowledging his presence, she shook her head, frowning: "Can you believe it? A week ago you were wearing shorts." But he had assumed a smiling, sympathetic face, taking her into his arms from behind and holding her gently—the way one might handle something delicate and rare.

Later, while they watched a rerun of *Law & Order*, Debra had shivered and said, "Lord, I've always hated this kind of weather." She was snuggled against him on the couch, draped in the same comforter she would eventually carry to their bed. "Pudding on a night like this," she complained. "Doesn't seem quite right."

Not right, Hollis had thought, when sun-washed vistas and mesas were promised in the sales brochure (astonishing views, sparkling air: *The morning's dawn another perfect day*), when the panoramic splendor of the Catalina Mountains loomed beautifully beyond the aquamarine waters of outdoor hot tubs. Then this morning—standing beside Lon on the buried golf course, gazing at the white expanse ahead of him—he truly felt displaced from where he actually stood, somehow removed from this region of cacti, diamondback rattlesnakes, and desert.

An insubstantial breeze roamed around, whisking up crystalline particles and spiraling them into sunlight as a shimmering, refracted mist. Yet it was a dry onshore wind Hollis was suddenly sensing, blowing cold from Siberia and southward along the Sea of Japan. Hidden beneath the layer of snow, he imagined, were the artifacts of warfare, a scattering of personal and military-designated debris. Like memories best forgotten, he thought. Like blank spaces in an old photo album where once images had existed. But how many discarded objects had been left behind as the troops concluded their tours of duty? What else had remained in that country where a heavy snowfall persisted, covering the hills and the mountains, sedating the hard fighting until, eventually, the storm had ceased?

4

Last week, while sitting at the kitchen table, Debra had said to Hollis, "Will you, please, tell me about us." She had, under completely different circumstances, said something similar many months before as they strolled around the block one evening after dinner. By then he had stopped writing every night, had been unwilling to face those earlier years, specifically those few weeks he had spent fighting in Korea. There was a lot he just wasn't comfortable recalling, he had told her, and although he was doing his best to do so, it would probably take some time.

"Then skip the war for now," she had suggested. "Why don't you write about us instead?"

"What do you mean?"

"Well, everyone likes a love story, right?"

"I guess."

"So write a love story, how we met and fell for each other, all that stuff."

"Who'd want to read that?"

"Christ, Hollis, I would."

"I don't know, Deb. You know, I'm sure I could write a little bit about my time in Japan."

"Okay, do that—and then you should write a Hollis and Debra epic. Tell me some things I might not know about us, and you, and how you view our life—because I'd really like to hear your take on our story. It'd likely do us some good, anyway."

"Maybe, we'll see."

But, to date, the book project had ground to a halt. With just over six pages completed, none of the self-assessment or introspection Debra had wanted was offered; nor was there an inkling of a wartime saga or a love story in progress—nothing at all which came remotely close to shedding any new light on their relationship, or his military service. He had, at least, begun an opening chapter for his autobiography—a chapter entitled "Where I Went & How I Got There"—in which he managed to write the following:

Japan.

You probably will figure out I'm writing all of this as things come to me and because sometimes I think of certain memories when I am in the middle of writing on something else. It has been three weeks since I wrote anything here, but today Japan popped into my head and what I mean by "Japan" is not the Japan of now. I don't know too much about what the country is like these days. No, it is the Japan of nearly fifty years ago, the Japan I knew for a small time as a soldier before getting myself shipped over to Korea. It was the U.S.-occupied Japan I experienced. Anyway, I can tell you I never intended to write a word on my military service, because it was a whole other life for me and doesn't seem worth the trouble of dwelling on. But a while back my wife said I had traveled from Tokyo to Tucson, and she said I was fortunate to have seen quite a few other places in between those two T's. Her saying that got me thinking of Japan again and I had the urge to set my thoughts down for her to read someday and so I will try to remember my days in Tokyo, 1950. Funny, it sure doesn't feel like I was ever really there, but I really was. At the time I was a kid of twenty, and in a flash I had gone from a hick American town to the streets of the largest city in Asia if not the world. I can't say there is a bunch to tell about the place. It's not like anything extraordinary happened while I was there on account of us not being at war yet. But I will write down what I can remember because it involved my early life and my wife wants to know.

While Hollis went on to describe post-war Tokyo in some basic detail—the poverty of a defeated and compliant people, a city in the bustling throes of reconstruction, the pleasure districts frequented by American troops at night, the little walkways lined by the large glowing red lanterns and the cloth banners of bars and eating houses—it wasn't the busy streets of Japan his memory readily gravitated toward. Instead, his thoughts always jumped ahead to places and people he couldn't yet invoke with written words; and when he found himself reliving that part of his past—when he reluctantly turned his mind to that brief but jarring period of his youth—it was never the battle-scarred terrain of Korea he first envisioned. Rather, he recalled the coast of Japan's southern tip and the Osumi Strait, where a convoy of four transport ships pitched upon breaking waves, forging through heavy gray sheets of rain and white, frothy spray (the iron hulls rocking, the bows crashing into the ocean before rising upward once more as navy flags continued slapping against the wind). Somewhere ahead loomed the lighthouse on Cape Sata, and beyond that—dotted here and there with tiny islands, the choppy waters swelling even higher—was the East China Sea.

Then it was the stench of vomit Hollis remembered, a disgorging fume hanging below deck, mingling with the body odors and cigarette smoke of the troops; the fresh-faced men were all crammed together within the dank, submerged quarters—breathing the stagnant air, uniforms wrinkled and stained by sweat—everyone swaying to the gyrations of the ship, some resting on cots, many sitting against partitions, while others waited in line for the head so they could retch out whatever else was left inside their churning stomachs. Soon the convoy would change course, angling northward, heading for the southern coast of Korea; but until their destination was reached, the troops were kept sequestered in their turbulent limbo, passing the hours with conversation or card games, or attempting to write letters home, or reading again those letters from loved ones which had been brought on board like precious cargo.

But Hollis had no letters to safeguard, nor had he written anyone or received a single missive since leaving Critchfield. There wasn't a hand-wringing girlfriend awaiting his return, not even a childhood friend anxious for news about him. The closest person in his life at that point had been his mother, and he hadn't yet felt the desire to inform her of his enlistment (she had last seen him walking from the house on an overcast morning, holding a suitcase, telling her only that he would be in touch once he settled elsewhere and found steady employment). Although he didn't comprehend it fully, he was—as the communal rabble loitered nearby, few giving him much attention while he remained on his fold-down cot and apart from the casual gatherings of his fellow cavalrymen—a silent, inexpressive individual, alone on the journey and without another soul for an intimate.

To kill time, Hollis filled several pages of a small notepad, fashioning detailed drawings which summoned less confining environs. A decrepit two-story farmhouse overlooking a lush valley. Two deer pausing at the edge of a creek—a doe with its snout reaching toward the water, an alert buck with its neck and head poised upright. A bowling ball floating through the atmosphere of interstellar space, drifting between twinkling stars and the bright glow of a distant sun. Finally, he sketched himself far beyond the ship's stifling quarters, placing his uniformed likeness on the moon's imaginary surface—where his ungracefully lean, tall body, his dark stubble of a crew cut, his long, gawky face took shape among craggy lunar boulders (the wide peeking eyes, dagger-sharp antennae, and skeletal fingers of tiny alien creatures made half visible behind each large rock); he gazed nervously from the page, his M1 clutched and ready, his mouth as round as the letter O, with a caption scribbled above him which asked: HOW ON EARTH DID I END UP HERE?

Yet even his drawings couldn't completely vanquish the caged-in, bustling reality of his surroundings, and periodically Hollis would set his pen and notepad aside, shutting his eyes so that sleep might guide him ashore. During those restful periods, his thoughts sometimes puzzled over the Korean peninsula, that Japanese stronghold before World War II now divided bitterly into northern and southern regions, whose separate governments were at odds with each other (Moscow having armed the north, Washington having done the same for the south): the communist North Korean army had at last pressed forward in a violent bid to unify the country; this was obviously a troubling turn of events for Douglas MacArthur's supreme commandership, causing the great general to deem the situation as being critical, an emergency which required the use of peacetime soldiers stationed in occupied Japan, as well as the need to extend all enlistment for twelve months, and, then, to herd hundreds of men aboard transports, and—with the sea lanes assaulted by thirty-foot waves, the typhoon weather nearly doubling the length of what was usually a three-day voyage—to send the troops sailing from Yokohama on a direct course toward frontline skirmishes.

More often than not, Hollis disregarded his uncertain thoughts of international police action and likely combat, eavesdropping instead on those close at hand, listening with eyes shut to a cacophony of voices—the bad jokes, the raucous laughter, the crass innuendoes—like a discordant choir accompanying the ship's creaking, metallic gyrations. The majority of them were younger men, most no older than eighteen or nineteen, while some had just barely reached seventeen, joining up after their parents had consented by signing the recruitment forms. Hollis, however, was already twenty, and although the age difference was minor, he felt displaced and out of rhythm with the quick, adolescent banter of his peers; they appeared, to him, like unruly kids left to fend for themselves, or perhaps wild things banded together by necessity and somehow holding one another in check.

"Look at that peckerwood, just look at him go."

"Goddamn, man, that ain't right."

"I fold, damn."

"Yep, I hear you. I fold."

"Hey, which one of your rotten crotches didn't ante?"

"Don't look at me."

"This is bullshit. Who didn't ante?"

One blustering voice was interchangeable with another—all their voices cut from the same cloth yet remaining singular—like the uniforms they wore, like the equipment they toted, like the similar rankings they were assigned and the robotic drills which were now performed as second nature; with rarely an exception, every soul huddled in the foul belly of the ship, including Hollis, was a trained rifleman for the army personnel parlance, each classified to an identical set of numbers. Except the faces and bodies were different, some more so than others, and among them was a particular oddity: a Chinese American private from Seattle named Schubert Tang—two of the darkest eyes Hollis had ever seen, coarse black hair cropped short, shiest kid in the battalion but a skillful poker player, wire thin and delicate, with almost a girlish appearance—whose three older brothers had served before him in the Second World War.

So while the men horsed around, or suffered from seasickness, or bantered with the tacky obscenities of soldiers, only a couple of them stood out perfectly in Hollis's memory—one of whom was Schubert, a Browning Automatic Rifleman, that solitary Asian in a den of mostly white faces. At the outset of the crossing, it became apparent that Schubert was very intelligent and very friendly, if not also rather quiet, and who, in spite of being Chinese, would have made excellent officer material in the future. But he looked like the youngest of them all, much closer to fourteen than his actual eighteen years—with smooth, unblemished skin which, to the amazement of some, had never felt the touch of a shaving razor. Moreover, it was Schubert who understood where they were going, who knew a lot about that place called Korea, who had even been able to locate it on a map well before the rumblings of civil war had begun. In the middle of playing cards, questions were thrown at him concerning the country, especially since many, including Hollis, had assumed the differences between the Chinese and the Koreans were negligible; and as he spoke, answering and then elaborating on what had been asked, the game would be put on hold for a spell—everyone listening to him, sometimes straining to hear him because his voice was so soft, then ribbing him afterward that only a North Korean spy could possess such information.

But with every question asked, Schubert would become unusually talkative, offering long explanations which were given in painstaking detail. He told them it was okay to think of Korea as a bridge for China and Japan, but that the country also had its own rich history which stretched back five thousand years. The nation, he said, was born after a god named Hwanung, who descended from Heaven and turned a bear into a beautiful woman; the woman eventually gave birth to Hwanung's son, and it was that son who, as an adult, ended up building the capital of Korea. Subsequently, as the hours passed with the chaotic, metronome-like sway of the ship, more would be gleaned from Schubert. He told of the Korean king who, in 1420, created a phonetic language for his people, using eleven vowels and seventeen consonants, forming the written language of Hangul. The same king invented the sundial and water clocks. Yet while he painted an alluring picture of that strange, unknown land, Schubert didn't avoid those recent junctures in history which, as a result, had set them sailing across the Sea of Japan: the annexation of Korea by the Japanese in 1910, the nation then humbled into a mere colony, a territory which remained under Japanese control until the Pacific War ended some thirty-five years later. And though he could go on endlessly and in great detail about where they were headed, the men did nothing to interrupt him, preferring instead to listen carefully to the shy Chinese kid from Seattle, perhaps regarding him as one who, by the sheer virtue of his otherness, might somehow hold the key to their survival.

There was, however, a soldier from Texas who truly stood above the rest—at least it seemed as such to Hollis—and whose gregarious presence was difficult to resist or shun. His name was Bill McCreedy, although he often referred to himself in the third person, saying things like "Boy, Creed sure wishes he could hunker down on a hamburger," and "Scoot on over, give ol' Creed a place to sit."

From his cot, Hollis spied McCreedy making the rounds, pausing to borrow a cigarette off someone, striking up conversations with those who crossed his path, or leaning for a while against a bulkhead and, exhaling smoke through his nostrils, coolly surveying the groupings of fellow privates as if they were under his stern command. But he was well regarded by pretty much everyone; in fact, McCreedy had an affable yet dominating nature which attracted others to him, and whomever he spoke with was given

the distinct impression they were, at that moment, his closest buddy. Moreover, he knew how to take the lead in any situation—playing poker, shooting the breeze, undertaking various work details—assuming the role of
team captain without really trying, smiling as he barked out instructions or
orders which were never questioned. His very aura suggested not only
power and cunning but, like those who seemed destined for grander heights,
an innate ability to get things accomplished his way, doing so with an effortless grin and a benign pat on the back.

Which was why Hollis steered clear of McCreedy, avoiding his over-
bearing proximity ever since they had all gathered on a Yokohama pier,
refusing to meet his dark blue eyes once they were finally secured below
deck. The two had brushed shoulders twice, and both times Hollis had kept
his stare either aimed forward or at the floor, simply nodding after Mc-
Creedy said, "Pardon me, friend." And while he recognized the inexplicable allure of McCreedy's personality, Hollis was also mystified by the
admiration it evoked; for he, too, was drawn to this slightly younger man,
casting discreet glances whenever that Texan drawl reverberated, watching
at a distance and hoping to remain inconspicuous. He couldn't deny or begin to understand the attraction for such a swaggering, cocksure private—
someone who, had the circumstances been otherwise, might have gone
unnoticed had Hollis passed him on the street. But he refused to believe it
was McCreedy's good looks which made him so appealing—the broad
shoulders, the above-average height, the golden-blond Mohawk haircut, the
muscular forearms. No, he eventually concluded, it was something else—
something primal and unique, something, possibly, which he had always
lacked.

Yet try as he might, Hollis could not escape McCreedy's unwanted attention, that vexatious need to make contact with everyone around him.
And so when half awake upon his cot—two days after the wavering voyage
began, resting despite the ship's continual turbulence—Hollis stirred to the
sound of a throat clearing above him, and before lifting his eyelids, he heard
that familiar lengthened tone asking, "Well—how on earth *did* you end up
here?" His vision was fuzzy at the second his eyes shot open, but soon he
distinguished the imposing figure looming over him, noticing first a thin

wisp of grayish smoke floating between him and McCreedy. "Sure didn't mean to spook you," said McCreedy, a cigarette bouncing in a corner of his mouth, staring down at Hollis with an amused expression.

"That's okay," replied Hollis—rising on his elbows, looking somewhat apprehensive—and noticed, then, that McCreedy was holding his notepad, the pages parted to the drawing of Hollis on the moon.

"You'd be the man on the moon, right? It's Hollis, right?"

"Yeah."

"I'm Bill."

"Yeah, I knew that."

"Guess I shouldn't be snooping, 'cept your book was on the floor so I couldn't help myself. Hope you don't mind none."

"It's fine," Hollis lied, resenting what felt like a calculated invasion of his privacy.

A short silence followed as McCreedy glanced again through the pages, smiling to himself.

"You some kind of artist?"

"No, not at all. It's only something I do to pass the hours."

"I hear that." McCreedy flipped the notepad shut, casually tossing it on the cot once Hollis had sat upright and swung his feet to the floor. "Say, you don't got a spare smoke I could bum?"

"I don't, sorry."

"No problem. Never hurts to ask a buddy, right?"

"Sure."

Instead of that being the end of it, McCreedy lowered himself to the cot, taking a seat beside Hollis, saying, "What's your story, then?"

The question caught Hollis off guard, perplexing him. He hesitated, staring ahead, thinking: My story? But it seemed there wasn't much to relate. He had been raised in a small midwestern town, an awkward and solitary boy. He liked hunting and fishing by himself. He had always been bookish, had few friends, and spent most of his free time under his widowed mother's complacent but watchful eye, keeping Eden company during the tough years which followed his father's malingering death from TB. After high school he had worked several part-time jobs to help make ends meet—

a short-order cook, a salesman for a Ford dealership, a gas station attendant, a cashier at the local five-and-ten—each business located on one of the four corners where the two main streets in Critchfield intersected. Five months prior to his enlistment, Eden unexpectedly remarried, bringing Rich into their home—a wine-bloated, needlessly quarrelsome little man Hollis immediately resented—a retired banker who, in turn, had found his bride's sullen, uncommunicative son rather impossible to like. With Rich's arrival, the house took on an oppressive quality, becoming an environment which, for Hollis, could no longer accommodate anything except the man's selfish, bullying whims—just the meals his stepfather enjoyed eating, the opera or classical music on the radio and nothing else, the disruptive childish tantrums which passed without apology and were only allowed with impunity for Rich; and, sometimes, when Eden wasn't present, the man delighted in taunting Hollis—throwing a cloth napkin at his face, flicking his earlobes with a finger after he had drunk too much—stating that he wasn't really very bright, that he was a full-grown brat who needed to grow up. Hollis always reacted to such unkindness with passive outrage, responding in his own discreet manner—often spitting in his stepfather's food before the man came to the dinner table, or running the bristles of Rich's toothbrush around the inside rim of the toilet bowl. As the acrimony increased— fueled by Hollis's jealousy toward this relative stranger now sharing Eden's bed, and Rich's assertion that his adult stepson was too old to live at home—Hollis, taking what little money he had saved, packed a suitcase and, on the cusp of his twentieth birthday, ran away from home one morning, Eden crying silently on the front porch as her son walked resolutely out of view.

"Don't really have a story," Hollis said.

"This fella says he ain't got a story," said McCreedy, as if talking to someone else. "Now that's a first. A man without no story to tell. You might just be my favorite person on this damn boat, Hollis."

And from that point on, McCreedy made it a habit to stop by Hollis's cot while doing his usual rounds, sitting down for a while and asking questions which Hollis felt uncomfortable answering.

"Hey, Hollis, tell me what your girl's like."

"What do you mean?"

"Your girl, what's she like? You got her picture?"

"I don't have a girl."

McCreedy squinted, cocking an eyebrow. He shook his head, saying, "Ain't buying that for a second. What, you worried ol' Creed will try and steal her away from you?"

"I'm being honest. There isn't any girl."

"Not even a little Shin-ju-koo honey going?"

"No."

"Well, what the hell's wrong with you? Horndog after it, boy. Life's far too short. Here, have a peek at this." McCreedy dug into a pocket, retrieving a slightly bent black-and-white photograph which he placed in Hollis's left hand. "That's my girl," he said, the animated clip of his voice becoming solemn. "She's waiting back home in Claude, missing me like tomorrow ain't ever coming."

Hollis lifted the photograph, inspecting it closely. What he saw brought a smirk to his face: the foreground was out of focus, showing the indistinct image of a dark-haired girl, her arms hanging at her sides, her cloudy features difficult to perceive, in contrast, the background—a wide field of high wild grass—was plainly visible.

"Don't get me wrong," McCreedy continued, his voice reanimating. "I mean, I've also got a gaggle of kobitos in Tokyo—but that one there, she's the real deal, my true gal pal. The rest don't really mean much when it really boils down to it. You know, I go to them others so I'll maintain my sanity while I'm away, if you follow. That one, though, nothing compares to her, God's honest truth."

"I bet she's pretty."

"Hell, yeah, she's pretty," said McCreedy, extracting the photograph from Hollis's fingers. "That's the mother of my children, someday."

The more Hollis got to know him—the more he learned about him, the more they talked to each other—the less bothersome the private from Claude, Texas, seemed. He had, in the course of the trip, chatted with several privates on the ship, except none were as friendly to him as McCreedy.

"Normally, I'd keep that picture to myself," McCreedy told him, "but

I get this feeling you're different. It's not that I ain't proud or nothing, just don't want these goons getting all worked up over what's mine, if you know what I mean. Some things just got to be treated with respect, if you follow, and I'm sure you do. Can't say the same for the rest of this bunch. But that's why I like you, Hollis. You got respect for the decent things, right? I could see it the moment I seen you. You and me, we're a lot alike that way. It's like we got the same birthmark or something, you follow? Anyway, we've got class, and that's what matters, wouldn't you agree?"

"Sure," Hollis said, nodding.

"We're too smart for this outfit, ain't that right?"

"I guess so. Sure."

"It's an undeniable fact."

Soon enough, Hollis would better discern the duality of McCreedy's personality, the two extreme and incongruous sides which were bridged by an irrepressible smile. And he would experience firsthand McCreedy's warmheartedness, as well as the sociable private's unexpected tendencies toward cruelty and violence. Only after leaving Korea, however, would he consider McCreedy as both an unwitting benefactor of the fortuitous outcome of his civilian life and the enigmatic symbol of his greatest shame. Then, at last, Hollis would also begin to comprehend his own paradoxical traits, his instinctive ability to appear as one kind of person and, just as easily, to behave as another. But four decades would pass before this realization fully took root, blossoming during the dawn of his retirement and springing forth on a sunny day while he cultivated his cactus garden; and months prior to that curious snowfall, he had stood alone in the backyard, gazing at what thrived under his constant attention, surprising himself there with a single word propelled from his mouth without forethought, evoking a name he hadn't uttered aloud for years and whispering it as if revealing a secret to the prickly pears.

"Creed."

5

"Where there is cactus," Hollis had told Debra last night, "there are sometimes snowflakes, too."

Even at this very moment—working here in the backyard, stooping beside his garden (a normally arid patch of earth running between the swimming pool and his tiki hut)—Hollis knows there will be days like today
which require a heavy jacket. Now bending forward with a spade in one
hand, he endeavors to blow snow from tangled, barbed spines—his breath
streaming through the garden like meager fog, grazing icicle-encased needles, dissipating past him amidst opuntia tunicata, mammillarias, and Texas
pride. Then he is amazed by where he and Debra had ended up, what was
meant to be their hard-earned detachment; how, finally, they had fled to the
Sonoran Desert from an increasingly overpopulated Los Angeles suburb,
and found themselves residing behind the high walls of a master-planned
resort for active adults: an exclusive community of championship golf
courses, gentle slopes, and seven distinctive floor plans (The Laredo, The
Lariat, The Montana, Ponderosa, Durango, Cheyenne, Santa Fe) with fifty
exterior design choices, all pretty much alike.

The tiki hut beyond the pool, however, was Hollis's own creation, something he designed just for himself. And while Debra couldn't stand the sight of the place, normally refusing to ever join him inside of it, she also understood that its construction was, in reality, a small price to pay for acquiring those interior flourishes she believed were essential to their house: she got the expensive no-wax sheet-vinyl flooring, the porcelain bathtub and ceramic tile surrounds, the single-lever chrome faucets, the oak-front cabinets; and, in return, Hollis got to build his little hut—handcrafted kiln-dried cypress wood, leak-proof thatched roof made of palm leaves, big enough inside for a hammock and two deck chairs, the ceiling fitted with a three-speed fan. It is a place where he and his buddy Lon could sip beer in hotter weather, nursing Tecate or Corona while they practiced golf swings, plotting certain victories at the weekly tournaments. So Debra had allowed him that hideaway, his backyard retreat—and if the majority of his drinking was done there (if he and Lon weren't too boisterous, if he shaved his back hair prior to lounging about in swimming trunks), then she never protested; she left him alone to split six-packs on summer afternoons and evenings. Truth be known, he has often felt more at home within his hut than within the house.

Lon, too, had once preferred spending long hours in Hollis's backyard, disregarding the upkeep of his own perennial garden and forgoing the thrice-a-week calisthenics class which his wife had expected him to take with her. On many of those summer afternoons, he would already be waiting at the hut, having already claimed a deck chair for himself, exclaiming as Hollis came outside: "You're running late, damnit. It's almost beer thirty. You better hurry."

"What are you drinking?"

"Everything, except water."

"Sounds about right to me."

It's not difficult for Hollis to envision his friend reclining nearby—snoring in the hammock with a beer can gripped by a dangling hand, or tanning himself away from the shadows of the thatched enclosure—although the hut has now become an empty, inhospitable haven; the roof is weighed down with thawing clumps of snow, water drips steadily from the palm leaves like rainfall. While the place had been intended as a whimsical symbol of Hollis's sunny leisure years, in its current state the hut appears more suitable for the black cloud which had unfurled over him and Debra some twenty-six months ago; for no sooner had they settled in Nine Springs— building the hut, landscaping the garden, completing the interior touches to the house—than Hollis received a phone call while Debra was out shopping at Costco Wholesale, hearing what at first sounded like a teenage girl's voice on the other end of the line: "Hi, this is Dr. Taylor from the Tucson Medical Center. I'm sorry to bother you, but I'm trying to reach Debra Adams. Is she available?"

He hesitated before answering, glancing toward the kitchen windows—observing the hot, bright midday sunlight reflected on the still water of the swimming pool, the sight of it underscoring the cool, unlit room he was standing in. "Debra isn't home right now," he said, absently coiling the phone cord around two fingers. "She'll be back in a couple of hours, give or take."

"Am I speaking with her husband?"

"Yes, that's me."

"Mr. Adams, I'm Dr. Taylor from the Tucson Medical Center."

"I know, you already said that."

As he pushed the receiver harder against his ear, the cord grew tighter on his fingers. What followed was at once surprising and, somehow, expected: the doctor requested that both he and Debra come to her office the next day, the meeting already scheduled for four in the afternoon. "Can you and your wife make it at that time, Mr. Adams? It's possible to meet earlier if it's more convenient."

"What's all this about?"

"I think it's probably best if we discuss everything in person, and with Mrs. Adams present, all right?"

He resented the matter-of-fact tone of her voice, how her words hinted at something tragic yet revealed nothing whatsoever. "It's serious, isn't it?" he asked.

"We'll discuss everything tomorrow, all right? So I've got your appointment down for four o'clock—"

"Can't we talk about it now? Is there anything wrong with my wife?"

But the doctor would not elaborate any further, telling him simply that it was important to remain calm, and concluding with, "We'll talk tomorrow. Four o'clock. Your wife knows where my office is."

"Okay."

"I'll expect you both then."

"Okay."

And as Hollis hung up the receiver, he thought he recognized a distant noise like the gentle evocation of wind chimes; it was, at that moment, as if he had stirred from a pleasant dream, only to realize the ground was collapsing beneath his feet. When Debra returned from shopping, carrying four grocery bags inside and setting them down in the foyer so she could close the front door, he was waiting at the dining-room table, his hands resting in his lap, his eyes following her busy movements even as he remained still. He addressed her from across the room, and without looking toward him she replied, "What is it?"

"Come here for a second, would you?"

"Hold on, let me get the groceries into the kitchen."

"You can leave them there, I'll take care of it in a minute. Just come sit beside me first, okay? Your doctor called."

Debra paused at the front door, her back to him, her hurried activity brought to a halt. "Dr. Taylor called?"

"Yes."

"When?"

"A little while ago."

"Was it about the sonogram?"

"I think so. She didn't really tell me anything. She wants us in her office tomorrow afternoon, at four. That's all I could get out of her."

"I see."

But she didn't turn to him. Instead, she remained facing the door, saying nothing else until Hollis stood and crossed the dining room into the foyer. He rested his hands on her shoulders and pulled her back to his chest.

"Did you hear the other side of the mountain is on fire?" she asked, tilting her head against his chin. "The Tucson foothills are covered in smoke. I drove home with the windows rolled up and the AC off because of it. It's awful. The radio said they're losing cabins in Summerhaven. My hair smells like smoke, huh?"

"It doesn't."

"I probably should shower anyway. That smell is stuck in my nostrils. Will you unpack the groceries?"

"Of course."

"Thank you."

Debra eased free of his mild hold, and—running fingers through her hair, releasing a prolonged sigh—she went from him without having once looked his way. Hollis started collecting the groceries; he hoisted the bags with both hands and trudged into the kitchen, lifting and then lowering the bags to a countertop—where, as he began removing plastic-wrapped bulk items (Lean Cuisines, Healthy Choice entrées, StarKist tuna cans). He suspected Debra was likely pondering those very things he had already considered while waiting at the dining table: Why did Dr. Taylor want them both there? What exactly was going on? And why had Debra's annual physical required a transvaginal sonogram and a CT scan, in addition to the usual pap smear and standard checkup?

The new doctor was younger than Debra's former California physician in Arcadia, and, as well, the woman specialized in internal medicine. "Maybe that's why she's so thorough," Debra had told him after receiving her exam. "She's certainly a breed apart from old Dr. Baker, that's for sure. Seriously, Hollis, I haven't felt that poked and probed since our honeymoon, I mean it."

"You sure it's not something else, Deb?" Hollis had asked. They were reclining near the swimming pool at dusk, seated in matching green deck chairs. "Sounds like an awful lot of trouble. I've had hundreds of physicals but never got sent to a radiologist."

"Well, your plumbing isn't as complicated as mine is, dear."

"Just doesn't sound right to me, all those tests."

"You know, it's my fault to begin with. I asked for a gallbladder exam and I guess she decided to give me the whole shebang. Could've done without that barium drink though. It's like I've been snacking on chalk."

Other concerns also had been at play, minor worries which soon felt greater than previously imagined. Upon settling in Arizona, Debra's weight had begun to increase, despite the fact that she exercised regularly, ate smaller portions, and refused fatty foods; the weight gain was most noticeable along her abdomen—"fluid weight," she had called it, "sort of like feeling waterlogged"—and she was convinced it had something to do with her gallbladder (a common source of discomfort for her throughout the years, the gallstones routinely getting purged with a fast which relied on a lemon juice and olive oil concoction). Then there was copious sweating, saturating her skin when she relaxed within their air-conditioned home and making her hair wringing wet, yet dismissed as a side effect of the hellish Sonoran weather while also seeming uncharacteristic for such a dry climate (the perspiration normally evaporating cleanly from Hollis's neck and forehead as he worked in his garden). Lastly, she had complained of an overall blahness, a general malaise since departing California; this indefinite ill-being, however, wasn't too terribly surprising, especially when put in the context of a stressful move, some weight gain, brutal desert heat, and gallstones needing to be passed. Nevertheless, it was difficult to perceive her as anything other than healthy.

But immediately following Debra's physical, Hollis couldn't shake that lurking fear of something possibly being amiss with her, although he never voiced those thoughts aloud—channeling his bothersome ruminations into gardening and a morning round of golf, while she continued operating in her upbeat manner, going about her errands and chores without a hint of despair. Even with Dr. Taylor's phone call, the typical pattern of their day didn't lend itself to panic. They ate dinner as always, saying very little during the meal. They watched TV together, saying very little during the commercial breaks. They went to bed together, briefly hugging and kissing before killing the lights. Neither one dared mention the imminent appointment, lest the conversation feed whatever irrational thoughts were brewing between them; yet their respective silences spoke volumes, and Hollis couldn't keep himself from gripping her hand for a second when they sat down to eat, or snuggling her against him while they watched TV, or enveloping her in his arms once the bedroom had become dark.

It was a restless night, to be sure. Hollis fell in and out of sleep, nodding off only to be stirred awake by Debra's gyrations, the sheets tugged this way and that, the pillow readjusted. "Are you all right?" he finally asked, rubbing a palm on her shoulder blade.

"I'm fine," was her terse reply.

"You want a melatonin?"

"No, it won't help. I already took one."

He slid a hand down the curves of her nightgown, stopping just above her plisse-covered abdomen, his palm pressing flat as his fingers fanned out. Prior to falling asleep again, he imagined he had the power to rid her body of whatever might be harming it. And as sleep resumed, he believed that that power had been effectively conjured, drawing the suspected ailment from her stomach, transferring it fully into his palm—where his hand entrapped it in a fist, and brought it to dangle over the edge of the bed, and, with fingers uncurling, sent it sailing to the floor. Sometime later, he woke to the sounds of her sniffling, her nasal passages emitting deep, punctuated inhalations.

"Deb?"

He felt her shift in the sheets, her body turning toward him. "You smell it?" she asked, and with that he realized she wasn't crying.

"What?"

"Can't you smell it?"

He lifted his head, sniffing the air. "Yes," he said, detecting a burning, somewhat aromatic odor.

"You know, I left the living-room windows cracked," she said, climbing from bed. "I'll go close them. I think the winds must've changed direction, or else the fires have gotten worse."

"Let's hope not," he said, a smoky, charred flavor materializing in his mouth like an aftertaste.

The next morning, they drank their coffee in the kitchen, sharing sections of a newspaper which placed the Catalina Mountains wildfires on the front page. But they didn't need to look any farther than their own backyard to understand how far the fires had spread overnight; for now a murky, whitish haze drifted where glaring sunlight and clear skies normally prevailed—floating among the gardens, hanging above the swimming pool area—recalling the Los Angeles smog they had left behind (a widening ring of pollution which skirted the wealthy beach enclaves and, instead, traveled inland to Riverside and the less affluent cities of San Bernardino County). The accompanying smokehouse aroma, too, had increased since dawn, tainting everything, mingling with the strong coffee, mixing with the frying pan's sizzling combination of eggs, chopped onions, diced ham, and chipotle sauce.

In due time, they entered that gauzy, scorched-smelling atmosphere, driving the thirty miles to Tucson as a classic-country radio station played. Hollis drummed his fingertips on the Suburban's steering wheel. Debra silently stared from the passenger window. Yet both were aware all the while of the plume of gray-black smoke rising like a mushroom cloud from the distant mountaintop, the desert landscape around them subdued and dull in color. With each mile the haze became more pervasive, as did their mutual, unspoken nervousness regarding the appointment. Then it seemed like the Suburban was being propelled forward by the smoke—the thickening vapor directing them beyond Oro Valley and the west end of the mountain range, speeding them past the Tucson Mall before ushering them across the parking lot of the medical center—and dissipating at last in Dr. Taylor's narrow examining room but still inhaled when the young doctor appeared wearing a long, thin face (longer and thinner than Debra remembered the woman's face being, somehow longer and thinner than faces ever were), saying right away the news wasn't good, explaining without a moment of hesitation, "You have ovarian cancer."

Hearing those words, Hollis sensed himself shrinking on the chair, becoming drawn up, shriveled, numb, blank—then momentarily deaf. He glanced at Debra who, in the same instant, glanced at him. But whereas Hollis felt stunned and immobilized by Dr. Taylor's diagnosis, Debra never lost her composure; rather, her intent eyes shot to the doctor, her head nodding confidently when she asked, "Okay, so what do I do now?" And with that, Dr. Taylor directed their immediate course of action: while sitting in the examining room, Debra was handed the doctor's cell phone and instructed to call her gynecologist to set up an emergency appointment; shortly thereafter, she and Hollis were sent racing to the nearby University Medical Center, where they retrieved her sonogram and CT-scan axial images from the radiologist; then they sped to the southwest side of town, entering the gynecologist's office twelve minutes ahead of schedule.

Dr. Langford, the gynecologist, was a no-nonsense, heavyset redhead, a woman who—as Debra had described her to Hollis—would have made a good detective on *Law & Order*; furthermore, she was also a gynecologist and surgeon, her expertise highlighted by the fairly prominent Phoenix medical family in which she had been raised. Behind her desk at St. Mary's Hospital, Dr. Langford studied Debra's axial images for a minute, lifting each one to the fluorescent light above her, expressing no emotion as Hollis and Debra sat on the other side of the desk holding hands. "Well, these seem straightforward enough," Dr. Langford concluded, peering through her bifocals. "It looks like we're dealing with ovarian cancer."

Hollis's stomach dropped. Debra released his hand and leaned forward, asking, "How bad is it?"

Dr. Langford shrugged and set the axial images down on her desktop. "Without the written report or an MRI scan, it's difficult to say for sure. What these show me, however, is that the tumors are clustered on the ovaries like clumps of salt, or like fistfuls of sand grains. Everything else— kidney, spleen, liver, pancreas—these appear unremarkable."

"Unremarkable? Is that good?" Hollis asked.

"That's good," Dr. Langford said. "As for mesenteric cancer, we won't know what we're really dealing with or what can be done about it unless we get inside you and see. To be totally fair, I can't accurately call it ovarian cancer until we take a look at it and pathology confirms it—and that's what I highly recommend we do."

"All right," Debra said emphatically, as if she were acquiescing to something no more complicated than a back rub. "Let's do that."

"Okay," Hollis mumbled, unsure then of everything which had just been said, hearing his own mouth speak but feeling apart from the situation. In hindsight, there was much he would forget about, much during those weeks which had flashed by him like an incomprehensible blur—various re-

ports, laboratory data, medical jargon. Yet even now, he remains aware of
his complete and utter helplessness throughout, watching when Debra was
wheeled on a gurney into surgery, half smiling while she joked, "If I die on
the table, put 'She wasn't ready' on my tombstone," and fighting tears once
the gurney had rolled beyond swinging metal doors. And, too, he came to
understand the havoc the disease had created within his wife, how it had
managed to spread into the peritoneum—to the uterus, the lymph glands,
the bladder, the gallbladder—how surgery could eliminate 95 percent of the
cancer, while the remaining 5 percent was inoperable (hundreds of microscopic tumors continuing to ravage the serous membrane of her abdomen,
seeking a home, some building a thriving colony on the delicate surface of
her bowel).

"Stage-III-C ovarian cancer grade two," was Dr. Langford's ultimate
determination, revealed in the hours following Debra's operation. "Ab-
dominal implants more than two centimeters in diameter and positive
retroperitoneal or inguinal nodes."

"I don't understand," Hollis had said. "It isn't making sense."

"Papillary serous cystadenocarcinoma," the doctor replied. "That's the
cancer your wife has."

"I still don't understand. What does it mean?"

But amidst that growing confusion, as he had felt overwhelmed by
cryptic terminology or frightened by the possibility of losing the person he
loved the most, Hollis brought his mind to the short-lived gray area—the
fleeting period between not knowing for certain and knowing too well (after Dr. Taylor's diagnosis and prior to Dr. Langford's surgery)—when he
and Debra had left Tucson at dusk and drove back to Nine Springs, and he
told her while they went, "It'll be fine, you'll see. We'll survive this."

"I have no doubt, dear," she had said, gazing ahead at a reddish-
orange-hued horizon masked behind a veil of smoke. "In fact, I'm positive
of it."

Several minutes later, Debra requested he stop at a roadside Circle K,
where she purchased a six-pack of Tecate and a bag of gummy worms. Arriving home, she surprised Hollis by avoiding the house altogether, preferring instead to walk the perimeter of their property, leading him along the

gravel pathway which guided them into the backyard. Soon they sat inside his unlit tiki hut as if in hiding, drinking beer and savoring the nighttime. She had never shown an interest in the hut before—nor had she done so since—but on that evening she seemed to regard it just like he often had: as a kind of a refuge from the larger world, a place devoid of fear or complications.

"This is nice," she said, angling to one side in order to pat his right knee. "I think I can see why you like it out here."

"Gives you a whole different feeling, right?"

"I'd say so," she said, her obscured form readjusting, moving upright on the deck chair.

And for a while they stayed there—finishing the gummy worms and Tecate, their fingers eventually interlaced—breathing the carbon-laden air, observing the jagged line of fire snaking across the far-off, imperceptible mountaintop and appearing like a savage fissure in what was usually a starry sky.

6

The long scar on Debra's body starts at her pubic bone—running about ten inches in length, its design zigzagging a bit—and concludes right below her belly button. But whereas the scar had previously looked inflamed and swollen, it is now considerably less raw and broad, appearing whiter than the rest of her abdomen's skin. Much to her annoyance, though, the hair which had been shaved away prior to the incision being made has never grown back, likely stunted—she decided—by the eventual rounds of chemotherapy which had shed every single strand of her body's hair. Regardless, Hollis has become strangely fond of the scar—fixing his eyes upon it whenever Debra undressed near him, occasionally bestowing it with a quick kiss—as if that injured tissue was a sort of cellular medal: an emblematic reminder of a hard-fought battle, one in which the war itself had never achieved an uneasy truce.

"We're almost twins," he'd told her once when they were in bed, bringing his left leg from under the sheets, pulling the knee toward his stomach while he traced a finger along his old war wound—a crooked, slender trail of discolored skin, a former gash which had cleaved the inner thigh to just above the kneecap.

"Almost," she said, regarding his wound briefly before returning her stare to the pages of a Sue Grafton mystery.

Yet Hollis can't quite forget his shock when first seeing her incision— the flesh all tender and red, the ragged seam stapled together—or hearing Dr. Langford's pragmatic voice telling him, "It's important you realize your wife has a disease that will probably shorten her life," while Debra recuperated from surgery. During her entire hospital stay he had kept a vigil beside her bed, half awake on a cot for four nights, listening to her labored breathing as air escaped around a drainage tube which had been inserted through her left nostril, taking note of what she wouldn't fully recall later on—the machine monitoring the draining of her body fluids, an IV bag sending drop after drop after drop into her veins, the electrical hum of an inactive hospital past midnight. Exhaustion overtook him on the third night, and he promptly submerged into the landscape of familiar dreams— that slow procession of cattle, then that formation of wandering, listless people—only to be jolted back by a handful of flung ice cubes grazing his neck, chest, shoulders.

"You'll wake the dead, Hollis," Debra said, lowering her head to the pillow, gripping a clear plastic drinking cup. "Lord, you're snoring something awful."

"Sorry," he mumbled, turning himself toward her, blinking lazily while she fished an ice cube from the cup and deposited it in her mouth. She chuckled for a second, closing her eyes, sucking the ice with cheeks drawn in, the cup still held tightly.

Now and again, the morphine played its tricks, sending her straight to sleep and, just as effortlessly, waking her—where she gazed about the room as if lost, as if she had suddenly been revived from a prolonged coma, sometimes addressing him with lucid words, sometimes uttering nonsense he didn't always comprehend ("It's in the drawer—better take care of it, okay?"); even so, she administered the drug herself, pumping it into the IV at those few moments when the pain rose to a level of recognition. The daytime hours at the hospital, aside from the day of the operation, were uniform, uneventful: they managed walks up and down the corridors, the IV bag and tubes in tow; they watched TV; they enjoyed small talk, avoiding the topic of cancer if possible; they slept within reach of each other, as had been done without fail since their honeymoon.

They were sent home on the fifth day, departing St. Mary's with a prescription for pain pills and their own uncertainty about what lay ahead. But upon returning to Nine Springs, Debra soon realized she didn't need the pain pills after all, simply because there wasn't any continual ache left to drug; in fact, other than the initial discomfort immediately following surgery, she suffered most in the minute or so that it took for the drainage tube to be removed—pulled from her stomach through her chest, through her throat, through her nostril, making her cough and gag. Eventually, it struck Hollis as being odd that the cancer hadn't immediately manifested in a clear-cut manner—no wasting away, no feebleness, no cinematic swift demise—odd, too, that the obvious signs of infirmity Debra had displayed were brought on by what was meant to help her: the surgery and, subsequently, the side effects of chemotherapy.

However, the presence of the cancer itself remained elusive, even as it continued to mutate, increase, and spread like dust motes transported in an afternoon breeze. Under such circumstances, though, she often conveyed greater energy on her worst days than Hollis did on his best days—driving herself to the library, shopping for wigs and eyeliner, refusing to let him do her laundry or fold her clothing. "I'm fine," she told him. "I'm not an invalid, you know." As if to underscore her resolve, Debra wouldn't allow herself an ounce of self-pity or a tearful outburst, although Hollis had succumbed to both emotional states on four occasions, always reserving his solitary breakdowns for his garden and the confines of his tiki hut.

Perhaps it was the absence of tangible death which bolstered Debra, to the point where she decided her sister in Texas shouldn't learn of the illness unless, of course, all her options had been exhausted and the endgame became imminent. But her innate fortitude was also tempered by the situation's undeniable gravity, not to mention the chemotherapy, and everything else she had researched at the library or was told about stage-III ovarian cancer. She knew, for example, the prognosis was far from good: seven of every ten cases were diagnosed after the cancer had already spread beyond the ovary; with stage III only one out of four women survived beyond five years. But—as Dr. Langford had repeatedly suggested—there was at least reason to believe Debra might join that 25 percent grouping.

Even so, nothing Dr. Langford said seemed real to Hollis, none of it seemed possible. The data and medical jargon, the new expressions and unheard-of treatments, the frightening odds of survival—all of it felt like some elaborate hoax at their expense, and a very cruel joke. There were a few other things which nagged his mind, things he was too ashamed to admit, not the least of which was his own ignorance about the purpose, exact physical location, and function of a woman's ovaries. So during one of Debra's library excursions, Hollis joined her on the ride, claiming he needed to do research for his autobiography. But rather than find books relating to Korean history, it was a long-out-of-print hardcover with a plain maroon cover which preoccupied his time, keeping him seated at a table away from where Debra read; when a page was turned, he glanced around to make sure she wasn't coming toward him, and then, discreetly, resumed studying the book he cradled against a forearm, hunched low over the text as if he were guarding answers to a test.

It was, in fact, the sole book found on the computer catalog which corresponded to the keywords "ovaries" and "female reproduction"— although the title raised an eyebrow, for it was called *The Illustrated Encyclopedia of Sex*, written quasi-anonymously by Dr. A. Willy, Dr. L. Vander, Dr. O. Fisher, and other authorities, published in 1950, with its almost bare cover using bold white letters to state: AN IMPORTANT CONTRIBUTION TO THE CAUSE OF SEXUAL ENLIGHTENMENT FEATURING A UNIQUE AND UNPRECEDENTED SERIES OF ILLUSTRATIONS REPRESENTING EVERY ASPECT OF SEX. Nevertheless, the book provided the information he had sought, doing so with a graphic series of antiquated drawings which looked more like 1950s science fiction than science fact. Spermatoza enlarged a thousand times. Fibrous coverings of testicles and epididymis. Sperm damaged by distilled-water irrigation. Sperm paralyzed by vinegar irrigation. Breast of a virgin. Breast of a woman who has had children. Menstrual blood in uterus due to obstruction. Six causes of painful menstruation. And then, on page 59, a woman's pelvic and sex organs shown in a transparent body, with the following page displaying a cross-sectioned ovary.

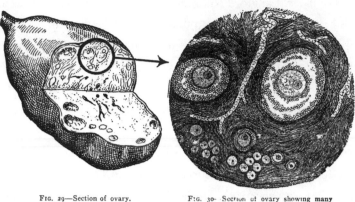

FIG. 29—Section of ovary.   FIG. 30- Section of ovary showing many unripe and two completely mature ova.

While staring at the ovary drawings, Hollis thought: So this is what you look like. This is what you are, and this is where you were hiding inside Deb.

Then he couldn't help but smile, especially as the book and its drawings were published the year before he had met and fallen in love with Debra. Those intricate drawings of male and female forms—the colorful sex organs, the facsimiles of naked and dissected bodies from a different era—belonged to their generation, striking him as lost representations of his and Debra's younger, healthier shapes and body parts. Only later, after leaving the library and heading home, did something else tug at his mind, a notion of humans as little more than cells in a larger social superorganism; and, as such, it stood to reason that individuals, like cells, might outgrow their usefulness, eventually withering and dying off. Maybe, he wondered, it was a myth about our evolutionary instincts being fully geared toward the survival of ourselves and our own kin—because if that were truly the case there wouldn't be cancer swarming within so many people as a preset, intrinsic suicide program. But if you remove the human disposition for war and destruction, he imagined, our cells would have no choice except to mirror such a change; they would adapt, evolve accordingly, shunning any self-destructive impulses. There would be, under those circumstances, a real end to sickness and human misery.

"We're the cure for cancer," he suddenly told Debra on the drive home. "People are."

"What?"

"We hold the cure—the human race, I mean. We need to change how we behave. I think it's important to reprogram ourselves, don't you? I mean, if we reprogram our way of thinking and behaving I'm certain we'll reprogram our cells, too?"

"Hon, I don't know what on earth you're talking about."

"I'm just trying to figure how we can get out of this mess we're in. And I'm thinking maybe if we alter our evolutionary patterns as a society—if we do that, in a positive direction—it seems like our cells will follow along."

"That's all well and good," she said, "but that kind of evolution takes a long time, more time than I've been given, dear. More time than any of us have. It's a nice idea, though."

"I prefer to consider it a concept," he said. "A new concept, not really just an idea."

"Well, you better write it down then, put it in your book."

"You know, honestly, I feel like I'm onto something here. I believe it might be the key to solving this problem for the world, Deb."

"You never know," she said, grinning to herself.

"At least it's something, right?"

But soon another new concept came into play—the notion of living with cancer as opposed to dying from it. A bizarre definition for living, Hollis felt. How better, though, to provide the hopeless with hope than with a useful oxymoron. And so it was hope he clung to, as surely as it was hope which fueled Debra's determination. And, too, it was a kind of singular belief in herself as an individual—as someone apart from those also suffering with the disease—which gave her focus. Shrugging off Dr. Langford's advice, she had little interest in looking into organizations such as the Wellness Community or Gilda's Club, in having her sickness treated like an analogue for the ovarian cancer of others. This was her fight, her life; she would manage.

"Who wants to be with a bunch of sick bald women anyway?" she balked, after Hollis mentioned he thought the support group named for comedienne Gilda Radner sounded encouraging. "Trust me, I don't need another thing to remind me I've got ovarian cancer. The chemo is bad enough."

"You're right," he said. "The chemo is bad enough."

So was the disease, he thinks now. So was the leaden, oppressive feeling which had consumed his gut—like holding his breath for months, like waiting for the other shoe to drop—and only relieved by a single refrain, those words Dr. Langford had spoken without expression: "We're not looking at a cure, just control. But there's still hope."

Now scooping away the slush which has settled among the cacti, Hollis can feel the pull of better months; tending to his garden here—discarding what the cold night had dropped upon it—he can bring to mind more recent days, when the sun blazed high, the ground burned hot underfoot, and his skin was of a darker tint. Then he smiles at what presents itself to him: a commemorative American Legion National Convention pineapple-shaped decanter, a 1962 Southern Comfort turquoise-and-gold jigger measure, two vintage Fabulous Las Vegas shot glasses—all curios purchased by Lon while on their monthly pilgrimages into Tucson, intended for use and displayed inside the hut, each item having been found the previous summer at the Tanque Verde Swap Meet.

"How much you think it cost me?"

"I don't know. Five bucks?"

"Are you kidding? The guy wanted seven, but I got it for four."

The swap-meet ritual became a kind of game, one in which the individual spending cap was twenty dollars (not including the steakhouse dinner which was always eaten prior to starting the return drive to Nine Springs). Parting ways, they had an hour and a half before rendezvousing again at the front entrance; during that time, both of them hunted rare deals to take home to their wives—antique picture frames, custom-made lampshades, collectable wall plates—with the month's winner determined by whatever was deemed the best buy for the least amount spent (the loser, then, required to pick up the dinner tab). Regardless of whether Hollis won a given month's hunt or not, he knew early on he had already discovered the greatest bargain the swap meet offered—something he didn't have to haggle over, something he couldn't carry home or claim as a victory purchase: a fifteen-minute, $6 massage from the expert hands of a blind Taiwanese masseur. So while Lon shopped elsewhere—exploring the dirt lanes of the swap meet, rummaging through milk crates—Hollis took a seat in Ah-Chun's little booth, waiting for his chance to stretch across the table.

Hollis had encountered Ah-Chun last May, when he observed the blind masseur sweeping the mat-covered floor around a massage table—tanned feet embraced by well-worn sandals, long gray-white hair tied into a ponytail, taut weathered skin covering a skull which looked large in relation to the small body it sat upon—whisking bits of trash, creating a pile the man couldn't possibly see. Frank Sinatra's recording of "Send In the Clowns" began playing from the swap-meet loudspeakers, and Ah-Chun paused, clutching at the broom handle, apparently moved by the melancholy and defeat expressed in the song. Wearing a white smock which was big on his slight, compact frame, the man remained completely motionless for a moment, his eyes hidden behind sunglasses. Then Hollis noticed the cardboard sign propped against the booth, its handwritten message fashioned by a black Magic Marker, stating:

TRUE BODY RUB, NO COMPARISON!
$4 ten minute/$6 fifteen minute/$8 twenty minute
RELAX BY GREAT BLIND MASSEUR ALL WAY FROM TAIPEI

That roughly made advertisement was enticing enough to lure Hollis onto the man's table—where, for ten glorious minutes, his skin and muscles were pulled, tugged, pounded, loosened. The following June he paid the fifteen-minute price, and those extra five minutes lulled him into a sublime, tranquil sleep which, after waking, left his body invigorated and limber for perhaps the first time since Debra's illness was discovered. It wasn't until July, however, that Hollis actually made an effort to learn about the blind man, asking his name and talking to him as one might do with a barber.

"How do you say it? Ash-hen?"

"Ah-Chun—"

"At-ch-ung."

"Ah-Chun—"

"Ak-chun—like action?"

"No, is Ah-Chun—my name very easy, you see, not hard. Ah-Chun—"

"Ah-shun—"

"Maybe—it's closer—"

Straining to comprehend the man's broken English, listening intently while pliant hands pressed against his spine, Hollis discovered Ah-Chun, like himself, had migrated to Southern California decades ago, and, as it happened, they had lived a few miles apart in neighboring San Gabriel Valley cities (Arcadia for Hollis and Debra, Rosemead for Ah-Chun and a now deceased wife).

"So how'd you end up way out here, Ah-Chun? What brought you to the Old Pueblo?"

He explained that his oldest daughter worked in Tucson for Raytheon Missile Systems. Another daughter was a university professor in Michigan—in Lansing—but the weather there was too cold for him. "I like hot," he said.

"Makes two of us," Hollis said, as Ah-Chun's fingertips changed course and slid toward the curves of his shoulder blades. "I've got a home out at the Nine Springs development."

With that Ah-Chun's hands paused. "It's Nine Springs where you living now?" he said. "Someone really call it that?"

"Yeah, just north of here, past Oro Valley."

The hands began moving again, and Ah-Chun spoke from above, mentioning that, in Chinese legend, another nine springs also existed, functioning as a gateway to the underworld. "Except no one wants to go there too long, you see." Because, he said, agitated spirits occupied that nether region in limbo, seeking justice for whatever wrongs might have contributed to their deaths, and wouldn't leave until recompense was made on their behalf.

"How about that," Hollis said. "And it's called Nine Springs, too?"

"Maybe not really same," Ah-Chun answered. "For me Huang Quan—something like Yellow Springs, you know—so not really same."

"That's good."

"Yes, yes, very good, I think."

But no sooner had Hollis become well acquainted with Ah-Chun than the heat of summer abated, as did the monthly swap-meet adventures. In late August, he entered Ah-Chun's booth for a final time—except the man never knew he was waiting there, nor did Hollis have an opportunity to rest upon the table (four customers were already ahead of him, each paying for an $8 rub). He took a seat on a foldout chair anyway, using his allotted massage minutes to finish a Diet Pepsi, watching as Ah-Chun was hunched beside the table—meandering digits at the corpulent, freckled neck of a young woman, faint Chinese utterances half whispered beyond understanding.

The vast, passive woman on the table seemed almost unaware of Ah-Chun's presence, and the man's mumbled speech was consumed by the evening crowds, the music and announcements piped from loudspeakers, the hawkers proclaiming specials, Tucson's tongue like a family's incomprehensible argument: Hispanic and Anglo voices melding—a cacophony of tones, though somehow not unpleasant, soaring upward above everything; it was that flow of language, life's currency, which Hollis believed Ah-Chun savored the most. Previously, the man had mentioned that his daughter's wishes to drive him were usually declined, and instead he opted to walk the sidewalks and the streets, to wander among the din of people. He also enjoyed riding transit buses, the portable table crossing the city with him to then stand inside the booth. The only blind man, Ah-Chun had proudly pointed out, offering his services at the weekend swap meet— the only blind Taiwanese man, he was positive, to caress and grasp local skin.

Ah-Chun quickly gyrated his fists between lax shoulder blades, warming flesh, and the woman on the table exhaled deeply, saying, "Mmmm— oh, that's good—yes—" How odd, Hollis suddenly thought, that one could give such pleasure to a woman he wouldn't ever know, an intimacy shared as teenagers, couples, and baby strollers streamed past his booth. "Right there—yes," the woman said limply, and never revealed more of herself than those short responses. How strange, an elderly man probably older than her father and prowling hands along her surface for cash—hands like a calming wind she could feel but wouldn't contemplate, hands which had traveled an ocean and throughout the years to relieve her body, pummeling rhythmically against her while something in Mandarin was spoken underneath his breath. Then how alien it must have been for Ah-Chun—ending up in a desert where dryness weathered faces, the ebbing fever of August hung like a vaporous gauze of wool, yet he couldn't discern the many phallic-shaped saguaros or accurately envision the island he had abandoned so long ago.

Still, the man ambled surely from bus to bus—slender cane tapping the ground, folding massage table held at his side—venturing twice a week to his booth, touching multiple forms which didn't usually address him with interest or wonder aloud about where his life had originated, where specifically he had gained the gift of softening hard muscles and pacifying tendons. But if asked, he explained as best he could, mentioning the narrow roads of the Taipei night market, the cheap tile walkways fractured by buried asphalt and, in spots, cupping puddles of rainwater. Hard to comprehend, he would still say, "Always work for me—I work there since I was small," and perhaps a body would find his story unusual, saying as Hollis once had, "Tell me more."

Then Ah-Chun's memory crossed the Pacific again, returning home; he inhaled the swap meet, steeping his nostrils with what lingered there—that carnival fragrance transporting him, placing him as a boy near the snake shops, the snake wine, the pickled snakes, the snakes hanging lengthwise at storefronts. About fifty years ago, it had been revealed, he was an apprentice masseur kneading bodies in front of a snake shop, pouring snake oil on shoulder blades and spines. Or maybe it was yesterday, he had said and chuckled—swallowing humidity, breathing a fusion of rain, fish, blood, noodles—hearing water slither into drains, flip-flops on the march, voices haggling; he could smell and recall it easily, could draw its vicinity there.

Now the woman emitted a faint moan as Ah-Chun wriggled an elbow on her thigh, then the two of them sighed together—she with eyelids shut, he with eyes wide open; although he wore sunglasses, even at dusk, and gazed in no particular direction, nor, Hollis imagined, did he often cast his mind toward the land which he had left behind for a better life in the United States, remembering it without any tangible clarity. The woman, too, was blind in her own manner; she couldn't conceive of Ah-Chun awaking from darkness into darkness and, thereafter, continuing outside like a somnambulist. She couldn't picture him shuffling on sidewalks until he slowed, his legs aching, or envisage him sleeping at bus stops, stirring confused amidst an abrupt fuming of exhaust, coughing and briefly unsure if he was conscious. No, Hollis thought, why should she care what it's like to come from someplace distant, a far-off homeland, settling in a remote desert, but not perceiving, either, where you've been and where you are—yet somehow finding yourself existing in both.

In spite of that, Ah-Chun's hands kept roaming, investigating, getting the lay of familiar terrain, the way the blind journey inside their apartments extending nimble, grasping fingers always ahead of themselves as if expecting surprises. And gradually the woman fell asleep while the drifting crowds floated through the evening; soon the booths and radiant avenues of the swap meet would turn vacuous. Until then, Ah-Chun continued mumbling to himself, perhaps he felt his own body desiring to stay longer—and from the sinews of that woman, perhaps he could touch the shapes of his past, understanding that today's skin was no different than yesterday's skin. In darkness, he had once told Hollis, a man can belong almost anyplace.

"That's true," Hollis had replied, shutting his eyes on the table. "You're right," he had muttered, before losing himself in an unprolonged though hardly insubstantial summer dream; for he was also beckoned elsewhere—departing once while stretched out there, slowly pressed back through time and across the Pacific—as fingertips urged him onward, as the warm elasticity of his skin, soothed in the evening, answered Ah-Chun's guiding touch.

7

There were pennies in every pocket of Private Bill McCreedy's olive fatigues, five pennies per pocket, treasured like amulets which could ward off bad luck—pressed by durable cloth lining, protecting his skin—as if, hopefully, the copper or steel-covered-in-zinc cents might deflect gook bullets. He liked bragging about the pennies to the other men who served alongside him, smirking while mentioning the importance of his American-minted trinkets and patting his pockets as he spoke: "These babies keep me more rooted than anything. They keep me reminded of why I'm here, what I'm fighting for." But even if he had never said a word, the significance he attached to the coins would have been hard to miss: before falling asleep at the bivouac spot southwest of P'ohang, the pennies were removed and counted and deposited inside a tin drinking cup; after stirring in that humid countryside—encircled mostly by teenage boys, half awake and scratching at their mosquito bites, lowering their feet to the green plastic groundsheets—the pennies were counted again, divided up into tiny stacks of five, and then, mumbling the Lord's Prayer, McCreedy slipped the stacks, one at a time, inside each pocket. Four of the pennies nearest his heart—he had told Hollis and the others—were engraved with the birth years of those waiting for him back home in the States (his mother, his father, his kid brother, and his young girlfriend), while the fifth penny commemorated the year in which he was born.

How distant the Panhandle of Texas must have felt to McCreedy—the cotton rows surrounding the family farm, the red-stone gashes of the Caprock canyons, the wide-open spaces which comprised the high, dry plains; how remote and dreamlike it all must have seemed when first riding by truck among South Korea's lush, mountainous scenery: the soldiers having caught glimpses of an impoverished countryside—village shacks tilting at the edge of hazy fields which were dotted with half-naked laborers, bone-thin dogs roving in packs on the roadway, sullen Korean faces watching as the military trucks rolled past—while far beyond the mountains, a hundred or so miles away, fellow soldiers were already dying beside the banks of a fast-flowing river, some drowning, too, when crossing the rushing stream to escape an onslaught of North Korean troops. For McCreedy, however, it wasn't yet the grim reality of battle which had immediately repulsed him, nor was it the possibility of a violent end which initially troubled his mind; instead, it was the ceaseless stench rising from the fields which wrinkled his brow, the noxious odor of human excrement combined with ash and used as fertilizer.

"This place is shit," he'd shouted while en route to the bivouac at dusk, waving a hand in front of his face as if he were shooing a fly.

"You got that right," another soldier responded, answering him from the midst of the identical shapes riding there.

Staring out at the darkening landscape, McCreedy had clamped the hand over his nose, holding it there as the vehicle proceeded—the bodies around him swaying or lifting with the bumps and turns in the road, the pennies sliding inside his pockets as they were all carried into the night. But if Korea was, to him, a foul land where its primitive people appeared unwelcoming—its water often contaminated, its mosquitoes surpassing the enemy troops in staging attacks—he at least found comfort in the little things, like writing letters to send home, counting his pennies, playing poker for matchsticks or cigarettes, and proudly speaking the password which had allowed entry through the bivouac perimeter: "Texas, sir! Texas!"

Hollis, on the other hand, didn't share his outspoken comrade's disdain for where they had been sent. In fact, he was quietly captivated by such a peculiar locale, a territory and culture so different from what had defined his life that he felt somehow transformed within its borders. To his mind, the southern part of Korea was like an imaginary place, a fiction, only to be discovered on the pages of novels, or spotted momentarily in grainy newsreel footage; yet presently the divided country unfolded—vividly, completely, replete with shades of green and blue and gray—and, as well, he was enveloped wholly by its otherness after a South Korean train soon transported the 2nd Battalion from bivouac to the war front (his rucksack destined for a march along winding trails, his darting eyes shadowed beneath a steel helmet and surveying the hillsides, his lungs breathing the heavy summer air when eventually moving deeper and deeper into that exotic, deceptively serene world).

Still, Hollis could agree with McCreedy that Korea was nothing like Japan, a nation which, by comparison, was more developed, more complacent in defeat, and, without question, cleaner. In parts of Tokyo, there was at least something resembling the leisure many of the soldiers had enjoyed back in the States; there were Japanese big bands playing American music at Ginza nightspots, and taxi dancers wearing evening dresses, and cheap beer. The Japanese, it seemed, were also more refined by nature than the dirt-poor Koreans, and because they had never suffered decades of subjugation and violent occupation, they lacked the hard, untrusting collective traits of a long-ago broken, scarred people. That being the case, Hollis fostered a greater feeling of sympathy for the Koreans than he did for the Japanese (the Koreans were, after all, really warring with themselves and not directly against the United States of America), while McCreedy— shaking his head beside Hollis during the twenty-hour train trip, scowling on his wooden seat at the shirtless women toiling in fields beyond the cramped passenger car—did little to conceal the contempt he felt for those he regarded as subhuman by default: "Like a bunch of pigs wallowing about in their own filth." And, he believed, their impossible language was coarse, distraught in tone, sounding like a wounded heifer echoing its pain. Furthermore, they lacked the fundamental and essential understanding of a Christian God, of the Lord's sacrifice.

"Honestly, Creed wouldn't fuck a single one of them, even if I wanted to—unless Christ himself ordered me to."

"I wouldn't either," Hollis had replied, sketching in his notepad and not paying much attention to his comrade's grumbling, pondering instead the warning their captain had recently made clear to each carload of soldiers: the enemy might be hiding among Korean refugees from the north, blending in without uniform, disguised as civilians.

McCreedy glanced down at Hollis's drawing. "There you go," he said, nodding resolutely at what he saw. A shaggy gorilla was taking shape on the notepad, standing at the center of a bean field, holding a banana in one fist and a hand grenade in the other; the caption above it read: WHAT KIND OF GUERRILLA ARE YOU? "You see, we're on the same page. We're like two sides of the same coin."

"Maybe."

Later on—once the steam engine had climbed the Autumn Wind Pass, chugging for Yongdong County and the front line—McCreedy stood in the aisle of the passenger car, his body rocking with the train's movements, and said, "Hey, you all give me your ears for a sec, will you?" At that moment conversations ceased, every set of eyes fixed on him, and, relishing the sudden attention with a grin, he held out his tin drinking cup, pivoting so all could see it. "Let Creed show you a little something about these folks we're fighting against and these folks we're helping out here. Let me give you a little insight about just how their kind of mentality operates." He produced three of his pennies, explaining that the Koreans named their newborns by dropping spare change into an empty can, the resulting clanking noises determining a child's lifelong moniker. "Goes like this, right? Listen closely, if you can." He shook the pennies from his hand, sprinkling them into the cup. "Park-Clink-Kim," he announced, bringing a few hoots and a smattering of laughter which were subdued beneath the train's continual rumbling. He sprinkled the pennies again: one after another after another. "That'd be a Clink-Kim-Park." Again. "And that's Park-Park-Clink."

Almost everyone, it seemed, was delighted by McCreedy's joke—everyone, that is, except Hollis, who, shifting his gaze to the window, ignored McCreedy's gleaming stare and recurring wink ("Now who's got a smoke or two for ol' Creed?") and beheld a rice paddy shimmering under the sun, then thatch huts, then a swift blur of oxcarts on a dirt road near the railroad tracks, belonging to what he suspected was a weary group of battle-fleeing refugees. Before long the voices of McCreedy and the other soldiers grew fainter to him, and the sound of the train became all embracing. In the distance, where sunlight reflected off more rice paddies, he saw the silhouette of a girl leaning against a parked bicycle and supporting herself on crutches.

When the 2nd Battalion began disembarking a few miles behind the Yong-dong front—filing onto the station platform, bringing C rations and full canteens, slouching under the weight of rucksacks, sporting eight-round M1 ammunition clips on cartridge belts—the soldiers they had come to replace stood waiting there, greeting the new arrivals without as much as a smile, posed haphazardly like a living tableau which depicted the aftermath of battle. It was as if they were being met by future visions of themselves, an opaque mirror image casting a grim reflection of what lay ahead. Stepping from the train in relatively clean uniforms, bright eyed and green, the young men of the 2nd Battalion were taken aback by their counterparts from the 24th Infantry Division: boys like themselves yet somehow made older than their years and now worse for wear—some bandaged about the head and arms, some on stretchers, most in grubby fatigues—each stubbled face looking beaten; but once the passenger cars were emptied, those tired expressions quickly betrayed varying degrees of relief as the men slowly ambled forward and started boarding the train.

"Here, pal, take this," a limping infantryman said, pausing long enough to fix a brown-eyed gaze on Hollis while pressing a fresh pack of Chesterfields against his palm. "I'm finished," he explained, moving on toward the train, his uniform dusty and frayed at the collar, his black hair matted and unwashed. "I've quit," he said, without glancing back. "I'm done." Tightening his grip on the pack, Hollis watched the infantryman recede, gradually losing sight of him amid the crowd readying for the return journey.

In hindsight, Hollis couldn't remember exactly when it was he began smoking (definitely not while stationed in Japan, undoubtedly after arriving in Korea), but he would never forget the morning he quit—just a couple of weeks later while dug in at the Naktong River, on his last day at the front. Nevertheless, he always associated that encounter with the infantryman as the beginning of an earnest, short-lived nicotine habit, soon hoarding his C-ration cigarettes at the bivouac near P'ohang, treasuring the packs where previously he had given them away. Moreover, there was smoke hanging in his memory, plenty of it—gray-white smoke sucked deep into his chest, regurgitated through his mouth and nose—as prevalent to his recollections as the grit which swirled about the cavalrymen, irritating their eyes, sneaking down the muzzles of their M1s.

Mixing with the summer heat, dust and cigarette smoke reigned behind the Yongdong lines, saturating the regimental command post, drifting above the 2nd Battalion while they took positions and established security posts; it wafted, too, beneath the moonlight when a patrol flank spotted the figures of northern refugees approaching, the white-clad shapes emerging like ghosts on a darkened road: the rumors of enemy infiltrators hiding among the civilians was enough to prompt fire from the jittery patrol flank, the rounds missing the refugees but successful in stopping the advance— the panicked villagers about-facing with heavy loads on their backs, reversing with their children or babies, scrambling backward into the night. And, in turn, it was to be the lighting of a cigarette which brought the regiment's first casualty, the fatal shots ringing through blackness and hitting a lieutenant when he struck a match before dawn, discharged from the semiautomatics of his own men (nervous Easy Company soldiers, inexperienced riflemen who jumped quickly at every sound).

Sometimes in the smoke-laden mornings, McCreedy's pennies were shown again to the jittery men who had returned from night patrol, those disquieted soldiers who sat tiredly beside one another, thoughtlessly nursing their cigarettes, saying very little while McCreedy tried bolstering their spirits by grinning his usual grin, smiling as if he possessed the answers to every problem: the pennies were stacked on his right elbow, balancing there until—with a deft movement of his arm—they fell away from his skin, floating for a millisecond, only to be caught by the swift-grabbing fingers of his right hand. Hollis had seen the coin tricks at least two dozen times; he had seen McCreedy's pennies rolled along gyrating knuckles, disappearing in fists, materializing soon thereafter like two round holes on someone else's forehead. Hollis had also heard more than once the usual spiel which marked the conclusion of McCreedy's display, memorizing the harangue in spite of wanting to forget it.

"I think some of you could use a dose of perspective," McCreedy always began, holding out a bulging prophylactic, the condom stuffed with pennies and dangling beneath his grip like a half-full water balloon. "Do yourself a favor and have a look at this here. This baby is pretty special, let me tell you. What I keep in here is my Indian Head cents, five percent zinc, ninety-five percent copper, minted by our own U.S. Treasury. This whole bunch was collected together by my grandpa. Seems kind of worthless, I guess, except they don't do these no more. Now, what sets this particular batch apart is every last one hails from the exact same year—that'd be 1876, and that'd also be the same year General Custer took that unfortunate tumble at Little Bighorn." He pulled a single cent from the condom, pinching it between a thumb and forefinger, turning the coin in the sunlight so that the front engraving, a Native American in a feathered headdress, and the reverse side, a circular wreath bound by three arrows, could be glimpsed. "So take a good look at it," he said, handing the penny to whoever was closest to him. "Have at it, go ahead, pass it on around, would you?"

The significance wasn't lost on any of the cavalrymen, nor did anyone appear dismayed while McCreedy went on to remind them that they were now the military descendants of a singular legacy: they belonged, after all, to the 7th Cavalry; they were also soldiers of the Garryowen regiment, named so after the Gaelic drinking song chosen by the 7th Cavalry's infamous lieutenant colonel—George Armstrong Custer—and still whistled or played on occasion by cavalrymen. As fresh recruits back in the States, they had each been given a pamphlet which glorified the 7th Cavalry's history as formidable Indian fighters, the cover adorned with a horseshoe-and-saber shield; their orientation had also included screenings of *They Died with Their Boots On*, in which Errol Flynn portrayed the fated commander, the film depicting the Battle of Little Bighorn and the massacre of Custer and his troops by Sioux Indians.

"Just don't ever lose sight of that," McCreedy said, his voice taking on a serious, melodramatic tone. "When you're feeling low or unsure of what's going on in this godforsaken country, you just remember you belong to the great Seventh Cavalry, and your role, like them what served ahead of us, is to clean the land of ignorant hostiles and pave the way to a better world. It's a true calling, I believe. It's our chance to settle an old score on behalf of those two hundred brave brothers that lost their lives to the savages at Little Bighorn."

However, it was apparent very few of the men, aside from Schubert Tang, actually had much regard for McCreedy (how they rolled their eyes or shook their heads behind his back, making fun of his pennies and loud, annoying big talk whenever he wasn't around), although he was tolerated out of necessity and, to a greater degree, because he was the single most intimidating, unpredictable one among them. Even so, it amazed Hollis that soft spoken, introverted Schubert had—since coming off the transport ship onto Korean soil—followed McCreedy like a devoted puppy, and, as a result, was offered a fair amount of kindness and respect, in spite of Schubert belonging to what McCreedy called the Mud Races.

The unlikely bond formed by the two happened early on at the bivouac near P'ohang, when four soldiers from another company gathered around Schubert as he walked alone to the mess tent, taunting him for being a gook, asking him what the hell gave him the nerve to join a white man's army. It was the sudden arrival of McCreedy—putting himself between Schubert and the soldiers, towering over all of them—who shut the foursome up with an extended, jabbing index finger, explaining he would thrash anyone who dared suggest that someone born and raised in the United States of America was a gook, especially if that someone was of Chink descent and was still willing to risk his life against the communist threat perpetuated by his own genetic background. The soldiers found themselves lacking the collective or individual wherewithal to respond, and thinking better of further provoking the wild-eyed Texan by uttering another word, they slinked sheepishly away like bullied children. From then on, Schubert and McCreedy were almost inseparable, eating together, playing cards together, swapping stories, loaning each other cigarettes or matches: the outspoken bigot and the only Asian in the group had become the best of friends. So however Hollis wanted to feel about McCreedy, there now appeared in his inward sight the image of a man at once brave and impossible to gauge.

While Bill McCreedy might have deliberately gone out of his way to be a kind of parody of himself, a one-dimensional hick archetype which had already become a common caricature in any number of B movies or war magazines, he would remain, to Hollis, a tangible person who had actually existed at one time. With that Mohawk which drew the scorn of their platoon sergeant, the expressive sunburned face shining beneath the dimmest of lights, he wasn't unsociable or withdrawn like Hollis, and so, by nature, he relished the lowbrow chatter which probably tempered his own fears— talk of women, tall tales from childhood, the mindless jests, general bull-shitting—the rite of strengthening ties with the brotherhood of soldiers. Yet for all his contempt and swagger and annoying bluster, McCreedy wasn't compassionless or incapable of conveying a genuine Christian demeanor, although, upon reflection, Hollis could only recall one other incident in which he saw McCreedy behave as the Lord would have done.

It was on a desolate road leading from Yongdong, where fleeing villagers and townspeople streamed southward to escape the fighting, the long procession repeatedly sent dashing to the roadsides when retreating U.S. Army vehicles barreled past them. Disoriented by the thick dust spun high by military tires, an elderly monk lost control of his bicycle and swerved into the path of a speeding jeep, his peddling left leg struck by the bumper, his body then thrown over the hood—airborne for a second, his gray robe fluttering, landing with a dull thud behind the braking jeep—as the bicycle continued wobbling forward without him. In the upheaval of dust and halting vehicles and startled onlookers, the monk was crushed beneath the front wheel of another jeep, his certain end occurring at the exact moment that the second jeep's horn briefly rang out. The bicycle, miraculously intact, veered several yards beyond the accident, crashing, at last, on the other side of the road—the contents of its saddle baskets dumped beside a sloping embankment, scattered near the boots of a twelve-man reconnaissance patrol from the 2nd Battalion. While horrified refugees on both sides of the road froze in their tracks, and the caravan of army vehicles rolled to a stop, a sudden quiet overtook the clamor, punctuated only by McCreedy's enraged voice rising among the reconnaissance patrol, shouting, "Son of a bitch!"

Before the dust swirling about the accident had fully dissipated, McCreedy lifted the bicycle, promptly turning it around. With his rifle slung across his back, he straddled the seat, and, shaking his head in disgust, proceeded to ride the short distance to where the monk's slack body was already being dragged from underneath the jeep. But it wasn't the stunned-looking young driver—wiping grime and sweat off his brow with a handkerchief, telling everyone, "Didn't even see him; it's like he dropped out of the sky or something"—who ultimately lowered himself to the body, nor was the monk held by the hands of the white-clad refugees who soon came running from both sides of the road, gawking at the tragedy in hushed voices; instead, it was McCreedy who cradled the old man, bending close to his shaved scalp, briefly uttering something into a bloodied ear, doing so as Hollis watched from afar, a cigarette fuming at his lips, the smoke curling upward into the brim of his helmet.

The monk's killing was, in fact, the first fatality they were to encounter during the conflict, and, in a way, it would be the most benign of all the deaths they were ultimately destined to witness. Yet many years since then, Hollis found himself wondering what it was McCreedy had spoken to the corpse, though at the time he had assumed it was a prayer, perhaps a blessing intended for the monk's departing soul. Or maybe—he considered when revisiting the accident in his mind—the words weren't as ecumenical or holy as he had imagined, maybe McCreedy had kept it simple, base, and impersonal: "Too fucking bad for you, buddy. Tough break." He would, of course, never really know, and, as such, he finally concluded that whatever had been said was irrelevant: the act of rushing to the accident—lifting that battered body, holding the dead man while others did nothing—was the meaningful part of the memory, if only because it served to remind him that McCreedy was, after all, a contradiction of sorts and, therefore, more human than Hollis had eventually wanted to believe.

And so on that road leading from Yongdong, McCreedy stayed for a while with the monk's body—shaking his head again and again, glancing up at the bicycle he left propped against the jeep and the driver who stood beside it with his eyes down. Before trudging forward to get a better look, Hollis finished his cigarette, blowing a final exhalation of smoke at a blue sky which was unfurling beyond fading currents of dust; just then the sun broke through that brownish filter, casting its rays to the ground, illuminating those items which had been in the bicycle's baskets and were now several feet away from the red cloth which had safeguarded them, two bundles wrapped in fishing wire: a packet of flat, slender lengths of polished metal; another packet of narrow, unfinished planks of wood; the metal and wood being of equal size—approximately twelve inches long and two inches wide, fifteen to twenty pieces per bundle—with hanja characters meticulously carved or etched lengthwise upon each one. A few metal pieces glinted brightly in the increasing sunlight, catching Hollis's attention and blunting his sight for a moment when he flicked the cigarette butt at them.

"Is he a goner?" someone in the patrol asked.

"If he isn't," someone else replied, "he's about to be."

Then while McCreedy held the monk, Hollis knelt in front of the old man's possessions, inspecting the bundle of metal pieces which glimmered back at him and reflected his ruddy face. Presently, he reached for the wooden planks, studying the ornate, scroll-like writing, the characters filled in with black ink—messages which would forever be impossible for him to fathom, as cryptic to his memory now as the words he once saw imparted into a fallen monk's ear.

8

"Wood and metal? What on earth is that going to do to me?" Debra had wondered, upon learning that her chemotherapy infusions were to be a mixture of two drugs: Taxol, derived from the bark of the Pacific yew tree, and carboplatin, from the valuable metal class used to create jewelry. "I'll probably become a robotic tin man with an ax."

"Surely a tin woman," Dr. Langford said. "But right now I wouldn't worry too much about that."

Then the autumn after her five-month therapy had commenced was passed in waiting, the slow, indeterminate days initially marked by the long strands of her hair discovered all over the house; sometimes the hairs ended up in unforeseen places—plastered on the TV screen, resting at the bottom of a coffee mug, hanging from the front doorknob—until, as an act of empowering herself, she decided to take control and buzz-trim her head to a fine quarter-inch stubble. "If it's going to happen anyway," she said, "why prolong the agony of it?" But soon the velveteen stubble also began shedding, dotting their sheets and pillows like benign, identically made splinters. In a further attempt at empowerment, she eventually stripped off whatever was left of her hair with a lint roller, emerging from the bathroom balder than she had been at birth, her eyebrows, too, no longer existing on her face. She stood before Hollis in an untied terry-cloth robe, her naked body lacking a single pubic hair (the absence of which, she realized soon enough, hampered her ability to use the toilet without making a mess—the thick, curling pubes having previously funneled the urine flow into a well-aimed stream). "Just call me Mrs. Clean," she told him, clutching the hair-matted lint roller in one hand, concealing her self-consciousness with a grin, even as he appeared mortified by just how thoroughly the job had been done.

"My lord," Hollis said, rising from where he had sat at the foot of their bed, walking gingerly toward her, his gaze traveling the circumference of her oval-shaped head.

"Well, what do you think?"

"I don't know," he said. "You look like you, but not like you." He extended a palm outward, bringing it to her tender scalp, letting it glide about on the smooth surface. "You look like a blank canvas, Deb."

"If only that were true," she replied, and at that moment a shiver shot through her body, producing goose pimples on her bare shoulders and arms, as if to signal the premature arrival of the dry, brisk winter months. Then the colder season found her coughing and sneezing more than ever before: surely a weakened immune system, she and Hollis had concluded; for a while, each abrupt wheeze from her mouth or nose—every single hack or sudden nasal eruption—was accompanied by an uncontrollable release of urine, to the point where Debra began relying on what she liked to refer to as adult diapers. "Never saw myself as the depending-on-Depends type," she'd told Hollis at Costco, after he had lowered two bulk-size packages of the moisture-absorbing undergarments into their shopping cart.

Since they hadn't yet formed any close acquaintants at Nine Springs, no one sought them out during that first winter, and, for the most part, the weeks between Debra's treatments were spent in relative solitude. Hollis whiled away the hours by doing landscaping in the backyard, cooking their meals, and strolling the aisles of Home Depot or Costco. There was also his increasingly questionable, slow-going autobiography, resumed now and then whenever Debra had urged him to keep writing, given the working title of *The Hardest of the Hard: A Young Soldier's Story of Adversity & Courage*

Under Fire; but with only a few pages completed, there wasn't yet the heroic wartime tale or narrative structure he had envisioned—that account of glorified half-truths he intended to composite from the published fictional accounts of others while omitting much of what he had actually seen or done in Korea. However, it was a return to drawing and painting which gave him the kind of immediate satisfaction writing just didn't provide, rekindling a hobby which had been dormant for decades and allowing him the opportunity to engage in an honest form of creative expression.

So on Friday afternoons, Hollis attended the two-hour Painting Your Life class at the local Funtivities Center, where—for a $58 monthly enrollment fee—he was supplied with colored pens, pastels, oil paints, watercolors, brushes, and large sheets of white construction paper. With a single assignment given at the start of every session (Compose a dream you've had—Depict your favorite place—Make a self-portrait—Sketch something you like to eat) and offering a minimal amount of instruction, the classes were reserved, meditative affairs set around four circular tables which could each seat five to eight participants. Under the roving presence of the soft-spoken and diminutive Mrs. Ambrose, a retired art-history adjunct professor from the University of Arizona, Hollis completed every assignment in less than an hour, always excusing himself before those around him had finished their pieces (his weekly creation carried across the parking lot in one hand, rolled up tightly as he headed for the Suburban, destined to be placed on a garage cabinet shelf).

But a couple of his paintings had caught Mrs. Ambrose's attention, bringing her to hover above his shoulders, her bifocals dangling from a silver chain and brushing against his neck. "Oh, I like this, very unusual," she had said while watching him add a light blue sky to a pastel-based image showing a half-naked man and boy, their heads concealed behind gas masks; and then, two weeks later, she repeated the sentiment when gazing down at a self-portrait which had Hollis surrounded by a purple-crimson background, arms at his side as he stood near a white cow and in front of a blackish tree with bloodred leaves. "Oh, I like this, Mr. Adams. I like what you're doing here—the symbolism of the tree, the colors you've used—figurative while also abstract. Now tell me what you're trying to convey in this?"

Lifting a red pastel he was using from the construction paper, Hollis regarded his self-portrait as if he were viewing it anew. "You know, I can't say for sure," he said, his words preceded by a faint sigh. "I guess I don't really know. It sort of just came to me, I suppose."

Mrs. Ambrose raised her bifocals, holding them at her nose like a magnifying glass. "Well, it seems rather personal, don't you think? Perhaps you're addressing something about your childhood, a longing for days gone by."

"Perhaps that's it," he said, lowering the red pastel to the paper. "It could be, sure," and with that he began working again.

Debra, on the other hand, occasionally took tai chi and ceramics classes at the Funtivities Center, although she usually occupied herself with escapist fiction, managing to track down and read the forty-six novels of Rex Stout's Nero Wolfe series; at the same time, she could not resist owning another escapist collection of sorts: shunning the typical line of chemotherapy wigs, she acquired instead various specialty hairpieces which added an elegant or humorous touch to her otherwise barren appearance (Illusion by Eva Gabor, Encounter by Revlon, Action by Raquel Welch, as well as a blond beehive, and a Princess Leia wig), wearing whichever one suited her mood when heading to the grocery store or into Tucson for treatment. But she quickly grew tired of such novelty items. In the latter half of that winter, she began leaving the wigs at home, deciding to venture outside adorned only with a bandanna or a purple Arizona Diamondbacks baseball cap, sunglasses, and a charcoal-filtered surgical mask to help protect her lowered immune system; although none of what she wore could hide the lethargy which had finally descended upon her—a deepening lethargy, Hollis believed, not based solely on the effects of the monthly chemo infusions but, rather, because she could also no longer deny a feeling of having been horribly betrayed by her own body.

Thereafter, their days and nights elapsed in quiet uncertainty, both waiting for the next round of treatment or some clear-cut sign that the infusions were working, hoping for a positive outcome to the ordeal, and for the colder months to conclude so they could at last open up the windows on warmer evenings. During one of those chilly nights when they were sitting together on the living-room couch—speaking very little while the fireplace crackled nearby, lost in their own thoughts as the TV played in front of them—Debra suddenly announced she wasn't the same person anymore, that she had become someone far removed from the woman he had married and the woman she had imagined herself as always being, saying this with the softest of voices.

"Why do you think that?" Hollis asked.

"Honestly, take a good look at me," she said. "Everything about me has changed. I'm not really me, not really me at all. I'm a complete stranger to myself."

Meeting her eyes, he shook his head; he wished to counter her view of herself, to let her know she wasn't any different, that she was still Deb, that once the cancer and chemo were gone she would feel like her old self again, that none of the physical manifestations of her illness, or its treatment, could ever completely alter her intrinsic qualities—except he wasn't sure if that was the case. In truth, she had changed dramatically during a relatively short period of time: as opposed to her usual energetic, outgoing nature, she'd grown increasingly listless and withdrawn, her movements were sluggish, she often spent more hours sleeping than awake; hairlessness aside, her skin, too, had a shiny, almost translucent veneer; from maintaining an irregular sleeping pattern, dark circles had formed like bruises beneath her eyes, her voice had a languid, detached tone—and mirroring those retirement-home shut-ins unable to tend to their own basic needs, there was sometimes a yielding look in her stare. Hollis placed a hand on her leg and returned his gaze to the television program, saying nothing.

Debra's debility wasn't entirely unexpected or alarming; in fact, Dr. Langford had cautioned them ahead of treatment about what was likely to occur. "Chemo brain," the doctor had called it, smiling wryly while the term was spoken. "The effect is real, but I can tell you now the medical community doesn't totally understand it." The cognitive condition was, as Dr. Langford explained, only temporary. "You might experience some forgetfulness—dull thinking, mental fogginess, that kind of impairment—most likely during chemotherapy, although some women have reported it lingering for a while once therapy was completed. What you might notice is a difficulty finding the right words when talking, or an inability to write or phrase sentences as quickly as you're used to. If it becomes a problem, my best advice is to keep your mind engaged. Continue doing work-related tasks, reading, whatever your hobbies are. Don't stop doing what you enjoy, that's the most important thing."

As it happened, the onset of chemo brain gradually made it impossible for Debra to fully absorb her mystery novels, or stick with the plots of her favorite TV shows, or concentrate while playing a simple game of Skip-Bo. Yet her sense of humor remained, illustrated by the Post-it notes she left scattered around the house—inside the refrigerator (*Buy Me Cheesecake Before It's Too Late*), beneath the bathroom mirror (*It Is a Good Day to Be Bald*), at the end of the kitchen counter (*Dear, Remove the Enya CD from the Stereo & Please Remind Me Again That "Sail Away" Isn't Helping Anyone Feel Better*)—and, much to Hollis's amusement, on the breast pocket of her own shirt: *Hi, My Name Is Debra. Who Are You?* Another saving grace was the absence of several afflictions commonly associated with chemotherapy— nausea, vomiting, constipation, diarrhea, loss of appetite—all of which were kept at bay by the antiemetic and antianxiety medication she received just prior to, and then directly following, every round of treatment.

Even so, for five or six days after each infusion, she experienced other side effects which had little or no remedy: fatigue, numbness in her fingertips and toes, difficulty picking up or holding objects, ringing in her ears, aching joints, blistering inside her mouth. Now and again, her limbs behaved spasmodically—her hands twitched violently for a second at the kitchen table, her knees jerked upward while she sat upright—as if her reflexes had been tested by a ghost. These instantaneous fits weren't without consequences: twice in one evening, the table was disrupted from the swift, hard bounce of her knees—a glass of water knocked over, the salad bowls sent wobbling, the plates and silverware made askew with the earthquake-like jolt she had delivered.

"Christ almighty!" she said the second time it occurred, pressing her hands against her legs to keep them anchored.

"It's all right," Hollis told her, going for the paper towels.

"This is so stupid."

"Don't worry about it."

"This is the stupidest thing I've ever known."

From where he now stood at the counter, Hollis glanced back at her, seeing a quizzical expression appear on her face, observing how, just then, her body trembled almost imperceptibly beside the shaken table. And so, too, there was an ineffable cold, infiltrating her marrow, keeping her bundled in jackets or sweaters throughout the days—even as the heater was set higher than what it should be, even as Hollis sweated indoors and often lounged in shorts and a tank top. Regardless of the heat, the sight of her shivering, the way she kept herself wrapped up, had a contagious influence. Later that night, he enveloped her on the couch, draping her like a blanket of flesh, warming her with his broad chest. But no matter how hot it actually was inside the house, he couldn't avoid her body's insinuation of winter, feeling his internal temperature drop and his blood thicken—like frigid soil shifting underneath a warmer layer of sand—while, at the same time, his brow glistened in the living room, his forehead reflected the flames coursing above the hearth.

That bone-deep, impalpable chill would shudder Hollis awake some weeks afterward, and—absently reaching an arm under the sheets for Debra, bringing his fingers to her side of the bed—he discovered a flat, coarse slab where his wife was expected to be resting. "Deb—?" In the early morning, as their bedroom remained shadowed behind drawn curtains, he explored the rough exterior his hand had settled upon; half conscious and with eyes still shut, his palm slid across rock-hard grooves, miniature plateaus and valleys: like a topography map, he thought while gradually stirring, like a landscape. "Deb—?" Turning his body toward her side of the bed, opening his eyes and blinking within the dim room, he first perceived her orthopedic pillow, observing the empty, curved space which hours earlier had cupped her head. He scanned the bedding, and, rising on an elbow, saw no sign of her sleeping body, or of anything else which hinted at the thing he had touched beneath the comforter. With a degree of apprehension he pulled back the sheets, revealing what appeared to be a shriveled, calcified form—a dark, asymmetrical puddle of a shape, perhaps two inches in height, three feet in length, his palm resting at its approximate center. "Deb——?" he said once more, quickly retracting his hand as if his skin had been grazed by fire.

A bedside lamp soon cast its light on the mattress, illuminating for Hollis a slender, reddish piece of flagstone—taken from a pile he had stacked by the back-porch door, something he had planned to use for the garden walkway—nestled now into the bedding like it had grown there overnight, spotting the sheets with flecks of sand and dirt. The fog of sleep lifted, summoning Debra's groggy voice in his memory, speaking aloud as she had wandered out of the room at dawn, "Can't take this anymore. I'm freezing to death." But he didn't recall her returning with the flagstone; he didn't feel the sheets being tucked, or yet understand—until after getting up to check on her, calling her name as he wandered down the hallway—she had hoped the flagstone might maintain a warm spot for her when she wasn't in bed.

Finding her awake but curled up on the living-room floor—covered by a heating blanket plugged into a nearby wall outlet, lounging like a cat where sunlight spilled through the window and brightened an area of the carpet—he breathed a dramatic sigh of relief before asking about the flagstone, mentioning the dirt in the sheets, eventually saying, "I don't understand. Why couldn't you use your heating blanket instead?"

She regarded him with confused and somehow questioning eyes and, giving the slightest of nods at his words, shut the mystery paperback she was reading, bookmarking the pages with an index finger, and answered, "That'd be fine, dear, except you forget I need my heating blanket here."

"I'll buy us another blanket, how's that?"

At this she frowned, saying, "You'd just be wasting money."

"Why would I be wasting money?"

"You just would."

She smiled involuntarily but, Hollis believed, she was trying not to sob. Only then did he become seriously concerned for her mental health—that, maybe, a full-blown depression was looming, fueled in part by the haze of chemo brain. And, too, he wondered—while preparing their breakfast, while boiling water for instant oatmeal—if they hadn't isolated themselves in a way which had been counterproductive to the cancer-fighting process.

As it was, he had kept his attention on the recognizable characteristics of her outward health—how much or little she ate, how tired or rested she appeared, how much energy she did or didn't have—that her fluctuating mind-set never really entered into his thoughts; she had, after all, always been better than he at keeping her spirits afloat. No, I'm not very good at this, he realized as the kettle began vibrating on the stove. You need someone else to talk to, another voice besides mine.

And later—it was afternoon, the sun was high above the backyard and the heating blanket she wore had been exchanged for a sweatshirt—when he nervously, haltingly brought up the idea of her seeking support ("It could be useful—I mean, if you felt like it would help—or not, I mean, I don't know—"), she replied without any pause at the dining table, as if she'd been awaiting the moment: "I suspect you're right. I've imagined it might take the edge off things, I guess." Then upon her face for the first time in weeks spread a genuine look of ease.

"So you've thought about it already?"

"I have." Between them was a turquoise-colored teapot, steaming with ginseng oolong, a souvenir they had purchased years ago in Santa Fe. She reached forward, taking hold of the pot's handle, and she repeated, pouring tea into his cup as if sealing a deal: "I have, yes."

"Fine," he said, spooning brown sugar from a matching turquoise bowl. "Fine," he said again, swirling the sugar around in his cup.

Soon enough the dining table would be cleared, the cups and bowl and pot and spoons placed inside the dishwasher by Hollis while Debra cradled the telephone against her neck, speaking to Dr. Langford—her right hand gripping a pen and jotting down information, filling several Post-it notes throughout the conversation. On the following Tuesday—having left Nine Springs near noon, driving under an overcast sky—she removed those same notes from her purse, sticking them to the dashboard as Hollis sped the Suburban toward Tucson. As usual, they said scarcely a word during the trip—Debra applying lipstick and eyeliner in the visor mirror, Hollis fiddling with the radio dial—and eventually they stared beyond the windshield, and watched the desert transform, the bare landscape bleeding into a more populous region of dying strip malls and brown-stucco apartment complexes, where, with the Post-it notes heeded, they arrived at their destination seven minutes early.

"Here you go," Hollis said, when pulling the Suburban along the curb, the passenger door slowly aligning with the front walkway of the Gilda's Club building.

"Isn't quite what I expected," Debra said, gazing from the side window, noticing a few small drops of rain which had begun hitting the sidewalk.

"Doesn't seem bad."

"I suppose."

Dr. Langford had told her the local Gilda's Club provided a homelike setting—a relaxed support environment for those with any type of cancer, offering group counseling sessions and educational workshops—but she hadn't expected it to be located within a converted one-story redbrick house (situated on a residential street, the front yard consisting of tall ocotillos and sizable agaves). For a while, she sat inside the Suburban, the brim of her Diamondback cap pulled discreetly down to her painted eyebrows, watching as a solitary, hunched figure in a hooded clear-plastic parka—it was impossible to tell if the person was a man or a woman, young or old—moved up the walkway with a portable oxygen tank, going like a snail toward the front door in abbreviated, labored steps. No sooner had the figure managed to enter the house when—appearing from nowhere, swooping behind the Suburban like a band of crows—four black umbrellas fluttered across the rearview mirror, startling Hollis for a split second before coming into full view on Debra's side: each held by a quartet of almost identical-appearing hairless, tight-lipped, middle-aged women (monks, was Hollis's immediate impression, a procession of monks), clenching the umbrella handles with both hands as if holding large crucifixes aloft, marching single file to the sidewalk and up the rain-spattered walkway.

"All right," she said, half sighing, "those look like my people. I guess I shouldn't tarry any longer."

"Want me to come?"

"No, no, I'm okay," she said, digging her surgical mask from her purse. "I'll brave it alone. Go do errands, just make sure you're back in an hour.

Don't forget to pick up the HEPA filter that's on sale at Home Depot. I put the coupon in your wallet."

"You sure? I don't mind coming with you. We can finish the errands on the way home."

"I'm sure," she said, sliding the mask over her face, affixing the elastic loops around her ears. Then she leaned forward and kissed him, her gauze-covered lips briefly pressing his cheek. "See you in a bit," were her muffled parting words, and with that she was out of the Suburban, holding her purse against her stomach, wandering away from him without looking back, the leaden movements of her legs conveying a measure of reluctance. He started the engine, but instead of leaving he remained there a little while longer, his stare trailing her into the house, lingering outside once she had entered the place and the front door was shut behind her: how absent of human activity the house suddenly looked—how desolate the empty walkway seemed to him, touched only by droplets which banished dust to the edges of their imperfect circles.

He returned in fifty-four minutes, parking at the exact spot. Already Debra had emerged from the house, loitering on the front porch in the company of two other bald-headed women (all three wearing surgical masks, all three speaking and gesticulating like old friends as the sky continued spitting rain). Impromptu hugs were given when Hollis was noticed, small slips of paper changed hands, and then Debra waved a quick goodbye while crossing to where he waited. Less than an hour had elapsed, yet now—it seemed to him—Debra's entire mood was elevated; her steps toward the Suburban were somehow light and confident, as opposed to the reserved gait which had taken her through the entrance of Gilda's Club.

"So how'd it go?" he asked, taking her purse for her as she climbed in beside him.

"Good," was her definitive answer.

He waited for her to elaborate further—the door closed, the seat belt was grabbed—but when nothing else was forthcoming, he, too, said, "Good."

As they headed home that afternoon, the invigorated spirit Debra had shown on the porch of Gilda's Club had faded by the time the Suburban exited Tucson's city limits. Hollis, feeling somewhat excluded from her new-found support, found himself wanting to know what had been discussed inside the house, but seeing her sitting rigid on the seat—the way in which she gazed ahead with an uncommunicative, absorbed demeanor—he decided it was better to hold off asking. And as their mutual silence took on an evasive air and the rain fell harder, an aura of gloom saturated the Suburban's interior—enhanced by the incessant squeaking of the windshield wipers, the blasts of static cutting into the radio signal—until, at last, she glanced at him, saying, "I think we should laugh more. I think it's important we do that, don't you?"

"They say it's the best medicine, right?" He had spoken immediately, eager to vanquish that indefinite sense of melancholy.

"That's right. And I could use the levity, and I think you could, too. We need to laugh at least once a day, okay? Can we do that?"

Can we do that?

He forced a grin, deciphering the true meaning of what she was requesting: You've always been good at making me laugh, he thought. Now you're wanting me to do the same for you. "I'll try," he said, nodding. "I'll give it a shot."

Nevertheless, Hollis had no illusions: he knew he wasn't a man with a humorous disposition, someone who could easily produce witty, pointed remarks—like Debra and Lon did—using an illogical, cryptic, sarcastic, or ironic statement to accentuate the underlying heart of a given matter, however grave it might be on the surface. Humor had never lurked in his gene pool; he came from reserved northern stock, stoic people—women who frowned when laughs were warranted, men who looked confused when wry comments were delivered instead of rote punch lines. Yet his desire to amuse wasn't fully muted, although his attempts were often expressed as the inchoate clowning of the unfunny: exterior displays which almost never went deeper than silly faces, farting noises, bad puns, jokes overheard on the golf course but retold without the appropriate context or timing.

"Say, Deb, did you hear what the upset inflatable teacher said to the irresponsible inflatable student in the inflatable school?"

"You've told me that one, dear."

"I have? Are you sure?"

"Listen, not only have you let me down, you've let yourself down, and you've let the whole school down."

"Oh, yeah, you've heard it already."

On some unspoken level Hollis believed humor was a luxury, an idle pursuit, but something not really suited for a planet which was, for the most part, deadly serious and historically devoid of cheap gags. A topical joke, a clever retort, farcical metaphors, oblique satire—these were modern human constructs, offered by those who, perhaps, dodged reality by enticing others to laugh aloud at their nonsensical utterances. As such, a physical act—an exaggerated facial expression of sadness, anger, fear, or a stumbling pratfall in a restaurant—was a lot funnier to him than a smug touch of verbal irony, because the overwrought gyrations of the body just felt more authentic and, therefore, undeniable. That being the case, he was usually funniest when he wasn't trying to be funny at all.

But it was almost a week following the Gilda's Club meeting—after Debra had awakened from a nap on the couch feeling morose again with no prospect of recovery and, subsequently, Hollis ended up standing within their large walk-in closet, having traced her path from the living room to the bedroom by collecting a trail of her discarded clothing and then depositing the sweatshirt, sweatpants, socks, and panties into the laundry hamper—before he made a deliberate effort to bring much-needed humor to his wife's day. Inside the closet, he could hear water hissing through the pipes concealed between the walls, the metallic grind of hot/cold knobs turning as Debra took a warm shower in the adjacent master bathroom; and, from where he stood, his eyes were drawn to an upper shelf, scanning the row of five life-size Styrofoam busts which stared down at him: the nondescript effigies being exactly alike save for a distinct specialty wig setting each one apart.

His long arms reached over the shelf, his fingers grasped the neck of a bust and—applying slight yet firm pressure on the Styrofoam skin, careful so it wouldn't slip from his hands—lowered it toward him. Now he was face-to-face with the disembodied head of what he perceived to be a woman (white skin, long narrow nose, white and pupilless eyeballs, sporting a blond beehive which towered above her pure white forehead). Soon the bust would be returned, placed back on the shelf among its other well-coifed sisters, but, looking now more akin to Debra, absent of the hair which had signified its uniqueness. He quickly made two round-trips from the closet: searching the drawers of his wife's vanity table for lipstick, browsing her coats and jackets hanging beneath the busts, studying his reflection in the vanity-table mirror, positioning himself just beyond the closet's open door and—upon hearing the shower knobs whine, the water's diminishing hiss—clicking off the closet light.

And so in semidarkness he waited, keeping perfectly still as he listened, monitoring Debra's movements through the thin plaster walls. She rattled the sliding shower doors. He envisioned her feet pressing against the fuzzy green bath mat—right foot first, left foot next—patting herself dry with a towel at the same time. Then she was wiping steam from the mirror prior to briefly running the sink. Then she stepped onto the scale—right foot first, left foot next—weighing herself. At last, she exited the bathroom, wandering slowly into the bedroom, the towel wrapped around her chest (covering her breasts and waist, concealing the scar which served as a bitter reminder). But she didn't go straight to the closet; instead, she crossed the room, heading for the window—where, pushing fingertips against her barren crown, she stared at the backyard, eventually cocking her head, and, from Hollis's vantage point, seemed to shift her gaze to the clear, sharp winter sky.

When she did turn, her stare settled on the closet doorway, except he wasn't certain if she immediately saw him or not. Presently, she eased forward, coming toward him, her eyes narrowing and her brow wrinkling, becoming aware of an obscured form loitering within the dim closet—something tall, imposing, yet barely perceptible. She wasn't sure if she was really seeing something or someone there; she would tell Hollis this later, she would explain that the chemo brain played tricks on her—the hazy, unfocused nature of the condition had produced its share of apparitions in recent weeks, half-glimpsed figures seen at the corners of her eyes which vanished whenever she glanced their way, shadows roaming outside and darting past the curtains, fleeting refractions of indistinct living things (Yes, I've seen them, too, he would wish to reveal but didn't. I've seen them for as long as I can remember, he would want to say but decided otherwise).

Now she hesitated in front of the closet, peering ahead, squinting. One arm kept the towel from falling while the other arm stretched for the light switch. But it wasn't her fingers which hit the switch; rather, it was Hollis who cast light on himself, illuminating in an instant what, to his mind, was surely a hysterical vision: a hulking she-beast made even bulkier by a full-length long-hair beaver fur coat—the shawl collar bunched along the neckline, framing Hollis's deliberately dour and absurd face (a thick layer of crimson lipstick shining on his mouth, the beehive wig camouflaging his thinning hair and tilting to one side like the Leaning Tower of Pisa). Except Debra didn't react as he had imagined she would; she didn't start at the looming, ridiculous sight of him and then cackle wildly. Instead, a gasp of true horror escaped her, released at the very second her body jolted as if she had received an electrical shock—her arms reflexively flailing outward, her eyes widening—and the towel dropped away from her body, exposing her pale, vulnerable flesh. Fixing him with an unforgiving glare, her entire body began trembling. "Don't you do that!" she yelled, seething at him as her hands curled into fists. "Don't you ever do that to me!"

"Sorry—I—it isn't—"

"Damnit, Hollis!"

In a way, it was Hollis who was the more startled of the two, for he had miscalculated badly, and, as such, he was promptly consumed by embarrassment and an increasing shame—as if he, too, were viewing himself like Debra was at that moment: a suddenly confused man stammering near his naked, sick wife, grimacing under a beehive wig, shoulders slumping beneath a fur coat.

"I didn't mean to—I was only trying—"

She shook her head while bending to retrieve the towel. Then she faced him again, her head shaking less and less, searching his flustered expression.

"I'm sorry," he said, steadying his voice, wiping the lipstick from his lips with the back of his hand, unintentionally smearing a crooked trail of red across his chin. "I guess I'm just not very funny today."

And that, for reasons which were completely lost on Hollis, finally moved her to laughter. "Deb—?" Her fingers clicked off the closet light, her hand pulled the closet door shut; her laughter continued for a while elsewhere as he remained standing there alone, frowning at himself in darkness.

9

So another year with cancer passed for Debra; the once bare surface of her head had gradually been replenished, sprouting fine, short gray-blond hair which never grew very thick or long. But the rounds of chemotherapy were already exhausted—various first-line treatments using Taxol and carbo-platin, Doxil, topotecan, carboplatin and Gemzar—allowing for just a single clinical trial as the last resort (the wishful belief in hope dwindling into the marginal territory of miracles). And now an early winter has come—arriving without warning like a presentiment of something inexorable, mak ing the backyard desolate—and Lon, as if not to be outdone by Debra, has also fallen ill with cancer, leaving Hollis wanting for his friend's summer companionship, that gruff humor and intoxicated bombast: the continuous derision regarding the clean streets they drove together, the monotonous homes they tenant, or—as was often the case—the other retired men who had regularly patted their shoulders on the golf course greens.

"Metaphorical fascists, most of them," Lon had said inside the hut, scratching at an earlobe with the rim of an empty Tecate can.

"How so?" Hollis responded.

"Lord, just take a good look at them sometime. Look how they act so damn smug, how they dress almost identically. Reminds me of ham actors all auditioning for the same lousy part."

Lon sighed with disgust, shaking his head amid the shadows as Hollis said, "What the hell are you talking about? That's how we dress. It's golfing attire, Lon. What else are we supposed to wear?"

Lon's head-shaking transformed into an emphatic nodding. "Exactly," he said. "That's my point right there. Hand me a beer, would you?"

In a way, they were like a pair of bothersome teenagers last summer, restless and hardly content, rippling still waters—withered adolescents racing their customized golf carts (Lon's black Humdinger, that prized miniaturized Hummer; Hollis's replica '57 Chevy, baby blue with canopy top, bucket seats, and coat frame), speeding on cart lanes, driving by parks where the only children they ever saw were attentive retirees strolling beside a feeble parent. Few streets were spared their wheels, their fateful bleating horns which created such a ruckus beneath the palm tree rows—the clarion call of two men intent on sailing kamikaze golf balls through the air, shooting them at the roofs of uninhabited homes, where the balls landed hard on reddish-tiled shingles and quickly dropped into yards marked with FOR SALE signs.

"How do you think they went, Hollis?" They had parked at the end of a cul-de-sac, bringing themselves to stand several yards away from three recently vacated homes—a Ponderosa, a Cheyenne, a Durango. Lon set a ball on the asphalt, squinting while he considered his target. "Think Alzheimer's caught up with them?"

"Maybe."

Taking a stance like a pro, Lon readied his hulking body for the shot. "Or a massive coronary?"

"Could be."

Coiling his knees, hips, and shoulders when turning into his backswing, Lon soon launched the ball neatly from the ground. "Or harboring grandkids without the association's permission?"

"Beats me," Hollis said, watching as the ball arched beyond them, curving downward, promptly striking the Cheyenne's roof with a *thack*— bouncing twice on the shingles, over the roof, out of sight.

"I'm putting my money on Alzheimer's. What about you?"

"I don't know," Hollis replied. Could easily be a stroke, he thought.

Could be a fractured hip. Could be death absolute—like the rapid demise of fellow golfers who had swung their clubs near them, like Jeff Turman who scored an ace just minutes prior to total heart failure, his final words being, "Oh, boy—man, this really smarts," before his eyes rolled back into his head and he collapsed while still clutching his five-iron. Or there was quiet, austere Chris Mayhew—complaining of a migraine during tee time, pressing thumbs against his temple—who had changed his mind about playing, deciding instead to return home; shortly thereafter, his wife found him in the living room while ESPN broadcast sports highlights, seemingly napping on his leather recliner chair but, in fact, quite dead (the migraine having apparently been the first rumblings of a cerebral aneurysm).

"Well, better him than us," Lon had insisted after Mayhew's funeral, unaware then—relaxing inside the hut, reeking of Coppertone and alcohol—of the disease already consuming his prostate, a malignancy which would inevitably lead to the gland's elimination; it was a rather minor impasse in comparison to the more troubling plight of Debra, a common ordeal for the men of Nine Springs: "A tonsillectomy for the aged," he would end up calling it. "A real pain in the ass, literally." But throughout the summer Lon had exuded an able-bodied, robust bearing—always maneuvering to get ahead of Hollis while driving their respective carts, clapping louder than everyone else when Anita Mann, a Peggy Lee impersonator, performed at the Sunpalace Arena (the melody of "Is That All There Is?" stuck in his head for days following the concert, piping from him as an off-tune whistle whenever silence prevailed inside the hut)—then mocking the Grim Reaper with deftly aimed golf balls which pelted homes he envisioned as modern, spacious mausoleums.

At least three evenings a week were spent in the indigo hue of Nine Springs' Starlight Grill, the pair sitting at the bar and cooling their sunburned foreheads with frigid swipes of dripping Corona beer bottles. They went on those nights when Mr. Tom Kat played his rhythm-laden Casio in the middle of the dance floor, taking requests and reviving the golden hits of yesteryear beneath a slow-turning mirror ball, crooning to the golf-tired patrons as his deep, often faltering voice was aided by repetitive, syncopated electronic beats. Only later in the summer did the small groups of college-age women breach the security gates of the community, appearing at the grill late into the evenings, dressed casually in cutoff jean shorts, tight T-shirts or tank tops; the girls were always accompanied by one or two tough-looking young men who kept themselves sequestered discreetly at corner tables—baseball caps pulled low or with the bills turned backward—watching apathetically as their female friends danced and sang and flirted with much older, more intoxicated men.

"See, look at that, there's the downside of Viagra," Lon had joked, motioning his beer bottle at one of the girls slinking her way across the dance floor. "Right there in front of us, the inevitable by-product of our reborn hard-ons."

"What do you mean?" Hollis asked.

"They're whores. We've got whores now."

"Really?" Hollis said, squinting to peer out at the dance-floor crowd. "I had no idea."

Another girl sang along to Tom Kat's rendition of "Moon River"— long black hair hanging past her eyes, skinny pale white legs illuminated with the streaking reflections of the mirror ball—as a retiree old enough to be her grandfather recorded her singing into a portable cassette player: the two swayed together on the dance floor, the man holding a microphone at her lips while she lazily wrapped both arms around his wide, hunched shoulders.

"My god, this town is pathetic," Lon chuckled, shaking his head. "What am I doing here?"

And if the answer hadn't been learned early on, Hollis might have then asked Lon why it was he ever chose Nine Springs to begin with. The serenity of the desert, Lon had already told him when they first met on the driving range, their friendship sealed immediately with the knowledge that they had previously served their country with distinction (Hollis in Korea, Lon before him during the Bikini Atoll atomic tests). Moreover, Lon and his wife, Jane, had picked Nine Springs because of the weather—seven glorious months, two cold months, three months of hell—and to improve Jane's overall health (the dry air did wonders for her rheumatism, keeps her in the pink) and, of course, for the fully stocked pro shop, not to mention the rare chance of having a well-kept putting green twenty-five feet from the back porch. Plus, their only child, Michael, lived nearby in Tucson, running an antique shop with his long-term partner. "My boy's gay—lovely kid, though, really wonderful, and so is his companion, Ben. Anyway, the way I see it is that evolution has had enough of my gene pool—mine and Jane's—and probably for good reason, you know."

But when it came down to the *elegant yet cozy* clubhouses, the fitness center, the *world-class amenities*—Lon couldn't stand any of it, especially after two or three drinks. "Contrary to what we want to believe, it's an America that never really was," he had said, resting on an adjacent deck chair, lounging with Hollis beside the swimming pool at dusk. "Just a fantasy of something imagined in hindsight, hallucinated by folks desiring safer neighborhoods, tidy lawns, no noise. See, I didn't know I was fighting a war for this kind of outcome, didn't foresee ending up in a modern version of what some developer thought my country was once like. You know, it's like Disneyland—it's a theme park we've invested in, that's all. I mean, you realize there aren't any springs near here. I bet they draw these names from a couple of hats. Oak—Ridge. Saddle—Springs. Nine—Oak. Saddle—Ridge. Nine—Springs. Really, honestly, it should be called Eighteen Holes."

The words of a Jewish liberal—Hollis had thought—spoken at a Sonoran oasis populated mostly by Baptists who, like Debra, zealously bought Kleenex, chicken tenders, melatonin, and Saint-John's-wort in bulk; they were the knee-jerk opinions of a cynical man who had more than once referred to himself as the Tin Robot God, because of the large collection of rare 1950s Japanese windup toy robots he had amassed over the years. Still, Hollis pointed out, their kind of escape wasn't anything new; and Lon, too, remembered well enough the suburbs of their younger years, the developments expanding for miles and miles from overcrowded city centers— updated army barracks, voguish, economical, affordable, and available to those returning as boyish veterans from distant battles.

"Fought a war too," Hollis said. "Glad I'm living anywhere, if you want to know the truth."

"Fair enough," Lon said, shrugging his shoulders, his face now darkened by the evening. "I'm sure William Levitt would be proud. That bastard isn't spinning in his grave, I'm positive of that."

They brought their arms behind their heads. Hollis scanned the sky for stars, but only succeeded in finding the full moon hanging above the desert. Lon farted and, at almost the same instant, sighed to himself before rising to retrieve another beer.

During the course of that summer, the subject of William Levitt had occasionally worked its way into their conversations, invoked by Lon who always uttered the famous housebuilder's name with a disparate mixture of reverence and contempt. But while Hollis and Debra had actually lived in a Levittown during the mid-1950s, Lon and his wife never did; his oldest brother, Joseph, however, had known Levitt, the two having become acquainted as sailors at the end of World War II. "My brother honestly felt that that guy heeded our best wishes, our fundamental needs and desires." So the story Lon was quick to tell concerning his brother and Levitt—the story he was prone to repeat with increasing degrees of hyperbole—went something like this:

Drunk one night from tequila shots yet clearheaded about what the future required, Levitt was surrounded by other Seabees at a bar, wondering aloud, "What's wanted when this war is done? You want a car. What else? You want that nice house. That's right." Beg, borrow, or steal the money, he urged them all before the night was finished, and then build and build. "Build for yourself, return to civilian life and build for those like yourselves. Our country is a bountiful pasture, we're so blessed. Go build!" From that night on, Joseph imagined Levitt as an avatar of noble plans, considering him to be someone touched by a great vision—someone who was so much more than a fellow sailor, more than just the industrious child of Russian Jewish immigrants.

After the war a handful of men joined Levitt, among them Lon's brother: converts like Christ's apostles, coming back to a homeland which was desperate for rooftops. They, too, lamented the housing crisis, scouting the countryside for suitable property to develop. Wearing gray flannel suits, they struggled up hillsides and gazed across open fields; they recoiled at the sight of trolley cars being sold as homes in Chicago, the antiquated brown-stones and packed apartment buildings, the undisturbed plains and bucolic meadows. They acquired their own machines to get the job started, burrowing under the land, bulldozing the soil into a uniform flatness; it was Levitt's decree: seventeen thousand new homes built on Long Island, the largest housing project in America; seventeen thousand reasonably priced dwellings, twenty miles from New York City.

"The will of mass production," Lon has called it. "The General Motors of the housing industry." And, as it happened, Levitt ruled benevolently as that general of the General Motors of the housing industry, triumphantly sweeping all the pieces from the Monopoly board, catching them and grasping them in a fist, and then sprinkling them like identical box-shaped seeds over the terrain—from Long Island to the outskirts of Philadelphia, turning potato farms into sprawling Levittowns; his homes never once varied, each floor plan design was exactly the same—seven color selections, trees spaced at twenty-eight feet (two and a half trees per house); every home was adorned with a stove, a refrigerator, a Bendix washer, and an Admiral TV.

"You don't have to tell me," Hollis said. "We were there, we know."

"How long did you stay?" Lon asked.

"Almost six years in Philadelphia, I guess. Then my job brought us on out to the West Coast."

"Six years, huh? That long?"

"Really, it wasn't so bad. Pretty ideal for newlyweds, actually. We'd put off any thoughts of starting a family unless we could buy a house of our own. Luckily, we found a Levittowner for around ten grand—before that we were stuck in a cramped little apartment on South Broad Street in Hamilton. In fact, that first house felt like a piece of heaven to us."

It was, Hollis had believed at the time, appropriate modern living for modern lives. Although the commandments were inflexible and absolute, the deeds unwavering: lawns must be mowed every week, laundry could only be hung on rotary racks and never on clotheslines. But most of the residents flourished adequately and multiplied in number; they had willingly entered Levitt's dream without any reservations and thereafter occupied that dream until it became a pervasive reality, as did their newborn children and, eventually, their children's children; this was William Levitt's vision, Lon asserted, this was the future he bequeathed—subsequent generations would know little else besides variations of that expansive, indistinct world of his. Yet, Hollis interjected, there was one man who had rebelled in his own way, who—amidst the many other ticky-tacky homes of Levittown, Pennsylvania—had taken it upon himself to mount a 16" × 12" × 16" gargoyle statue above his porch awning: the stone-chiseled grotesque existing as a unique expression of singularity, so much so that families from other streets hiked blocks out of their way just to stand on the sidewalk, pointing and marveling at it.

"That man wasn't a Hollis by any chance, was he?"

"It's possible," Hollis said, grinning in the light of a full moon.

And it was enough to bring laughter, an incredible guffaw bursting from Lon—such a contagious racket was created, instantly penetrating Hollis's woolly belly button, working its way up to his throat: two balding, hysterical Buddhas, sunburned and intoxicated with something other than just beer, two deck chairs shaking with hilarity on a summer's night. Hollis wouldn't conceive of that inevitable frost, that swirling snowfall, winter; he wouldn't yet feel the cold devouring the heat, that swelter which had nourished his garden while he vacationed inside or near his hut. Nor would he be prepared for the laughter to stop, to trickle into an uneasy silence—a hush made more formidable by the nighttime and Lon's then motionless form.

But Hollis had experienced his rowdy friend's sudden silences before, had glimpsed Lon's squinting, insolvable stare in broad daylight (bloodshot eyes peering above rooftops, aimed for a while at the vacuum of blue sky). Those momentary lapses, he concluded, were probably the result of too much beer and too much heat; for the cumulative aftereffect of both alcohol and Arizona sunlight remained potent even when dusk had passed, capable of inducing a lethargic, insensible state at any time. It was a kind of stupor Hollis associated with gratification, a lulling sensation he had also felt in country club sauna rooms (wrapped naked inside a woolen blanket following a good massage, the sweat oozing like sap from dilated pores). And, indeed, Hollis relished the silent minutes—surveying the backyard or gazing toward the sky—thinking nothing whatsoever, his mind free of preoccupation, his body warm and relaxed. Only with Lon's vague mumbling did conversation resume—"Oh, well. What a life, huh?"—the same words often slurred and spoken as a sigh.

Except the words were different on that summer night, surprising Hollis by how morose they sounded. "Was terrible," Lon had muttered. "What a mess," he whispered into the darkness, his beer-saturated voice hinting at something lingering beyond the confines of Nine Springs. Aside from crickets and a breeze rustling in mesquite branches, little else was heard or forthcoming. With the silence continuing, Hollis now discerned an oppressive quality in the air which made it difficult for him to say anything. Instead, he sipped at his beer, turning his attention toward the crickets and the breeze—and the tiny ripples of water spreading out on the illuminated surface of his swimming pool. Then he pondered the words Lon had said, drawing his own conclusions while his friend remained stock-still beside him.

Maybe, Hollis decided, it wasn't William Levitt's vision Lon was calling terrible. Maybe, he thought, the mess wasn't the sprawl of suburbia; rather, it was, perhaps, the inapprehensible sight Lon had witnessed as a young sailor aboard the observer ship USS *Mount McKinley* (Baker Day in the Bikini Atoll, July 25, 1946, at 0835 hours, nine miles from zeropoint), the subject of which had been mentioned from time to time since meeting on the golf course, discussed beneath the punishing sun, brought up by an inebriated Lon without prompting but addressed in a detached, guarded manner as if it were the gravest of secrets: because what Lon had seen on the deck of the *Mount McKinley*, what had erupted before him in an instant—pure white, brilliant, awe-inspiring—was the first post–World War II nuclear disaster, unleashed by an underwater atomic bomb which shot a massive column of ocean water nearly a mile into the Pacific sky, decimating a fleet of abandoned battleships which were deliberately positioned at the zeropoint ("target vessels," Lon had called them, "thrown about and sunk like toy boats").

In truth, the human eye wasn't capable of processing the entire phenomenon, nor had there been appropriate definitions available beforehand to explain it. As a result, two months following the bomb test, scientists organized a conference—reviewing the data from Bikini Atoll, analyzing military film footage—whereupon a vocabulary of thirty expressions was developed, including terms such as "cauliflower cloud," "dome," "base surge." For Lon, however, the recollection of the detonation seemed crystal clear: the monstrous dome which rose immediately before him on that day—geysering among the target fleet and blanketing the ships all at once—stretched upward and upward, briefly usurping the natural firmament during its white, expansive birth. In fact, the explosion was so incredible—so immense, so much greater in scope than anything his mind had expected—that it left Lon gazing openmouthed, even as others around him could not suppress their loud gasps or ecstatic shouts of delight. No intelligible thoughts seized him, and he was moved to the point of tears; for it looked as if creation itself was at play, as if he were glimpsing the beginnings of a new world: mutable mountain ranges swirled within that dome, snowcapped peaks shimmered in the light of a second sun.

At the very moment the explosion propelled millions of tons of saltwater toward the heavens, an enormous crater fractured the ocean floor, extending two hundred feet deep; as surrounding water filled the gap, the ocean lifted and fell for several moments, and a series of huge waves were set into motion—swelling and churning and sweeping forward, abruptly rocking the observer ships. The largest waves known to mankind were created that morning, rivaled only by those which came with the eruption of the island of Krakatoa in 1883. My lord, Lon found himself thinking as the high waves approached, someone made a mistake, someone miscalculated. About forty seconds after the blast an otherworldly, demonic roar swept over the *Mount McKinley*, inciting a newsman to shout, "Why doesn't the captain get us out of here?" But already the massive column of water had begun to collapse, settling into a circular cloud of radioactive material, carrying its lethal spray, mist, air downwind for more than seven miles. With the column's disintegration, a heavy fog–like bank of steam, some two thousand feet high, rolled across the target fleet, enshrouding the ships.

Three and a half miles away from zeropoint, on the recently evacuated island of Bikini, coconut trees swayed violently when the shock wave jolted the deserted island at a rate of 3,500 miles per hour. And standing not far from Lon on the *Mount McKinley*—snaggletoothed, dark-skinned, compact, wearing Marine Corps utilities (khaki trousers and shirt, black navy-issue shoes and no socks)—was His Majesty King Juda of the people of Rongerik, formerly of Bikini, observing the spectacle without amazement while others beside him grimaced or smiled, watching impassively as his tropical kingdom was laid to waste and, Lon realized in hindsight, seemingly no longer shocked by anything white men could do to him, or his people, or his beloved islands, or themselves.

"It was an awful sight," Lon had once told Hollis, "and it was so beautiful, too. I've never been able to reconcile that disparity. You've never seen anything like it. Trust me, the movie footage doesn't do it justice. You couldn't even begin to understand what it was like to see something that unimaginable unless you were there."

You don't know what you're talking about, Hollis had wanted to say but refrained, hoping instead Lon might manage to hear the voice of silence. I've seen things just as awful if not worse, he thought. Smaller-scale indicators of the apocalypse, lacking the impersonal grandeur, the sublime aspects, the disquieting majesty of a single nuclear explosion beheld from afar. No, he thought, I've stood before macro destruction, the slow-moving, close-range, tangible mechanisms of human annihilation—and none of it, regardless of how he had tried recasting it in his head, offered a remote hint of paradoxical beauty or unexpected reverence.

"Yep," Lon had said, "it was something else, and I'm surprised I haven't paid for it yet. God knows plenty already have. I knew a guy there who ended up having a malignant tumor removed from his thyroid, and another one who died of a rare kind of adenocarcinoma, and another from chronic leukemia, not to mention all the ones who got colon and liver cancer, or lost their entire immune systems, or that bunch of others who became sterile. But, you know, I've been lucky so far, pretty damn lucky.

Doesn't matter much now, though. Not many remember all that stuff these days, no one talks about it anymore. But I'm fairly certain I saw the very beginning of our undoing—that exact second when the world started losing its mind for good."

Realizing his wordless communication had failed to pass between them, Hollis had simply nodded, casting his eyes to the concrete ground. Fifty-three years ago for you, he calculated. Forty-nine for me.

10

The place where Hollis's cactus garden now grows was once square, lifeless, about five yards of hard earth. Whenever wind swept through the backyard, small brownish gusts rose from it and blew out over the swimming pool, like the futile encroachment of a miniature desert. While still setting up the house, they would go there, he and Debra, to ponder the garden they had talked about building with mostly wildflowers, some rocks, maybe a prickly pear or two. They would go there even at night—often in the night, so that they could avoid the summer sun   when the concrete was tolerable to their bare feet and the dirt patch before them was dissipating the heat it had absorbed during the day.

Debra would recline on a deck chair set away from the future garden. Hollis, shirtless and wearing Bermuda shorts, would remain standing while considering the possibilities; it was always he, never Debra, who strolled the concrete perimeter of the patch, where—upon reaching the other side, the dirt between them like a void—he would offer his thoughts: "I'm thinking we can fill it in with gravel, but only when we get everything planted. How about that?" A shrug of indifference would bounce from her shoulders, as if her mind was on something else. He would nod his head in response, suddenly unsure of what, just seconds ago, had seemed like a decent idea. Soon enough, though, Debra would forgo any involvement in the garden planning, encouraging him instead to landscape the area as he saw fit, while also freeing herself to decorate their new home without his input.

"I've spent the better part of my life watering flowers," she explained one evening, having begged out of surveying the empty patch yet again. "It's a lot of work, you know. And now that you've got plenty of time on your hands, I believe you should assume that duty for a spell. You'll see, it'll do you good getting plenty of sunshine, getting your hands a little muddied. Anyway, I think you're more suited for desert botany than I am, wouldn't you agree?"

He gave her a sort of agitated look, at once amused and perplexed. "Really? How do you figure?"

"Well, you're certainly pricklier than me, and nowadays your belly strikes me as fairly succulent."

"Oh," he said, wrinkling his brow and glancing down at his broad, inflamed stomach. "I guess so."

Then, for him, developing the garden became a singular preoccupation, if not a somewhat protracted affair; its progress was labored over in the cooler morning hours, its design revised from day to day: no gravel, no flowers, nothing which required an inordinate amount of watering, but rather something indigenous, something which might thrive by itself should he eventually fall ill or become too enfeebled to maintain its care. At the kitchen window, Debra would spy him out there, crouched on his haunches, finally cracking the dirt with a spade and digging narrow, shallow holes for the eight tiny barrel cacti he had bought at Super Wal-Mart. His gloved hands—which she knew were thick, rough, and calloused from his lumber-industry years—would reach for a single two-inch-wide barrel, carefully extracting it from its temporary planter, balancing it gingerly on his palm and sliding it upright into a hole.

Those initial plantings rooted successfully, although the landscaping was approached methodically and even now continues as an ongoing project. Hollis marked off sections of the patch, intending each section to display a different variety of cactus, but ultimately the concept was abandoned in favor of naturalistic, scattershot groupings. Then one day—it must have been right after planting the first barrels—his spade unearthed something other than centipedes or grubs or fire ants. The ground was stabbed. The spade pushed deep, striking what felt like a pebble. He made several jabs with the spade, tossing dirt aside, and scooped out a hard olive-green clump covered in soil, which he sifted into his fingers.

"Take a gander at this," he said, and Debra—sunbathing on a deck chair, her face shadowed beneath a visor cap—opened her eyes, leaning forward as he briefly held his discovery high.

"What is it?"

"It's an army, man," he said, lowering his hand, contemplating his find for a moment: a small plastic toy soldier, a rifleman with his weapon aimed.

"Good lord," she said, sounding bothered.

Digging nearby he exhumed a second soldier, then a third and a fourth soldier—until, at last, six plastic figures were scattered about him, filthy and strewn around several holes, like men thrown to the ground by mortar blasts. He said, somberly, "Just look at you—you didn't see it coming at all—you weren't expecting this," as if he were repeating it to himself. But the soldiers weren't the only toys he had discovered there. Previously he had found several opaque-orange and black-swirled marbles, a purple Hot Wheels cement-mixer truck, as well as a tiny blue sock made for a toddler.

"It isn't right," he heard Debra say. "Those kind of things shouldn't be in our yard, not way out here."

Turning his head, he caught sight of her face as she climbed from the deck chair to go inside; it was very serious and very pale, as if she had seen something awful. He then understood her consternation: prior to their house being built, he realized, there must've been another house on the property. Prior to Nine Springs, he thought, another community must've existed there, and someone else had once wandered and slept and played and dreamed on the same plot of land where they now reside. Thereafter, his fingers behaved like God, organizing the soldiers into a crooked formation, righting them on such broken, dusty earth: a firing rifleman, a grenadier, a rifleman using the butt of his weapon to strike at the air, a running rifleman with an M1 carbine, an advancing rifleman with a bayonet on his weapon, a G.I. charging forward with a tommy gun—none of them larger than three inches, each poised yet somehow fighting an unseen battle. As cicadas rattled in mesquite trees, he evoked the soldiers' names without speaking aloud—*Buddy, Jimmy*—an index finger swooping down on the toys like a precision-guided missile—*George, Mikey, Mark*—flicking the plastic helmets—*Schubert*—knocking the men to the dirt. Standing upright, he gazed at the bodies far below him, as if observing a distant, foreign landscape from a bird's-eye view. You're the boys that didn't make it, he thought. You're the ones that fell in my presence.

"Sorry about that, Schubert," he said, bending to pick up the soldiers, recalling the Chinese American kid who had idolized McCreedy, laughing at the Texan's jokes when no one else would. "That's rich," Schubert would say, nervously looking at his feet, grinning uncomfortably as if he assumed everyone else was staring at him. "That's a hoot, that's pretty funny." Schubert's eyes often shifted to McCreedy while they were on patrol—fixing on the sunburned neckline, that rugged profile—instead of staring ahead or monitoring the hillsides. While there was little age difference, McCreedy seemed older than Schubert, much older; and, as such, he treated the kid like a younger brother, giving him obvious advice ("Remember, keep your head low, otherwise you'll make for an easy target"), admonishing him now and then ("Godamnit, Schubert, don't you piss out in the open like that, you'll get your pecker blasted!").

Ultimately, though, there was nothing McCreedy could have said or done to keep Schubert Tang alive—not when enemy mortar and machine-gun fire erupted indiscriminately, not after a bullet tore through the kid's skull, and blew away a portion of his nose, and removed most of his right jaw, and threw his teeth and strips of flesh into the air like confetti. As others scrambled for safety, it was McCreedy who rushed to Schubert, promptly rolling the splayed body this way and that—his boots stepping in the kid's waste, creating bloody tracks on an exposed hillside trail—taking a dog tag, retrieving a billfold, wristwatch, and a pack of cigarettes from the corpse; all of it, except the cigarettes, would be given to the division's graves registration unit. Upon leaving the body behind, dropping beside

Hollis as machine-gun rounds zipped above them, McCreedy said, "Tough fucking luck," with hardly a quiver of regret.

But Schubert wasn't the first casualty McCreedy had readied for the medics or the graves registration unit, nor was he the last. Buddy Campbell got hit in the chest, an inch or so from his navel. Fleeing down a hill, George Martinez had both arms blown off by a mortar blast. Jimmy Shurlock was shot in the left eye, and to everyone's amazement burst into laughter shortly before dying. It was a tree which killed Mikey O'Brien, a tree struck by a mortar—the wood splintering apart, jettisoning like bullets, and gouging open O'Brien's stomach. But Mark Neiman took the cake: one second he was sharing a joke about a legless pig, and a second later he was completely legless, writhing on his back, reaching a trembling hand toward the two bubbling, red stumps where his knees, shins, and feet had just been.

In hindsight, it only seemed right that those deaths would have an impact on McCreedy, continually tempering his affable manner and drawing his personality further inward, allowing the more sullen, acerbic parts of his nature to emerge (qualities Hollis had sensed lurking below McCreedy's exterior from the start). Then it was to be a tougher McCreedy marching forward, a colder character with his weapon ready, taking the lead without needing to assert himself, remaining unfazed whenever they happened upon the horrific: bloated, discolored corpses stacked alongside a narrow trail; a dead infant with flies swarming about its face; a woman's head flattened like a crushed grapefruit in the middle of an unpaved road, her long dark hair spread out in the dirt as if it had been combed that way.

"Tough fucking luck. Too bad for you."

No, no, Hollis thought, don't think about it anymore. Leave it be.

But even after disposing of the toy soldiers—dropping them into a mass grave and covering them with soil, sealing them beneath a small piece of flagstone—he was unable to shake what he had tried for so long to forget. How strange, he considered, that a single day—or an hour, or a minute, or a second—could drastically change the direction and outcome of someone's entire life. One man's sudden misfortune, he knew well enough, might be another man's salvation. He turned his eyes from that piece of flagstone, and surveyed the barren ground on which he stood. Just then, the garden became transformed in his mind, ceasing to be a place of pleasant diversion but, rather, now an expansive grave plot for memories which refused to stay buried.

In all—once the days of 1950 were tallied up and relegated to an increasingly remote past—Hollis had spent less than a month fighting the North Koreans, from the last week of July to early August, with the majority of 7th Cavalry deaths he witnessed occurring while en route to the Naktong River (the 2nd Battalion retreating southward as advancing enemy tanks, snipers, and artillery shells chased them in rain and sun to the base of the Sobaek Mountains). How indescribable his time abroad sometimes felt—how abrupt and hallucinatory—like a blur which had swept through a brief portion of his life, taking him from rural America to urban Japan to the hills and valleys of South Korea, and bringing him back home to Minnesota from what, upon reflection, could have been described as a whirlwind vacation to hell. Yet it was early on—just before Schubert's killing, before McCreedy stopped smiling and began gritting his teeth, while everyone still believed the conflict was to be a short-lived affair—that he experienced his own grim turning point, a moment when, as it would soon happen for McCreedy, the war took on the attributes of a debased and needless game; except, unlike McCreedy, Hollis recoiled from the horrors he glimpsed (averting his stare if possible, hesitating at times to pull the trigger of his M1), attempting to keep himself somehow separate while also perceiving many of his fellow cavalrymen as nothing more than willful children set loose on a massive playground, becoming promiscuous with their weapons and the disposal of human life. Nevertheless, he knew his autobiography would skirt these amoral, vexing aspects of the war, and in some manner, if he got around to actually writing it, he would need to revise certain facts, censoring moments of his own history by deliberate omission, shifting much of the story into a fictional parallel universe just so he could sleep at night.

The maddening reality, however, refused to transform itself in his memory, regardless of how he intended to modify events with the aid of words and a computer. For it was only five days after setting foot on Korean land, during their first full operation at the front, that the 2nd Battalion of the 7th Cavalry regiment found itself positioned in the hills above a curving railroad line—the bare tracks beneath them cutting over a small double-arched concrete trestle near the village of No Gun Ri. On that Wednesday, the sun blazed high, enhancing the humidity, reflecting off of rifles and binocular lenses. Cicadas purred within acacia trees. Long-necked herons were spotted at times, flapping across a sky which was dotted with clouds. Down below—close to the trestle, gathered under acacia trees and in the shade beside the railroad embankment—were exhausted, frightened refugees: six hundred or so weary souls (elderly, middle-aged, young, entire families who had been evacuated from the Chu Gok Ri valley), wearing billowing white clothing and walking on rice-straw sandals, hauling livestock while making their way to the village of Hwanggan, but resting now among the cool shadows before proceeding with heavy packs or children on their backs—aware all the while of the Americans scattered around the hills, yet feeling secure in the relative stillness of a bright midday.

Hollis has always had difficulty placing himself there in a hillside fox-hole, or accurately remembering what actions he took as the events of July 26 unfolded. In some regard, his recollection was not unlike the per-spective of the herons which swooped above everything—the rice paddies, the distant pine groves, the valley, the railroad tracks, the refugees, the Americans—gliding for the jagged slopes of White Horse Mountain. Yet he knows other soldiers blew whistles at the moment three air force planes emerged through the clouds, roaring from the horizon, and sailed low toward the refugees. And he knows, as the refugees paused and gazed up-ward at the planes, the valley below him suddenly exploded in a deafening thunder—again and again and again, shaking the ground with greater anger than any earthquake he would experience in Southern California—throw-ing stones and trees and bags and bodies into the sky, blasting limbs apart, tearing clothing away and turning the day to night amid a storm of dust and dirt. Cattle bellowed in chorus with human screams. The wounded briefly moaned for help or gasped last breaths. Then more bombs and rockets fell, machine guns rattled from the planes, as survivors ran in every direction, stunned and panicked—some dragging children, some pressing hands on their ears, some incapable of moving—while pieces of people and livestock crashed hot to the ground.

When the planes retreated, careening beyond the clouds, they left in their wake an appalling aftermath. The tracks running parallel to the embankment had become a twisted, fractured mess of steel, and craters fumed where just previously villagers had rested on rice-straw mats. Shrouded by the heavy smoke which obscured the destruction, the wounded lay dying, either motionless or writhing near burning baggage and smoldering carnage (bits of fingers, severed heads, naked torsos, a dead man's legs pointing straight up at the heavens). Weaving through the mortally injured and the remnants of bodies, its entire brown hide set ablaze, a solitary cow managed to reach the perimeter of that hellish scene—the black smoke unfurling there ahead of it, faintly revealing faraway mountains and blue sky—and heaving a prolonged cry of misery, its legs buckled and it collapsed into a silent, fiery heap.

The refugees fortunate enough to escape the attack had fled for the hillsides, while others found shelter inside the narrow, 200-foot-long passageway of a culvert underneath the railroad, or beneath the twin tunnels of the trestle. But many of those clambering along the hills, striving to find safety, soon ran out of options; when word came through the line to open fire on them, it was McCreedy who, without any hesitation, immediately discharged his M1 after catching a small girl in his sights and, upon striking the child, exclaimed, "Got her!" And though Hollis tells himself no one was murdered by his weapon, at least not on that day, he is fully aware of having aimed his rifle—perhaps at rocks, maybe at those who were already killed—and pulling the trigger. Then what's lodged in his mind isn't so much his participation in the action, but, rather, freeze-frames of memory capturing the untested teenage cavalrymen who stood or knelt closest to him; only days previously they had entered dank Tokyo bars, fondling taxi dancers and requesting sake or beer, yet, with the passing of a week, they were gripping their weapons in Korea and shooting, for the first time in their lives, complete strangers. How quickly they had all adapted—launching mortar shells at defenseless groups of refugees, spraying machine-gun rounds into the culvert and the trestle tunnels, killing villagers even as they understood they were there to fight for them, firing simply because they were ordered to do so.

Presently, the rifles and machine guns led the soldiers from the hillsides, bringing them to where smoke enveloped that confounding terrain, the dark plumes drifting over corpses like souls ascending. Boots pushed at bodies, checking to see if anyone in the air-strike zone had lived, while, at the same time, surviving villagers were being herded together—brought from the hillsides, the surrounding fields, the tracks—and ushered slowly toward the trestle. Either weeping aloud or too stunned to make a sound, parents held their children, just as others helped the wounded ones who couldn't walk; the rifle muzzles and soldiers guided them forward—past ravaged limbs, their feet stumbling on the fallen—sending the villagers into the two cavernous tunnels beneath the bridge. But for the injured ones who had been unable to stand or move forward, they were promptly dispatched with point-blank shots, yet were fortunate enough to receive a swifter death than what would eventually befall those crowded inside the tunnels. The gunfire would sporadically echo there during the afternoon of the twenty-sixth until the morning hours of the twenty-ninth, hundreds of rounds ricocheting from the concrete walls at dusk, the heavy shelling, tracers illuminating the pitch interior at night as meteor-like bullets ripped into huddled figures.

Even after the survivors were crowded into the tunnels, McCreedy continued roaming above them near the tracks, stepping through the smoke with Schubert trailing close behind, ambling casually from corpse to corpse; when Hollis came upon the pair, they were standing on either side of an elderly woman who must have died from fright rather than injury: she lay perfectly intact among the ruin, spine against the ground, eyes fixed wide, legs straight, slender arms outstretched but with her thin fingers curled inward as if they were clutching at air. Without a trace of emotion, McCreedy leaned toward the woman—one hand gripping his rifle, the other hand gliding across her face—and, like magic, an Indian Head penny materialized on each of her eyes, covering her wide brown pupils.

Knitting his brow in bewilderment, Hollis shouldered his rifle as Schubert snickered and said, "Sleep tight." Then he followed the pair for a while, watching the two bend down here and there, placing Indian Heads on the faces of the dead (the pennies soon dotting the eyes of dismembered children and charred men and mutilated women in what seemed, to Hollis, an irrational attempt to even out history). With the incomprehensible mass killing of the refugees not yet fully processed, it was the behavior of Schubert—enjoying himself beside fresh corpses whose faces superficially mirrored his own features, acting nothing like the shy, thoughtful young man on the transport ship—which initially mortified Hollis; it was as if he were recognizing in the kid the signs of a potent malady which had begun spreading quickly from man to man. Pausing by the blackened, fuming trunk of an acacia, Schubert snickered again while McCreedy poured more pennies out of the bulging prophylactic, replenishing their palms.

"Here you go," McCreedy said, thrusting the condom at Hollis. "I haven't forgotten about you."

Hollis hesitated. He half closed his eyes, which were irritated by the smoke, and, very slowly, said, "That's okay. I'll pass."

McCreedy was stunned. Schubert snickered uncomfortably. They both stared at him with the same perplexed look; then they glanced at each other and, once more, stared at him.

"Now come on," McCreedy told him, his voice barely masking annoyance. "You can't pass on an opportunity like this. You got an obligation here to fulfill, right? We all do. Come on."

"It's okay, really," Hollis said, stepping back from the condom. "I'd just rather not."

A stern expression surfaced on McCreedy, even as he tried speaking calmly, his tone conveying the kind of urgency which was meant to change another's position: "Look, you better climb on board, son." He reached forward, pressing a single Indian Head into Hollis's left hand, where it was kept within a fist. "You need to start seeing the bigger picture, or you might not get a place at the table, got it?"

Nothing McCreedy had said made sense, but Hollis still burned with an immense hatred for him; and when walking away to go elsewhere—upon catching the sound of both soldiers whistling beyond him in the veil of smoke, humming the old Gaelic drinking song which George A. Custer had adopted as the 7th Cavalry's marching anthem—he felt sickened by Mc-

Creedy and harbored a great sadness for those whose eyes were sealed beneath such cruel pennies. After depositing that single cent on a crooked rail track, hoping it would eventually get crushed flat, Hollis turned around, gazing back to glimpse the murky, receding figures of McCreedy and Schubert (stooping and rising, stooping and rising). Someday—he sensed it at his core but was never able to articulate it clearly to himself—there will be more of your kind than mine. Someday, he was sure, the world will be governed to accommodate the exclusive cupidity, unfounded fears, and willful inanity of people like Bill McCreedy.

Here in the backyard, the cacti now recall melting snowmen, globular and icy shapes thawing as Hollis scoops with the spade—clearing slush, tending an untenable garden which has somewhat relieved his conscience of the massacre he had witnessed: the refugees huddled beneath the railroad trestle at No Gun Ri, the men, women, and children seeking shelter there, but dying instead underneath the large twin arches, falling from bullets fired by his battalion; what horror he's conjured when sometimes shutting his eyes in the garden, like an incubus arising through memorial and continuing onward with him, a thread of regret keeping him beholden and disrupting the tranquillity of his hard-earned retirement.

And, as well, there is that other vision—the listless figures in gas masks, the stray herd of cattle—entering his sleep during the night. Upon arriving at Nine Springs, with the beginning of his newfound leisure, it had come to him more readily, more vividly, as persistent and pervasive as the cancer which had begun to spread unnoticed inside Debra. While the meaning of the cattle had always mystified him, the symbolic procession of restless souls had not: early on, he'd recognized them as a manifestation of his own guilt concerning No Gun Ri, a visitation from those who sought resolution or amends for their unjust deaths. Out in the garden they also started coming to him, weaving through his mind, distracting him. Yet the planting of a single cactus could stifle the recurring thoughts; when digging a new hole, when lowering the roots of barrel into the earth and patting down the soil, he saw nothing but life and creation, and, with time, the vision grew less and less troublesome, appearing infrequently at night while becoming nonexistent in his waking hours.

All the same, nobody has heard him address this grievous memory from the war—not Debra or Lon, no one he's ever met. He hasn't spoken of these crimes, of rifles fired at mothers holding babies, villagers digging under corpses as gunfire ricocheted—a wholesale slaughter issued discreetly by the 1st Cavalry Division headquarters, stating that refugees crossing the front lines should perish in case they might be the enemy hiding behind peasant clothing. Except he never saw the enemy at No Gun Ri, simply terrified bodies rushing about below him, screaming from one end of the bridge tunnel to the other, scrambling to avoid the shooting which rained through both sides—until body lay upon body, everything unmoving but blood and the faint, shallow breathing of the mortally wounded (how awful ebbing between man-made arches, how tragic greeting death where safety at last seemed palpable). Yes, he had pointed his rifle, had fired too—although, he feels certain, only the ground and the bridge supports took his bullets; even if, possibly, his bullets had ricocheted into the innocent and caused fatalities, Hollis remains proud of the fact that he didn't directly kill anyone, and, in the intervening years, he has never allowed that belief to waver.

For that matter, he is also proud of his garden, because it has become a remembrance of sorts—as thorny and forbidding, to his mind, as any reliquary. How right, then, for his skin to get punctured on occasion, his own blood dripping into places his fingers can't touch. So he is pleased with his efforts, his mornings spent planting. He doesn't shudder whenever the flesh is pricked, or curse himself; he can accept the pain easily, dutifully in fact, as a tithing offered to this soil where so many spines blossom (now more needles flourish here than bullets expended at No Gun Ri, soon a cactus will exist for each person who died). In fashioning the garden, he has begun to settle his burden, attaching that vexing recollection to something beneficial: a slow transformation which, in time, he prays will alter the darker ruminations—hopefully placating the restless procession within his dreams, the straggling forms signifying his culpability—ushering forth pink spring flowers nestled in the midst of cacti spines instead of the living turned abruptly dead, irrelevant, discarded by history yet present to him still.

At some future point, he believed he would sleep contentedly in his bed and nap warmly inside his hut, untethered from regrets, free to enjoy his days while anticipating flawless golf swings—doing so as the sun nourishes his garden and shines down on this ever-widening, arid development. Then he would never again doubt the choices he has made for himself, even should Lon recline beside him, muttering, "It won't stop, Hollis—won't stop until there's no desert left. Not so long ago this was wilderness—the last spot on earth we would've inhabited." No, he had planned to avoid any second guessing after the garden is completed; he'd already told himself it was meaningless to think much about the past, or to contemplate how these streets and homes and golf courses were simply blueprints in an office somewhere, a design requiring cheap property. He has made himself forget that all of this real estate, not long ago, was once farmland owned by a sole Mexican family (probably a large family, with at least one child who saw fit to bury a handful of toy soldiers in shallow, fortuitous graves), disregarding whatever leftovers are evident at the fringes—orange trees beyond the development, cattle gnawing along the outer limits like exiles from another place in time.

"Look, everyone gets their moment under the sun," he wanted to tell Lon. "They've had theirs, we're having ours. You know, maybe everything is just exactly as it's meant to be. Have you considered that?"

But while he may wish to think otherwise, Hollis will always be conscious of rarely encountering few colors other than his own pallid blush, his very wrinkled kind. And, too, he can't envision last night's snowfall as anything less than an emblematic one, a paradoxical showering, covering what, in its origin, was meant to be brownish and coarse yet has since been concealed by good roads, consummate planning, gated uniformity—that snow chilling Nine Springs with its inexplicable arrival, hinting at the impermanence of those now sequestered here; how it descended with such assurance, claiming the earth—how, then, it faded almost as quickly, melting away, disappearing into the ground, turning the loamy soil to mud, and offering precious little else before finally departing.

II

SAFE PLACES TO DIE

11

Before her chemotherapy began, Debra had made up her mind: she wasn't going to start treatment with any reservations or the slightest amount of dread, nor would she deceive herself by pretending the chemo wasn't destined to underscore the magnitude of her illness (surely quelling whatever sense of control she had had over her own fate, at times producing vast feelings of discouragement). So, she had decided, there wouldn't be an internal struggle against what was about to occur; rather, she had accepted the therapy as an essential step toward recovering her health, while also relying on a practical-to-a-fault, no-nonsense mental inclination which—she reassured herself—was befitting of a West Texas woman. "You should know by now, we're pros at separating the meat from the bone," she'd told Hollis. "We've got bullshit scrapers embedded in our souls." That pragmatic side of her was key, for she believed it gave her a better opportunity to rise above the vagaries of her situation and tolerate the fact that her life was evolving in a manner which she could have never predicted. Moreover, she wouldn't allow herself to entertain hysterics—not even when she recognized twinges of panic or anxiety in Hollis—because she knew the treatment was inevitable and that she must be wholly resigned to its assault on both the disease and her body. As such, she had understood beforehand that the chemo was, in the very least, a wayward ally of sorts, albeit a horribly toxic and draining one.

Then while sitting for hours on end at the Arizona Cancer Center—relaxing in an open, brightly lit space, tended to by a small staff of attentive clinical and research nurses—she and Hollis had been relieved that the Patient Treatment Suite wasn't like the place they had secretly imagined. Without saying so, they had each shared a similar fantasy of a sterile yet archaic ward, a cramped environment lined with stretchers which were partitioned off by white plastic curtains—where stoic nurses strolled from patient to patient, filling out charts as the very ill grew sicker following the administration of chemotherapy. But, in truth, the cancer center had four modern treatment areas (three with reclining lounge chairs and a television mounted on a wall, one with stretcher beds for those who wished to rest throughout the therapy). Instead of voicing discomfort or writhing from pain, the other patients around Debra passed the hours in relative peacefulness—eating potato chips and pizza slices and hamburgers, watching afternoon talk shows, listening through headphones to portable CD players, flipping the pages of newspapers or magazines, talking and playing board games with family members, napping—while the drugs went into their arms as if dripping from a leaky spigot, the chemicals burned up their perfectly good veins, and the IV bags hung above every seat.

It was, for Debra, like a large communal living room, or a weigh station occupied by people who were replenishing themselves amid the dubious journey none of them had asked to embark upon; although what was evident to her during the first rounds of chemo—what she could easily discern from her lounge chair—was that while all of them were there together, many had been on the journey longer than she had (her husband didn't need to help her to and from her seat, the nurses hadn't yet begun searching her arms for undamaged veins in which to stick the IV needle). Still, there was something calming about the suite, boring even. The drugs, too, weren't much of an ordeal; she had assumed she would feel the chemo entering her system, except, as it happened, she felt nothing whatsoever—other than the slight prick of the needle breaching her skin.

And so—with Hollis sitting beside her, his chin tilted upward at the television—she read a Nero Wolfe mystery novel, or worked crossword puzzles. In those weeks when chemo brain finally hampered her ability to concentrate on words, she would choose a chair near the wide, expansive windows, surveying the mountains and sky, often studying the patients and staff who came and went across the center's parking lot. She and Hollis also took walks, bringing the portable IV along with them as they stopped at the nurses' station to chat, or headed down the hallways, or, on occasion, paused inside the clinic's quiet, simple, and usually empty chapel (the two rarely ever speaking there, preferring instead to keep silent beneath the vaulted silt-cast ceiling, the stained-glass window, a cascade of bells). Yet after months of chemo, Debra had never lost sight of the fact that the twenty-nine other chairs in the suite displayed the various shapes of men and women who were praying for the same outcome; as a result, she knew she wasn't alone, and from that understanding she had gleaned a modicum of solace. For just like her, they had left their daily routines behind, and, once a given round of treatment was done, they could again resume a fairly normal existence.

Hollis, too, had been mindful of the patients which filled the suite with Debra—several he had grown fond of encountering, others he recognized but hardly acknowledged. More striking to him, however, was the diversity of the continually changing group. Aside from retired, middle-aged, or university material—male or female—there were white and black patients, mainland Chinese and Mexican locals, a Japanese housewife and a Saudi Arabian graduate student. A handful of different languages were spoken in that room, a cross section of the world had somehow found its way into the desert and past the sliding doors of the cancer center. But over time—as Debra's illness progressed, as the chemo only slowed its advance—new patients began appearing in the places where familiar bodies had previously sat; then it felt like a lethal game of musical chairs was being played out, one in which the names of the winners and losers weren't divulged. Yet few, if any, it seemed, would be spared the ravages of the disease; fewer and fewer were bound to circumvent its wrath, and so everyone, he now believes, will have their lives altered at some point by the infernal lottery of cancer.

Even so, there were no conversations of possible death at the Patient Treatment Suite, no end-of-life issues brought up during commercial breaks or between bites of food, as if an implicit vow to avoid the subject had been sworn by the patients, their families and friends, and the nurses. The treatment alone reinforced the idea that cancer wasn't an automatic death sentence, and as long as therapy continued, both the afflicted and their loved ones might survive with the disease for months, sometimes years (the end result—that final act where the chemo had either succeeded in eliminating the disease or failed altogether—was more akin to an abstract concept than a certainty). In this way, death refused an obvious personification; it wouldn't hang about in the form of an archaic, lingering, black-hooded specter, nor would its onset produce crucifix-like stigmata upon the flesh of the doomed. Instead, it was a kind of death which had an intangible presence, manifesting by degrees rather than all at once—covertly building upon itself like a creeping paralysis, spreading here and there—with the telltale signs becoming cumulative and, to those expecting its imminence, undeniable.

Now without the advantage of much hindsight, Debra's cancer months had already relegated a number of the recently deceased to memory, acquaintances met early on at Gilda's Club—five or six faceless women to Hollis—which his wife mentioned only after each had passed away. "We lost Dianne this week," she'd tell him, saying so in a direct, unemotional tone—as effortless and nonchalant as if she had just uttered, "We're out of toilet paper again." Since Debra began attending the meetings, the club had also lost a Rebecca, an Alice, a Martha, a Kelly, and—because Debra always referred to her by her full name—one Tina Archuleta. With the exception of Tina Archuleta, the women died from complications brought on by their advanced ovarian cancer (bowel obstructions, fluid collecting in the lungs, tumors pressing on key organs). Ms. Archuleta, on the other hand, was a stage-I survivor who had been free of the disease for six years; a seemingly healthy, muscular woman, an avid cyclist and jogger, she frequented the meetings whenever possible, encouraging newcomers to "thank Mother God and surrender yourself and the temple of clay you live in to Her care," while giving everyone a good look at the overly enthusiastic, beatific face of remission.

But it was Tina Archuleta's unexpected demise which altered Debra's normally impassive response to such losses, dismaying Hollis with a sly grin even as she somberly explained that Tina had been killed in an off-road accident (thrown from an open Jeep when the vehicle lost control, her body sent tumbling down a prickly pear–covered hillside before coming to rest at the rocky edge of an arroyo). "It's pretty tragic," Debra said, shaking her head. "I guess her temple of clay got busted to pieces."

They were driving back to Nine Springs from Tucson, and Hollis—right hand on the steering wheel, left hand turning the radio dial to his favorite country station—glanced at her, discerning then from her expression that it was sarcasm he had heard and not simply a bad choice of words. "That's awful," he said, returning his stare to the road. "Why'd you say that?"

She shook her head again, as if she wasn't so pleased with herself. "Who knows what's gotten into me," she said, maintaining the same somber tone yet doing nothing to suppress her grin. "I think I'm in shock. It must be shock. At least she's with Mother God now."

"Stop it. Why are you talking like that? Why are you smiling?"

She shrugged her eyebrows once, and with that the slight grin disappeared for a moment—only to reemerge seconds later as a full-blown smirk: "You know, we all die someday of something, dear. It's not like getting past cancer means you'll live forever. But promise me one thing, will you?"

Somewhat hesitantly, he answered, "What is it?"

"Considering everything I've gone through with this disease—it doesn't matter if I get flattened by a bus or crushed under a boulder—you better make sure my obituary says ovarian cancer is what did me in, okay?" She half chuckled at her own request, but her levity was unnerving to Hollis.

"Deb, don't talk like that," he immediately responded. His forward gaze drifted across an abandoned strip mall and the parking lot of a Tony Roma's. "And please stop smiling. It isn't funny."

This is how you're coping, he had thought afterward. This is how you're dealing with what's happening to you, and us. She would tell him again and again that Gilda's Club had been a blessing, that its support had lifted her from the melancholy and haze of her ordeal (even as her cancer remained, even as the treatments had failed to bring beneficial results). The other Gilda's Club members she joined every week—those who were sharing her fears and sickness—had instilled the importance of positioning one's self to be a survivor; they had, in fact, added color to her life under the bleakest of circumstances—not just with humor, or counseling, or reliable information, but also in a more literal fashion: she was advised to avoid muted shades, encouraged to wear clothing which was vibrant, warm, and positive.

Then gone were the gray sweatpants, the black sweaters; gone, too, were the black ceramic dinner plates, and the light-gray bedroom walls and ceiling (a color she had originally picked for their room, a color Hollis had blotted out over the course of a weekend by covering it beneath a thick, smooth veneer of pale yellow). Soon the bedside table was lined with a row of small, brown-tinted bottles, each containing a different oil and scent which—according to the aromatherapist who had visited Gilda's Club one week—were excellent for activating the olfactory nerve cells in the nasal cavity, sending impulses to the limbic system (the part of the brain commonly associated with emotions and memory), as well as relieving various physical maladies by stimulating the immune, circulatory, and nervous systems. At any given hour, the bedroom became fragrant with eucalyptus and wintergreen (aiding congestion relief), jasmine (calming depression), lavender (reducing anxiety and improving sleep), citrus (elevating mood and increasing mental sharpness), peppermint (helping with digestion while reducing nausea), rosemary (easing pain and providing muscle relaxation), or the single best oil for evoking a surge of happiness: cherry. At last, Debra would take it upon herself to symbolize happiness with her own hand, using Hollis's paints and brushes, climbing a stepladder in order to design a bluebird on the bedroom ceiling—its wings widened amid a flat yellow sky, its arrow-like beak aimed at the doorway. "It's our bluebird of happiness," she had told him while lowering herself from the stepladder, blue paint spattered on her fingers. "Everyone should have one, don't you think?"

"Of course," he answered. "Of course," he repeated, his voice sud-

denly trembling, watching as the bluebird became diffused with the welling
of tears and seemed to flutter above him.

The spade acts as a snowplow, clearing the precarious spaces between
golden barrels, succulents, and old man cereus. The funneling system which
Hollis designed along the rooftop gutters—a series of black plastic tubing
and sheet-metal rivulets—is hampered by blockages of ice. Below the funneling system—close to where he is working—the fifty-gallon tub which
normally collects rain during the summer monsoon season now contains
slush, as does the five-gallon bucket he uses for retrieving water from the
tub to irrigate his flowering plants (scarlet betony, yellow bells, columbine).
The trailing rosemary near the back patio is nowhere to be seen—lost
beneath a melting stratum of white—yet a single cottontail rabbit sniffs
at the ground there, unconcerned by Hollis's proximity while it searches
for something to gnaw on. Taking a break to stare beyond his property,
Hollis is aware of the rabbit but gives it little notice, for he has previously
encountered more impressive kinds of free-roaming wildlife behind the
house—a covey of quail, solitary coyotes, a pack of javelinas, a hawk, and
an owl.

As no walls or fences enclose the yards of Nine Springs, he can peer
into neighboring gardens, observing the mini-oases growing around his
own refuge—backyards which, in warmer months, showcase bougain-
villea and cape honeysuckle vines, wide-spreading palo verdes and hybrid
mesquites for cool summer shade, creosote bushes, prickly pears, cholla
cacti, and red yuccas whose clusters of bright flowers entice both humming-
birds and butterflies; he can, when surrounded by such subtle desert shapes
and colors, perceive this gated community as a kind of barren paradise, a
well-deserved reward for almost forty years of service to the Dusenbury-
Soper Lumber Company (that majority of his lifetime spent overseeing cutting rights, production, and processing in Pennsylvania and, then, Southern
California).

In truth, Hollis's thoughts concerning Nine Springs rarely waver, nor
do his concerns usually align with Lon's mixed feelings about the place; he

has never been able to equate his retirement here with some exclusive theme park for the aged, a present-day dystopia built from antiquated, homogenous ideals. Instead, he feels the community is not so different from the valued destinations of his youth, holiday retreats like Palm Springs or Lake Tahoe—unique getaways which allowed couples to leave the steady drone of urban motion and, for a brief period, find peace in wide-open, slower-paced environs; without such halcyon alternatives made available, he believes many decent people might find their twilight years to be somewhat less fruitful.

Debra, too, had sought contentment here, while also embracing the motto of "living with cancer" as a personal mantra. Shrugging off the cruel timing of her illness—the late stage of her disease, the exhaustion of chemotherapy, her declining health—she, like Hollis, was still determined to enjoy what was supposed to have been prolonged recompense for those laborious, gainful decades. As she saw it, his retirement signaled her retirement, at least to some extent; so it wouldn't be all pain and sickness for her, nor did she continue to play the role of a restive and childless San Gabriel Valley homemaker, or that of a part-time sales associate at Mervyn's. Rather, she quietly redefined herself upon leaving California, seeking an appropriate analogue to her husband's almost daily rounds of golf, finding her answer inside the meeting rooms of the Funtivities Center—where she attended a weekly lecture series on the religions of the world, engaged in several lively debates regarding current events, and learned how to research the genealogy of her family tree.

Immediately following her surgery and prior to becoming too weak to participate, Debra often passed entire days at the Funtivities Center: mornings practicing tai chi, afternoons doing ceramics, and, for a short while, evenings rehearsing with the Ol' Settlers Drama League (the effects of chemo at last preventing her from performing as Mrs. Gibbs in *Our Town*, or realizing the dream of tackling Rosie DeLeon in *Bye Bye Birdie*). And although she had once fostered a desire to raise her own children—a desire left unfulfilled due to the double-edged revelation that her body had been overloaded with androgens and her husband's sperm were abnormally shaped—Debra tended to herself at Nine Springs in the manner which,

Hollis imagines, she might have done for a child raised under her supervision: balanced meals, regular exercise, hours devoted to reading or studying, and plenty of extracurricular distractions to keep negative influences and ennui at bay. Nevertheless, with the disease's progression, she couldn't help but view her premenopausal infertility—the abundance of male hormones complicating her system, the irregular periods, the difficulty she had had ovulating—as being, in hindsight, a clear warning for what lay ahead.

Yet only after Dr. Langford's diagnosis did Debra learn about the studies which suggested a connection between ovarian cancer and never having children. Still, she had remembered sensing minor pangs while ovulating, that mid-cycle sensation her gynecologist at the time had called Mittelschmerz—that moment when a single egg expanded, bursting beside the ovary, awaiting either fertilization or to be flushed away with menstruation. Not until her cancer was discovered, though, would she consider the damage inherent to such a routine, commonplace function: for with every egg which ruptured near the ovary came a division of cells—a shifting, a multiplying, a regrouping along the surface lining to seal the gap; and it was that mechanical, automatic dividing and subsequent repair which could allow rogue cells to go astray, producing the microscopic starting point for cancerous beginnings.

"You know what I really hate, what I really can't stomach?" she'd said to Hollis, as they paced the hallways of the cancer center. "It's knowing my body is operating on its own internal clock. Early on it decides I shouldn't have a baby. Then it decides to change my hair color. Then it decides to wrinkle me all over. Now it wants to kill me, and there isn't a damn thing I can do to reset it, or make it stop tick-tocking my life away. That really pisses me off."

But at least she had her mind, he countered. At least she could control her thoughts, in spite of what her body was doing.

"You're right," she said. "I guess I can still evolve in a positive direction, even if the rest of me is rapidly decaying. So if nothing else, my brain is on my side."

"Me and your brain," he reminded her.

"Forgive me. I stand corrected."

A fairly recent development in Debra's ongoing evolution was the avoidance of beef and fatty foods, relying instead on a diet of soy products, organic vegetables, chicken breasts, and brown rice. This conversion began when she watched a CNN special report about mad cow disease; soon afterward, while she was asleep in their bed, the disturbing images of infected, spasmodic cattle and humans repeated in her mind, jolting her awake beside Hollis.

"No more beef," she had announced, nudging him with an elbow: "Hey, no more beef. We can't eat it anymore."

"What is it?" he said, only half conscious.

"Bovine spongiform encephalopathy."

"What are you saying?"

"It's cannibalization. They're using meat in stock feed. They're feeding them to themselves."

"I don't understand."

"Cows are eating cows, and we're eating the cows that do that, and it's coming back to haunt us. People are dying because of it, and they don't know why for sure. But it's pretty obvious, we're paying a price for toying with nature. Stuff like this always happens when we go against the natural order of things, right? So, please, promise me—no more beef."

"Okay," he mumbled, "I promise—no more beef."

Later Hollis wouldn't confess to the steakhouse dinners which he and Lon consumed during their swap-meet pilgrimages, nor did he point out to Debra that their dormant sex life had been reinvigorated by purely unnatural means: a small 100-milligram pill taken before intercourse, increasing blood flow into his penis, providing an erection which lasted for more than three hours. Although such a laboratory-designed gift wasn't enjoyed without a few minor side effects, including shortness of breath, flushing of the face, and a slightly upset stomach. The drug also brought temporary changes to his color vision, casting their lovemaking in a blue-green tinge ("Viagra vision," was Lon's nickname for the condition—as he, too, had endured that aquamarine, swimming, goggles-like sensation). The side effects, however, never prevented Hollis from using the pill, and—until she was rushed into surgery—he and Debra had attempted sex on a weekly basis upon arriving at Nine Springs. Then, as opposed to her younger self, she made few excuses whenever the old urge had arisen in him—a headache wasn't claimed, cloying shyness wasn't feigned now that age had banished her modesty.

But if Viagra had sexual side effects, so did ovarian cancer–related surgery. Except no one had addressed the sexual component for Debra—none of the doctors or nurses had brought up postoperative issues involving vaginal dryness and atrophy from a loss of estrogen, or the possibility that the quality of her sex life would change dramatically. Nor was she prepared to exit the hospital with more than a complete hysterectomy and, weeks thereafter, discover that her libido had somehow also been removed. Perhaps, she had explained to Hollis, her lack of sexual interest resulted from a combination of stress, chemo, and an altered body image: not to mention the pain which accompanied intercourse, or the scar which defined her pale-white abdomen, or—as she would ultimately conclude—the fact that the organs she had always identified with her womanhood were forever gone.

"You're still beautiful to me," he told her, reaching for her breasts. "You're still the most beautiful woman I've ever known."

"Well, I better be," she said, giving his hands free rein, closing her eyes when his lips pressed against her neck.

Yet following her surgery, in the moments succeeding their halfhearted attempts at intercourse, Hollis sensed her dissatisfaction—not so much from the lazy aftermath of sex, or from the heightened pleasure their bodies had endeavored to reach; rather, it was a vague reproach, a kind of indirect longing for something he couldn't know, an absence, expressed with the shifting of her figure, how she had turned her back to him, sighing or yawning prior to napping, the sheets becoming a warm membrane which then separated their skin. Once they were finished—wads of Kleenex dotting the carpet, the K-Y personal lubricant set aside—silence frequently overtook her; on occasion, however, she spoke, saying things which seemed out of context to his lingering ardor: "It's double coupons at Safeway this Thursday, don't let me forget."

"I won't."

He felt he hadn't touched her, hadn't touched her at all.

"And remind me to call Viv to get her sand tart recipe. It'd be a nice treat for the drama league's potluck next month."

"Okay."

Or, lately, she summoned people and places which rarely entered his thoughts, evoking memories of their old ranch-style home in Arcadia, wondering if the new Taiwanese owners were taking good care of its gardens: "Do they have birds-of-paradise in Taipei?" Maybe her deceased family members were discussed, maybe a trifle concerning her only sibling: "Jackie's a mess. She phoned this morning, looks like Fred is off the wagon." Or she didn't turn from him at all, although she avoided his gaze—propping herself up with pillows instead, taking an aromatherapy bottle from the bedside table, a vexed expression crossing her face while she inhaled the cherry oil which conjured the cough drops her father had sucked like candy: "How strange. Daddy keeps popping into my head these days, and I'm not sure why. I guess I keep thinking he never had anything like this, you know. Just that same old house, pretty much those same rooms from start to finish. I wish him and Mother had settled somewhere else. It might've been a lot better for them, if they'd had something like this to look forward to. I think Daddy would've appreciated the desert, don't you think?"

"Probably," Hollis said, the cherry-oil scent filling the space between them, his deceased father-in-law then appearing in a haze of cigarette smoke (Marlboro fuming at the man's chapped lips, crossword puzzle book folded across the lap of faded jeans). "Can't see why ol' T.J. wouldn't."

And Hollis knew that Debra, too, was remembering the man exactly as he was envisioning him—alone in the living room of a West Texas farmhouse, sitting upright on the right end of the couch, empty Lone Star cans by his slipper-covered feet, a cluttered TV tray before him, the Magnavox flickering several feet away with the volume set low. The No. 2 pencil held by his liver-spotted hand slowly deciphered the puzzle—jotting an answer, or erasing a wrongly chosen word—but presently the pencil stopped moving and the man's head slumped forward, eyes shutting while a cigarette continued to be savored, his thoughts propelling him elsewhere for a little while; then her father shuddered once and coughed, startling himself. Raising his head and eyelids, exhaling more grayish vapor, he returned from whatever daydreams were just experienced to the stagnant room where his body resided, the pencil soon resuming its methodical work.

12

At the outset of their first proper meeting, Hollis had readily perceived his future father-in-law as a recondite, intractable soul. Just prior to being introduced in the large backyard of Debra's family farm—an isolated homestead named What Rocks, buffered by thirty acres of land, surrounded by cotton fields and, beyond, the limitless sweep of West Texas plains—he watched the man loitering among brittle, yellow grass. Not wearing any pants but clad with a plaid bathrobe which didn't fully conceal a white undershirt, black dress socks, and red slippers, Debra's father watered a lone mesquite from a green hose which snaked through the grass to where he was standing and had been lifted up between his pale, hairless legs, hoisting the rear hem of the bathrobe; the tree in front of him was gray and looked barren save for a number of empty Dr Pepper bottles someone had slipped over branch ends (the durable bottles often set in motion by the fast winds coming off the plains, clanking hard against one another at times like a primitive wind chime—yet never shattering).

"Nobody around here calls me *sir* anymore," the man would soon tell Hollis, crimping the hose while extending his free hand. "Mostly they call me T.J., so you call me T.J., all right?" And that brief overture revealed

more than Hollis had expected: for the words were flavored with midday alcohol and stale tobacco, spoken lazily by a mild-mannered, clean-shaven
face harboring an unkempt head of thinning brown hair; the surprising
firmness of the simultaneous handshake had loosened the man's robe, displaying the inelegance of a lean body impregnated by a hefty beer gut and
the garden hose pressed against the crotch of baby-blue boxer shorts.

"Pleased to know you, T.J.—"

"Said you're Hollis then?"

"Yes, Hollis—Hollis Adams."

Nodding slightly, and with a degree of wryness, T.J. said, "Well, that's
fine—nice making your acquaintance, Hollis—Hollis Adams," resuming
his watering, showing no concern that his bathrobe had now completely
unfastened.

In truth, not everyone had called him T.J.; to his two daughters he
would forever be Daddy, to his wife, Ida, he was Father (she was Mother to
him), while others knew him redundantly as Junior Jr.: the enterprising son
and heir apparent of Junior, a rancher who had inherited his own father's
thriving cattle ranch—more than eight hundred head of cattle by 1926,
about twelve hundred head by 1929—until the black blizzards of the dust
bowl years rained long-term ecological and social devastation on the Panhandle, that protracted drought abetting the near-simultaneous collapse
of the American economy. When, finally, there was no more feed for the
starving cattle, no more grazing found on the dirt-swallowed prairie, Junior
reluctantly sold his entire herd to the government slaughter program, taking $15 per head for young cows, $10 per head for old cows. Thereafter, he
paid all his ranch hands and employees a decent parting wage, temporarily
closing shop—he assured them—in full expectation of better days on the
horizon. Still, the dusters continued rolling across the plains, along with
countless bankruptcies and foreclosures; fearing he could lose everything,
Junior divided the ranch into nine parcels, selling most of his property at a
loss while keeping thirty acres and the stately Victorian family home T.J.'s
grandfather had had built. But that sacrifice didn't prevent him from cursing such bad fortune, from assailing the sandstorm consuming his dimin-
ished land—bounding outside as his wife and son sat mystified at the dinner

table, shouting obscenities in the midst of the blinding abrasive swirl—and, overcome by hopelessness, dropping on his knees while pressing the barrel of a Colt revolver against his jawbone; the resounding crack-shot then echoed back from where he had come, surpassing the wind's low hum, signaling his departure to the grit-tainted rooms and hallways of a lonesome, darkened house which hadn't been graced with sunlight or sky for nearly a week.

But in its heyday, the huge, neglected three-story house—erected on a grassy hill overlooking the plains, a crumbling monument to the decorous age of cattle barons—and its run-down bunkhouses had provided shelter for more than thirty people, although by the time Hollis arrived there in early 1951, the sole occupants of What Rocks were T.J. and his family (the individualistic foursome having plenty of space in which to carve out their own territory, navigating around one another with a curious mixture of intimacy and disregard). Adopting Queen Anne styling—the exterior consisting of brick, sandstone, and marble, the interior fashioned with mahogany and oak mantels, coffered ceilings, cornices, and parquet floors— the house was already a grand anachronism when compared to the newer, efficiently sized homes springing up in nearby towns and distant cities. As such, at least half of the interior wasn't utilized—the doors of some rooms kept shut year-round, several passageways dulled by unbroken, thickening dust layers. Behind a given entrance could be a gloomy, musty, vacant bedroom which needed mousetraps and a fresh coat of paint, and yet the adjacent living quarters might be bright, clean, furnished, with the wood floors shining.

Eventually, as both daughters married and moved away, less than a third of the What Rocks house became used (most of the ground floor, a bathroom on the second floor). While Ida maintained a regular workweek at the county courthouse, T.J. found it harder and harder to venture past the gates of the property, shunning the weekly domino games he had once enjoyed in town, arranging front-door delivery for his beer, gin, cigarettes, cough drops, crossword puzzle books. Subsequently, he was no longer encountered anywhere, not appearing at Ida's side when she repeatedly won elections as county treasurer, or attending the funeral services for departed friends. Some of those who had known him throughout the years began discussing T.J. discreetly, exaggerating him in a manner which made children wary of the imposing residence outside of town, the eerie hilltop house where the human spook named Junior Jr. crept at night. He would, in fact, creep out the remainder of his life inside the vacuous home, growing old faster, it seemed, than his peers, sometimes mumbling continually but addressing no one—often crossing from one room into the next with eyelids half open, as if he were trapped within a dream he couldn't escape.

Yet decades before T.J. died, Hollis had recognized something of himself in his reclusive father-in-law, had, in his own way, experienced similar lapses which likely summoned a disparate mix of mental imagery: the vast cotton fields T.J. had helped farm since the dusters subsided and the maze of two-lane backroads running for hundreds of miles through endless, unambivalent prairie—interwoven with lush, dense tropical islands abruptly seared black and left smoldering by the contrivances of warfare; the inability to reconcile such polarized worlds had irrevocably shaped him, Hollis was positive. But only after T.J.'s passing did Debra, too, begin to contemplate that lurking disparity, suspecting then that his visions must have gradually consumed him like an incurable malady while, at the same time, he had quietly resisted them without much success. So, in hindsight, she concluded he had started drinking to moor himself to the present—among the clutter of the living room, on the couch, with the TV rarely turned off—doing so to lose consciousness of the widespread battles which had urged him from his small town, enticing him overseas with the kind of heroic possibilities which could rouse those who truly longed for peace: YOUR COUNTRY NEEDS YOU, the posters on Main Street had importuned; and T.J. answered the call, leaving his young wife and daughters behind, going westward in his Rambler, sporting new blue jeans and shined leather boots, inhaling exhaust and cigarette smoke as the flatlands stretched out ahead and ultimately guided him to the ocean.

As the Second World War approached its atomic conclusion and T.J. returned to What Rocks upon receiving the Purple Heart (a bullet having torn away the top joint of his right thumb, a minor injury in light of the graver wounds sustained by many he had served with), his earlier border-

line alcoholism soon became a full-time vocation. Yet he pretty much limited his drinking to the living-room couch, the TV tray functioning like a
desk and holding the few items he required. On occasion Hollis had drank
beside him there—the two men sucking cough drops, sipping from Lone
Star cans—but while both were veterans, the fifteen years between them, as
well as T.J.'s uneasiness with small talk, made any casual rapport difficult.
Still, Hollis had wanted to somehow engage his father-in-law like a confi-
dant, to ask, "Just how awful was it over there? Was it as terrible for you as
it was for me?"

Except they never would speak of their wartime experiences, would
never utter more than what was required in the moment—the television
usually prompting their unsustained remarks, laughs, nods of agreement, or
halfhearted cheers. Nothing stirred up the man's ire. Nothing provoked de-
bate or notable commentary. The closest they ever came to sharing an in-
sightful exchange occurred while watching a network documentary about
Martin Luther King Jr., the black-and-white program flickering through a
bluish, fuzzy glow. "You know, King was an amazing man," Hollis had re-
marked at the start of a commercial break, attempting to gain his father-in-
law's perspective.

"Yep," T.J. replied without hesitation, eyes fixed on the screen. He took
a thoughtful drink from his beer can, then added: "There's one nigger who
had something going for him."

All the same, Hollis—like Debra—had viewed him as a tolerant man,
not as someone inclined toward hatred; T.J.'s head had often shook at what
the nightly news reported—the Tet offensive, the assassination of Bobby
Kennedy, Soviet tanks invading Czechoslovakia to crush the Prague
Spring—resigned sighs escaping like a kettle's first shuddering gasp. Before
secluding himself at the big house, he frequently drove down to Nigger
Town, playing Chicken Foot well past midnight, nursing gin and orange
juice with grizzled black men who were fated to pause in front of his un-
sealed coffin (put to rest late one March, months after his failing liver had
become a pitiful filter, his dribbling urine turning redder than wine). When
seeing him inside the casket—rosacea-tainted skin retouched by the em-
balmer's garish palette, eyes now permanently shut, arms placed at his sides,

wearing a brown polyester dress suit—it was impossible to glimpse a handsome sailor upon that emaciated, inanimate form. During the war, however, he was an attractive man in uniform, bearing a superficial resemblance to Tyrone Power—although his luck wasn't as good as his looks: separated from his naval unit while fighting the Japanese on the island of Tinian, forced to take refuge with frontline marines, witnessing innumerable variations of death in the southwest Pacific which, later on, he avoided talking about, hoping instead to dismiss it all from his mind even as he never could. Those final weeks of his life unfolded at the V.A. hospital in Amarillo, where—after seeing a news report about HIV-tainted blood reserves—T.J. refused any transfusions out of fear he might contract AIDS, pleading instead for cigarettes while remaining oblivious to the fact that he was already a dying man.

Shortly following his passing, Hollis and Debra assumed the chores Ida didn't have the will to perform, entering the guest bedroom where T.J. had slept alone (an untidy sanctuary near the living room, down the hallway and, seemingly, a long distance from the much larger bedroom he'd previously shared with his wife). On a brisk spring afternoon, they packed his belongings, dusted the furniture, polished the floor, washed and folded the linen. Then they tackled his mothball-steeped closet, sorting through clothing—what to keep or throw away, what to donate—climbing atop a stool in order to retrieve cardboard boxes stored well beyond their reach. One box held homemade fishing tackles, one was stuffed with issues of *Life*. Another box contained hundreds of photographs and negatives, most bound by rubber bands yet given a rough chronology; there were various shots of T.J. as a ranch kid, as a high-school quarterback, as a farmer, as a smirking entrepreneur in a community not yet made anxious by combat reports (sharply dressed outside his Ford dealership, his gas station, his Bobcat Bite diner—the businesses he divested himself of at the end of the war); portraits of him wearing his navy attire, the spotless uniform appearing as white and smooth as his skin; images of him at a port tavern, hoisting a beer bottle, laughing.

And there, finally, there: her father huddled with tougher-looking men—marines—on a beach somewhere, crouching together, posing like a football team above the opposing dead. What breathless shock seized Debra then, as if she'd stumbled into frigid water but was unable to cry out, when contemplating a Japanese soldier's severed head clutched by her own father's hand, a hand which had held her hands and had stroked her hair; the boyish soldier's face was savaged on the left side, a rent eyelid hanging over a hollow Asian socket, the black hair coiled around the same fingers which had gently patted her shoulders. "This didn't happen," she said, abruptly tearing the picture in half. "We didn't see this." How could Hollis have told her such human desecration was commonplace for the victors of battle— that he, too, had also stood above the fallen, his rifle aimed toward the lifeless? Instead, he kept quiet as the picture was torn again and again—the bits fluttering, sprinkling about the floor. Better, then, for her to collect the pieces without hesitation, depositing them in the trash—better returning that particular box to the highest closet shelf, shutting the door, and not dwelling anymore on what she couldn't fathom. "We didn't see that," she repeated, and, as her father had also done, never spoke of it further.

But while Debra refrained from disagreeing with her mother's or younger sister's postmortem resentment concerning T.J.'s alcoholism, in time she concluded that it was her father's right to have anesthetized those assaulting memories; he earned the privilege, and none of them should have expressed reproof for his indolent excursions out of the living room— bare feet shuffling along the floorboards, taking slow, deliberate steps toward the kitchen, going to where another cold Lone Star could be fetched. In hindsight, she wished she had shown deference as he had ambled past her like a purposeful sleepwalker, understanding him as one in need of forgetting so thoroughly he'd rather drink himself to death than remember. Even so, she'd always loved him very much—she whispered this to herself at his funeral and knew it was true. She had grown into an adult alongside his calm intemperance, had gone from his little girl to Hollis's wife while he inhabited the sagging couch; she had accepted his vague presence since childhood, had maybe sensed his days melding into the manifold of dreams—where his decades of casual dying, to her now, somehow felt like a cloud's broad shadow winding across an unbearable terrain, dissipating by degrees until at long last it was nothing more.

Debra was next to him, propped up in bed, as Hollis lay there with his hands folded behind his neck. Her eyes were blankly staring forward, the bottle of cherry oil held below her nostrils. He was looking at the yellow ceiling, squinting, while discerning something else altogether: that big hilltop house on the West Texas plains—an ominous, creaking silhouette rising high beneath moonlight, a black hole shaken by itinerant winds, doors and windows boarded, panes shattered—abandoned and, at last, truly haunted since Ida had died, his mother-in-law succumbing to pneumonia some ten years ago.

"Come to think of it," he said, turning his head to her, "I'm not so sure your dad would've liked Nine Springs. I mean, I suspect he wasn't meant to leave Texas, don't you?"

Debra glanced at him with an expression of such melancholy on her tired face that Hollis thought tears were imminent, but she was only readying herself for a yawn. "Who can really say," she said, her mouth gaping. "You could be right, I guess."

"Oh, what do I know anyway. It isn't like I think about him all that often these days."

Hollis had never imagined he would find himself off in an exclusive desert community recalling the life of his late father-in-law, or remembering the solitary Victorian house which had remained standing after the majority of its former residents were deceased. Yet whenever pondering his own life, however briefly, he had assumed his demise would come well ahead of Debra's end—although he hadn't given much thought to how she would survive without him. There were, of course, stock investments, his life insurance, and their considerable savings. The vague supposition lurking somewhere deep in his mind was that she would be able to take care of herself, just like her widowed mother did following T.J.'s passing. In any case, it seemed, for him, the natural order of things: wives rarely preceded their husbands to the cemetery. His mother, too, had buried two husbands by her seventy-third birthday, spending her final years in a Critchfield retirement home while keeping herself busy with bingo and origami. And where Debra had grown up, the men were always inclined to go beforehand—from drinking, heart failure, mental decline, hard living—and, ex-

isting beyond their spouses, the widows banded together, becoming attentive to their friendships and Jesus. Rugged cowboys and stoic farmers aside,
West Texas was, in truth, a land governed by strong, independent women.
But then again, he'd reminded himself, ovarian cancer wasn't part of
Debra's gene pool; her disease was a fluke, the sole exception to the rule,
and he couldn't have foreseen or ever conceded the possibility that he might
now outlive her.

She tightened the cherry oil's lid, setting the bottle on the bedside table,
and, without hesitation, picked a different aromatherapy bottle, shaking it
for a few seconds before unscrewing the top. Then, as she began inhaling
from the bottle, it was sleep-improving lavender replacing the lingering
scent of cherry. "What about Bill?" she suddenly asked, between sniffs.

Hollis rested his right hand against his forehead. "Who?" he said,
glancing furtively at her.

"Bill McCreedy. Do you think about him at all anymore?"

For a time nothing was said. Debra kept inhaling and exhaling, and he
stared at her, taken aback by the question. His expression was so unlike his
usual attempts to force a smile that he seemed like a separate person. "I
don't know," he said, his voice almost a gasp. "I don't."

"You don't know? Really?"

He nodded, a look of utter consternation on his face: "I suppose I think
of him. What about you?"

"Not so often," she answered, frankly. "Only sometimes."

"Me, too," he lied. "Not so often."

And that was that. Debra put her hand to her mouth and yawned once
more. Presently the room would fall dark—the pillows adjusted, the lavender scent then diminishing with the increasing tenor of Debra's snoring, the
sheets bunched around her shoulders. But sleep would elude Hollis for a
while. Instead, he tried to picture what it was Debra saw whenever her
memory invoked McCreedy—but, despite his best efforts, little was revealed to him. How many years had it been—he found himself wondering—since they had last spoke of Creed? Ten, fifteen years? And why were
the long dead recurring to her now? Gripped with anxiety, Hollis gazed into
the pitch of the room until the darkness surrounding him made his body

shudder and eyes close. A distant scent came to him there, a pleasant mingling of odors which weren't within reach or distilled in bedside bottles of
oil—apples and pears and muddy earth and tall, fragrant reeds, transporting him elsewhere, sending him far from where he lay with his wife; and,
too, while aware of her sonorous breathing, he was observing a broad river
coursing near groves of apple and pear trees. He was, in those tugging
moments just prior to sleep, somewhere else—somewhere he had never
wanted to visit again, a valley where the rushing, shifting water now sym-
bolized only loss and the transience of living.

13

There was, on that quiet August night, no light save for what came from the stars above, or from the sporadic bursting of flares discharged into the sky. The moon didn't rise over the craggy Sobaek Mountains to cast its reflective glimmer across the brown waters of the Naktong River. Yet crickets were heard among the meadows and reeds, and the river made a low, continuous murmur as it moved between fruit groves, elevated pastures, crooked hillsides (winding toward the sea, cutting a two-hundred-foot-wide scar which halved South Korea into eastern and western portions). In a nearby apple orchard, the rows of shadowy trees were—when viewed at the magic hour of dusk—like a postcard image from home, a welcome sight for American soldiers who had grown sick of seeing rice paddy after rice paddy after rice paddy.

Earlier Hollis had wandered beyond the orchard and away from the two-man listening post he was supposed to share with Bill McCreedy, holding his M1 in front of him while patrolling the eastern shore. He continued down a narrow dirt path until arriving at the high grass and tall reeds which grew abundantly by the water's edge—then he pushed inside the dense overgrowth, his encroachment silencing the crickets around him. A few feet past the screen of reeds the currents burbled and the other side of the river appeared blacker than the heavens. He crouched, letting the overgrowth envelop him. As the crickets resumed trilling, he kept his body still while slowly pivoting his head this way and that, resisting any urge to stand up, or urinate, or stretch his arms. Sweat began dripping from his helmet, wetting his ears and eyes and mouth, tasted by his tongue. Shortly he felt tired, and, eventually, very tired. However, he managed to stay awake and didn't move himself an inch, listening for the slightest alteration of sound, blindly peering out—at the path which had brought him there, at the field of rice stalks behind him, mostly in the direction of the terrain across the river—certain all the while that unseen enemy counterparts were doing the exact same thing on the western shoreline of the Naktong.

Before long Hollis knew sunlight would breach the darkness, allowing him to emerge through the reeds. He would trek back along the dirt path, regrouping with the rest of the night patrols and scouts; the weary, nervous men glancing about—the river, the paddies, the brightening hillsides ri fles gripped as they returned to the defensive line which had been dug along the Naktong's eastern banks, crawling into foxholes, briefly finding much-needed sleep beside or within the illusory tranquillity of the apple orchard. But, for now, the night remained present, and while his body was rigid—his senses on high alert—his thoughts strayed restlessly during his watch, defying what he had chosen as his own personal combat mantra: let memories fade, let instinct take over. Yet how effortless it was for a willful thought of not thinking to become deposed by more potent thoughts somehow born of themselves, flashing his mind elsewhere, manifesting recent scenes which already seemed like fragments from a previous lifetime.

Thirteen days, Hollis calculated, since they retreated from No Gun Ri in summer rain and fog, soon pursued like bandits by North Korean tanks. Thirteen days, almost fourteen, during which mortar fire struck along slippery roads, and mud guided jeeps and ambulances toward ditches; the cavalrymen fled southward on foot or in trucks, exchanging rounds with advancing enemy units, setting fire to every village or hut they happened upon, carrying the wounded and, sometimes, leaving their dead to spoil. Thirteen days of constant fear and persistent inhumanity, distinguished by hills and valleys strewn with the corpses of strangers and fellow soldiers—by vultures descending through swarms of flies to pick at rotting flesh. Only such repeated carnage could distance No Gun Ri, surpassing those who were killed beneath the bridge and temporarily absolving those who had killed them so flagrantly. And why, he wondered, should it have mattered anymore? Why did he care? For the score had been quickly settled in the duration of thirteen miserable days, thirteen uneasy nights.

But on this peaceful, moonless night nothing hinted at what the troops had endured to reach the provisional safety of the Naktong, having crossed the river more than a week ago, demoralized and fatigued—machine gunners, riflemen, recoilless riflemen, mortarmen, scouts, clerks—digging in for the final battle which was drawing closer by the hour. There would be no more pulling back in daylight, no more cowering behind the veil of nightfall while flares erupted in the skies like meager red, white, and green fireworks, and artillery shells exploded the ground and men from out of nowhere, and the North Koreans raced after them as if they were easy game. The horrors which had recently befallen the regiment had, at some point, ceased to unnerve Hollis; betraying a casualness now and a detachment whenever stepping through the configurations of mortally wounded, he scarcely noticed the irretrievable forms marking the earth. His long legs maneuvered forward without reservation; his once darting, blinking eyes had turned into a squinting, encompassing gaze—as if he had been fighting in Korea for years instead of weeks. Then, for Hollis, the greatest horror of all was how mundane death ultimately began to feel—becoming an almost non-event, a commonplace occurrence which was less unique than simply picking apples off an apple tree.

He was not alone in this regard. Few, if any, among the survivors had made it to the Naktong lacking a hard, remorseless thousand-mile stare. Each soldier had witnessed his share of the unimaginable, each man contained a mental catalog of both heroic and repugnant deeds. They had all been left frozen at the sight of familiar faces torn apart, riflemen or gunners or medics speaking aloud and then, a second later, having no head or chest or recognizable shape. But they had also heard tales of exceptional bravery: the three F Company men who had taken cover on a railroad embankment, using four rocket shells and a single bazooka to destroy a North Korean tank—or the solitary H Company commander who, following the annihilation of his platoon, stayed put under fire and single-handedly phoned in the artillery coordinates of approaching tanks.

Yet valiant and nightmarish acts were often the same. When Private Mark Neiman was fatally wounded by an incoming mortar round but continued writhing hopelessly in shock—fingers trembling toward the mangled, grisly stumps where legs had been—it was McCreedy who ran to him and eliminated the private's agony, doing what a nearby officer couldn't bring himself to do, mercifully pressing his rifle barrel against Neiman's forehead, squeezing the trigger. Afterward, McCreedy frowned at the private, as if annoyed by him. He straddled Neiman's remains, stooping to claim a dog tag before feeling inside pockets containing no more than half a pack of cigarettes and matches. While another mortar round sent men scrambling, McCreedy finished lighting up one of Neiman's cigarettes, savoring it for himself. Unharmed by the ensuing explosion—the mortar having overshot its intended targets, striking a rice field to their rear—he slowly walked away, tapping the ground with the butt of his rifle as he went. "Smokes left for the still breathing," would then become his maxim, although only he was willing to risk life or limb to pat down bloody uniforms, procuring cigarettes from just-killed comrades: those kids who had never once expected the sudden civil war which would soon end their lives, or who had never really known anything about the divided country where their limp, ragged bodies would be lifted onto stretchers and shipped home in coffins.

Like the rest, Hollis had known little concerning the history of Korea and its people, yet in spite of that, he believed he understood the fiber of the country too well. It was, to him, an ambiguous land, a contrary region which accommodated the absurdities of war. Nowhere else could he imagine birthday gifts being delivered by the army postal service to besieged foxholes—chocolate cakes with cherries, handmade cards, corn whiskey masked by mason jars which also contained preserved fruits, all sent from the States, somehow arriving even when needed supplies couldn't reach the front—or white-garbed refugees rushing toward the Americans who were there to help them and, depending on the moment, either would be allowed safe passage or get gunned down. So what was then gleaned seemed nonsensical, devoid of clear reason other than a kind of tactical logic he didn't always comprehend.

But the intensely surreal two weeks at war did teach him an undeniable lesson regarding the spurious nature of first impressions: the serenest-looking valley or flower-rich hillside might possibly be the most dangerous area to cross through, harboring enemy snipers or probes. And, too, he had caught the distant shrill of birds, had angled his gaze upward, spotting four sparrow hawks gliding far above him which, upon second glance, had transformed into air force jets flying northwest on a four-plane mission. He had loitered along the edge of a grassy field at dawn, surveying endless clumps of clothing and discarded belongings left behind by refugees, and with morning's expanding sunlight was amazed when the clothing began shuddering to life—the disheartened men and women, the old people, the hungry children gradually rising from the thick grass like phantoms, here and there, before resuming the southward journey as a mass procession of white.

That lesson, however, had gone unrealized for many refugees, the unfortunate ones who—rather than submit to a violent, opposing army of their own kind—perished while counting on the benevolence of their mercurial American protectors. Had the moon graced the sky, Hollis could have stared downstream from where he hid, making out the contorted outlines of girders, a heap of mangled steel which had formed a bridge over the river but was destroyed after the U.S. Army had reached the Naktong's eastern shore, blown up with charges in order to prevent the North Korean troops from coming across; in an instant the blasts had jolted the bridge, flipping it sideways, twisting girders and propelling lengths of steel through the air. Now the skeletal ruins littered the banks yet bore no traces of the human toll accompanying its destruction—the refugees who had packed the bridge from one end to the other, unaware of the charges set on the supports and roadway, never expecting the deafening explosions which would then swallow their bodies and oxen and luggage, hurling them all to the passive waters below. A bridge, after all, was supposed to be a bridge.

Let memories fade, let instinct take over.

Finally, a subtle gradation of hues began separating the eastern mountains from the night, but it would be a while yet until Hollis could leave his position. Concealed among the reeds and near the rice stalks, conscious of every flutter of movement, he was well attuned to his surroundings—the varying tempo of the crickets, the steady flow of the river, the natural plops and gurgles and crunches around him—expecting the sudden, inevitable emergence of North Korean infiltrators: for the recent dry spell had lowered the Naktong by several feet, creating shallow places where the enemy might wade safely through the water. Nevertheless, since they had dug in along the eastern shore, the fighting had settled into a lull, disrupted periodically by skirmishes from the western side of the river. And with the daily rattle of cicadas, the restless downtime meant letters could be written and received, and home could be missed again (the girlfriends, the parents, the friends, and the food, especially the food).

But for Hollis there wasn't anything back home he recalled fondly or found himself missing. His father was deceased. His mother was content with her new husband; she had no idea he was in the army, let alone fighting the North Koreans, although he believed he should inform her just so the news of his conceivable death wouldn't be of such a great shock. While others wrote loved ones, he, too, had tried writing his mother a letter—except he didn't know how to begin or what to tell her. Pages were torn, crumpled up. In frustration he drew pictures, sketching the apple orchard, the mountain ridges, the rice stalks. At times he eavesdropped on the conversations of those sitting nearby, taking note of familiar sayings which were uttered like grand epiphanies, jotting them down instead of writing his mother, adding a few lines he had heard or read elsewhere: *In God we trust, time flies, rest in peace, peace be with you, peace on earth, good will toward men, one for all and all for one, home sweet home, God bless our home, don't tread on me, give me liberty or give me death, all or nothing, you can't take it with you, all men are created equal, for God and country, what's worth doing is worth doing well, don't give up the ship, don't fire until you see the whites of their eyes, remember the Alamo, remember the Maine, remember Pearl Harbor, our Country right or wrong, hew to the line and let the chips fall where they may, praise*

*the Lord and pass the ammunition, put your trust in God and keep your powder
dry, abandon hope all ye who enter here, to err is human to forgive divine, make
hay while the sun shines, Pike's Peak or bust, e pluribus unum, amen.*

While out on patrol or manning a listening post, Hollis sometimes
whispered the lines to himself, memorizing the expressions like a prayer.
And although the Naktong front was exposed, he always felt a real sense of
security after reciting the litany, using it for his own charm—the way others wore crosses around necks, or kept photographs of mothers and girlfriends, or carried lucky pennies in pockets. In fact, nothing usually
happened when he uttered the words—no mortar shells came his way, no
one came under fire, and the war seemed to be somewhere else. Still, casu-
alties happened, some men were killed or wounded in the brief exchanges
across the river, but otherwise the lull prevailed without a major attack. In
midday heat the men found shade, relaxing together throughout the uneasy
afternoons, and prior to sundown there were card games and long conversations which invariably ran the gamut from God to the *Stars and Stripes*
pinup of August's Miss Morale.

It was during the afternoon card games that McCreedy routinely
brought up sex, using any unrelated topic or offhand comment as a segue
for what was a group preoccupation. What the military needed to do, Mc-
Creedy once suggested, was enlist a unit of Tokyo mama-sans, putting them
on active duty inside the foxholes, a little something what'd help release the
tension of combat. The men laughed, and one said, "I'd murder every single son bitch here for a lick of poontang," and somebody else chimed in,
saying, "Damn, man, you know it's been too long when the mud starts
looking good, know what I mean?" Cards were dealt, bets made, cigarettes
bartered. The topic changed in due course, evolving from pussy to sports
cars, from sports cars to football—then, invariably, circling back to sex
again. The cards were shuffled.

And through the laughter and small talk, it was McCreedy's stealthy
eyes which landed on Hollis (never sitting with the group, always close by
yet never joining the conversation), glaring at him coldly while talking or
cracking jokes, letting him know that he wasn't really one of them; and Hollis didn't flinch, didn't look down but rather met the stare and held it, as if

to say: I've already seen too much, you don't impress me anymore. Since No Gun Ri they had avoided each other's company or conversation, and since Schubert was killed McCreedy's gaze had turned toward Hollis, perhaps, at first, imploring his friendship and then, perhaps, admonishing the indifference he was sensing while also dissembling an overall amiability which didn't exist in the depths of him. But when assigned to a two-man listening post, whatever mutual dislike was quietly fostered could no longer be kept at a respectable distance.

Located several yards from the apple orchard, adjacent to a rice paddy, the listening post was built entirely of sandbags—with a large, dying pine tree used for the rear barrier, the base of its trunk reinforced by more sandbags. Sequestered in the cramped space for three nights, the two men hardly spoke, both keeping silent while monitoring the river. Then last evening, having paused to urinate, Hollis arrived at the listening post following McCreedy, and discovered him sitting there—a hand on his rifle, a hand on the sound-power phone—using a sandbag for a cushion. "What, you're still alive?" McCreedy said, not looking too pleased.

"Sorry," answered Hollis, stepping over his boots.

"Ain't nothing to be sorry about," he said, with a sardonic smile. "Anyhow, you might as well get in on the bet some of us got running. I'm wagering my tinned biscuits that tomorrow night the gooks will come across the river for us. Tyler and Sims are betting their chocolate bars it's tonight, and ol' Parsons has put his toilet paper on the line that we'll get evacuated before the gooks can start anything serious. What you say, you in?"

"I'll think about it."

"Don't think too long. Clock's ticking."

Hollis looked out at the wild grass and reeds. His stare crossed the river; he scanned the Naktong's western side, letting his gaze travel the shoreline. Green strands of waterweed rippled off the banks like ribbons, waving along the brown undulating surface. Soon McCreedy had risen, propping himself next to Hollis, gazing beyond the sandbags, bitterly saying, "Damn river has gone down again. Wonder how shallow the stupid thing is by now."

"Can't say for certain," said Hollis, "but it's pretty shallow. On this side the water is probably waist high, but on the other side I've heard it's deeper."

McCreedy sighed needlessly as Hollis spoke, then responded with: "Sure, sure, you're a real reliable source of information, aren't you? I suppose you've waded that river dozens of times yourself, you fuckin' peckerwood."

Even after everything they had been through at the front—when cynicism, sarcasm, and profanity had flavored the collective tongue—Hollis was taken aback by the harshness of McCreedy's words. He kept silent for a few seconds, still staring ahead before glancing at the smirking, brutish face hovering beside him, saying, "That's what I heard, all right? I couldn't care less if you believe it or not." Just then he wanted to be anywhere else but near McCreedy. "Honestly, I really don't give a damn!" Without thinking, he turned around, moving unsteadily to leave the post. Except his exit wasn't allowed, at least not yet: for he was promptly grabbed from behind and, loosing hold of his rifle, thrown sideways against the sandbags— where McCreedy managed, while wearing the same smirk, to deftly pin his shoulders back with clenching fingers and an arm bracing his chest. "Let go," was all Hollis could muster, his heart racing, his body incapable of resisting the weight pushing into him. "You'd better let go."

McCreedy sighed a couple of times, deeply, finally saying, "You're one queer customer, you know it?" Hollis blinked impassively, barely suppressing the fear and anger he was feeling, and lowered his gaze. "How come you don't like me, huh?" The smirk became a straight, tapering line; he brought a hand under Hollis's chin and forced his head up until they were eye to eye: "I thought we was buddies, right? What'd Creed ever do to you?"

Then, for once, Hollis registered something like hurt in McCreedy's voice, a perplexed tone betraying vulnerability. But there was nothing he wished to explain, nor had he completely grasped his inherent aversion for McCreedy. He thought: You expect me to laugh at your dumb jokes when I don't want to laugh. You want me to agree with you when I don't agree with you. You decided I was your friend when I didn't want to know you. I always hear you talking, and you talk too loud and too damn much. I've seen the things you've done. You put pennies on the dead. You have no shame or regrets about anything, and I just don't like you. You're not worth fighting for. "What the hell difference does it make?" he said, shaking himself free at the very moment McCreedy eased the bracing arm off of him. "Let go of me!"

"Suit yourself," said McCreedy, drumming fingertips on Hollis's neck, " 'cept I won't be watching out for you once the shit hits the fan, okay?" Then, patting the fingers to the stuffed breast pocket of Hollis's shirt, he added: "Anyway, if you're deserting me here, I'd best get a little compensation, otherwise I'll have to report you, and we don't want that, do we?" He gave Hollis a sly wink, extracting a pack of cigarettes from the breast pocket and, the smirk reemerging, transferred it to his own shirt pocket. "I guess we're almost even—"

By then Hollis was sweating heavily, his skin glistening in the twilight. Slipping around McCreedy, he stooped for his rifle, taking it with a trembling hand, and kept going, aware of the hard stare trailing him. At last escaping the listening post, he felt his hot heart pumping underneath the fatigues—as if his chest had absorbed some of the sweltering, radiant heat of the bright summer day and was releasing it back into the night. He continued along a narrow dirt path—away from the listening post, beyond the orchard—until arriving at the high grass and tall reeds which now camouflaged him. Once cloaked at the river's edge, he grew mad at himself for having been bullied so easily, for not standing his ground any better than he had done. Thereafter, he entertained fantasies of killing McCreedy, of lobbing a grenade at the listening post or demanding his cigarettes be returned before opening fire. But the long night eventually mellowed his anger, subduing it with immediate concerns: the possibility of enemy attack, his own survival.

How baffling, Hollis later considered, that that brief confrontation at the listening post had upset him more than the grand-scale violence and ruin he had witnessed since No Gun Ri. How vexing that such an insignificant yet personal affront could outrage him more than the sight of an infant being shot in its mother's arm, or of a fellow Garryowen blown apart. Except, he reminded himself, nothing made much sense there. Everything was misplaced, thrown out of kilter. Nothing there was exactly as it should be—and he had ended up in the middle of it, cast alone among crickets, mindful of the river and the nearby listening post he could no longer see.

The dawn preamble had commenced fading the stars, and at first light, faint yellow and blue, gave vague form to the reeds and grass, the shorelines and trees. Hollis inhaled the air, which felt cooler and smelled sweeter than it had during the interminable night. Already the crickets were lessening their volume, the chirps punctuated by longer and longer intervals of silence; soon the morning became extremely calm—the water flowed almost noise-lessly, the whir of insects and the occasional rustle of nocturnal creatures had ceased—although the environment alongside the river was still danger-ous, more so now with sunrise. The canopy of darkness turned luminous, and overhead the cloudless, transparent sky was tinged with color. Then glowing cloud billows began swirling up behind the mountain ranges, and the sloping hillsides were becoming green and golden.

Hollis brushed aside the reeds in front of his face, peering cautiously round him. But it wasn't the western shore ultimately drawing his attention, nor that of a solitary crow gliding downward to the rice paddy, releasing a caw which was echoed by something else unseen; rather, he caught a flicker of movement in the corner of his eye, just up the trail from where he had come last night. Turning his head, he let the reeds sway back into place, ad-justing his stare with the wavering of stems.

The listening post was now visible—some twenty yards away, much closer than Hollis had estimated—and McCreedy had emerged past its sandbags and dirt, M1 in hand, scrutinizing the area while half circling the dying pine tree, putting the grayish trunk between his body and the Nak-tong, shielding himself there. Upon leaning the rifle against the tree, Mc-Creedy undid his pants, tugging his penis out through the fly, and, as the sun angled a ray within inches of his boots, started urinating on the ground, ex-posing himself in the way he had once warned Schubert never to do (yet he was nothing if not cavalier regarding his own safety, unflinching in the be-lief that the pennies in his pockets would keep him secure). When finished, he didn't fasten his pants, but instead left his dribbling penis open to view while fishing a cigarette from a pocket, eyes darting here and there, careful not to let his guard lapse and, perhaps, also searching for the whereabouts of Hollis. Behind him sunlight crept along the river, stunning the banks.

Then with McCreedy's exhalation of smoke, the previous evening's anger and humiliation stirred inside Hollis like bile. No damn good, he thought. Worthless. Lifting the semiautomatic, easing the barrel through the reeds, he fixed the sights—the smoldering cigarette, the head in profile, the muscular neck—taking careful aim: McCreedy's right hand slid into his fly, bringing his penis with it, doing so while lowering himself, back pressed against the tree, legs set akimbo; puffing on the cigarette, the heedful gaze now cast toward the crotch of his uniform, McCreedy's right hand squirmed around within the pants, making a wrenching motion which bulged and gyrated beneath the fabric. Hollis, too, suddenly felt an unexpected charge of arousal mixing incongruously with his desire for revenge, the extreme sensation becoming heightened with the spasmodic jolting of McCreedy's boots, the acceleration of motion underneath the uniform— even while he steadied the rifle, finding McCreedy weaker and more assailable than he had ever seen him previously. You'd never know what hit you, he told himself. You'd be gone like that.

And as if it had been impelled from his own mind, a single shot burst forward, terminating the morning calm and stunning the hearing in Hollis's left ear; then, simultaneously, down the length of the rifle he saw McCreedy transfigured into the autonomous, undeniable world of the dead: the round struck him at the neck, ripping apart a jugular vein—splitting bark after passing through him, cracking the trunk of the pine tree—and briefly jettisoned blood up and out like a geyser, giving the illusion of McCreedy's head having just exploded, accompanied by a fine red mist which shimmered for a moment in the air before dissipating into the cascading sunlight. With his head violently jerked to one side and the neck partially severed, the weight of McCreedy's helmet pulled him over, slumping his left shoulder and torso to the ground, raising his bent right knee a few inches—his hand now motionless inside his blood-soaked pants, his boots no longer twitching with pleasure.

Indistinct voices began yelling from the apple orchard. A whistle blew on a hillside. Serves you right, Hollis might have thought, had McCreedy's impromptu demise not confounded him so, robbing his breath, making him senseless. You weren't really that special, you had it coming. But his finger hadn't been at the trigger; he hadn't fired, nor had he truly planned on vengeance: he simply wanted his cigarettes returned. In his left temple, a pulse started pounding against his brain. "In God we trust," he whispered with the lowest of sound, regaining himself, apprehending then that the lethal shot had been discharged within feet of where he was hiding: "time flies, rest in peace, peace be with you, peace on earth." Someone tore through the overgrowth several meters behind him, a hunched figure obscured by reeds and bolting for the shore. "Good will toward men, one for all and all for one—"

What happened immediately thereafter would forever exist in Hollis's memory as a mostly bleared, unfocused event, meshed with sparse flashes of clarity. Without thinking twice, he scrambled from the reeds, uttering words which didn't reach the air, and, McCreedy's tilted corpse burned like an after-image, rushed along the bank, chasing a small figure in a mustard-drab uniform. His boots twisted in sand, across rocks and stones—that much he remembered—yet he couldn't recall if he had fired first, knocking the North Korean soldier to the sand, or if, in fact, the boy had tripped and, with Hollis drawing near, the M1 poised, rolled over, squeezing off a haphazard shot which still hit its intended target. Regardless, they had quickly exchanged fire, striking each other at close range: five rounds from the semiautomatic M1, a single round from a Japanese-made bolt-action rifle. And then, in what had seemed like the fleeting passage of mere seconds, it was all finished; the war had concluded for him, McCreedy, and a young North Korean whose name or short-lived history he would never know.

Subsequently, Hollis scoffed while watching cowboy movies or TV police dramas, frowning whenever a character was struck by a bullet and seized their chest, staggering dramatically, grimacing, and, all of the sudden, collapsing. His personal understanding of being shot was quite different; for he had remained standing on the bank, staring at the dying sniper who lay faceup at his feet, the Japanese-made rifle cast aside. Where did you come from? he wondered. Why didn't I hear you any earlier, or you me?

The boy gasped like a stranded fish trying to breathe and oozed red foam between quivering lips and then, producing a slight gurgling noise, stopped living: the brown eyes reflected the sky; the face was round, smooth, hairless; although stained with blood, the mouth and chin were untouched; the coarse black hair was groomed, cropped short; there was a mole on the right cheek, a mole on the left earlobe; the hands were slender, the fingers long and unadorned, the fingernails dirty; the torso was a mess, the uniform oily and glistening with sanguine fluid—the five shots having struck millimeters apart, punching a fist-size hole in the narrow chest; the boy appeared younger than twenty, older than fifteen.

Fueled by adrenaline and panting hard, Hollis glanced at the Japanese rifle and noticed his left leg, saw the blood cascading from a massive gash in his fatigues, wetting everything below his knee. "Son of a bitch," he said, his voice less enraged than irritated. "Goddamnit." Like a waterfall, he thought. Like a crimson waterfall, pooling in the sand around his boot. But he didn't stagger about on the bank or use a hand to cover his injury, nor did he panic or feel anything other than numbness; instead, he promptly used the rifle like a crutch, pushing its butt into the ground and gripping its barrel for support as he sat himself in front of the boy, extending his sodden leg outward, waiting to be helped. Presently, he lay down on the sand, filling his view with a pure expanse of blue ether, and all at once his body grew perceptibly lighter—a point of fraction, as if an unknowable part of himself had risen up, escaping the riverside, choosing to stay in Korea even while the rest of him was bound to be rescued.

With his consciousness now ebbing, he heard a burst of machine-gun fire from the apple orchard and a single explosion somewhere else, perhaps across the river. He had the impression that major combat was resuming, although he didn't trust his ears anymore. "In God we trust," he began again, "times flies," but was unable to continue. Later, when he reflected on it, the conclusion of the incident seemed anticlimactic to him, because he was strangely at peace, somewhat relieved; the resentment and anger he had harbored toward McCreedy had been eradicated—and rather than transfer those emotions to the boy, it was an odd kind of gratitude he experienced instead, especially since he had survived circumstances which should have easily killed him. Then just as a wounded animal or insect might die quietly in its own environment, so had the boy. But Hollis had never belonged there, and, as such, he wouldn't allow himself to expire beside the Naktong; he wouldn't rot on the shore or get sent floating downstream: two lives may have been claimed at dawn, yet his life was about to begin anew; that was how he felt. Conceiving this to be his outcome, he closed his eyes. He heard the sound of multiple footsteps approaching, pounding the rocks and pebbles and sand—and, he knew, they were coming to save him, to carry him away from the river and, hopefully, ship him home alive.

14

When did Hollis awake again, buoyed in a sanctuary of whiteness? When did he open his eyes again, perceiving his surroundings through a drug-laced filter, believing then that everything charitable in the world—everything benevolent, clean, and restoring—was pure white? And how often had he woke, straining his groggy mind for answers he had already been told? No, he hadn't gone to heaven, nor was he somewhere in Korea: "I can't be dead, right?"

"Far from it, dear," she had said, hovering above him like an angel in her spotless white attire—an indistinct navy nurse resting gloved hands upon his body. "You're at Yokosuka," she'd revealed, her soft voice saturated with comfort, assurance. "You're safe now." She had bathed him that night, dabbing and wiping his skin with a sponge. She had shaved his chin, throat, and cheeks; she had made his skin glow. With the aid of a corpsman, she had put white pajamas on him, and then she had rolled him in a wheelchair to a ward with wooden floors and white walls, bringing him to a bunk amid a row of other bunks—where wounded soldiers slept, their uniforms now pajamas. He had wanted to know her name, her full name; she had repeated it more than once—yet he had still forgotten it and her face, remembering only the white of her clothing and the soothing touch of her covered hands. After administering his painkillers and tucking him in, she had asked if he wanted anything. "Milk," he'd heard himself say—and she had obliged, leaving him and, minutes later, returning with a tall glass of milk which grew warm on his bedside table, staying there because he had already drifted off again, falling asleep in white sheets. But what was her name? And how long—he wondered now—since he had arrived at the hospital in Japan?

His mind worked backward from that first night. He had been awake when the ambulance brought him to Naval Hospital Yokosuka, half conscious while a pair of Japanese orderlies pushed him on a gurney, sailing him down corridors which seemed endless. Sometime before that, he had stirred elsewhere—not at the naval hospital, not anywhere he had recognized— glancing around at what looked like a vision of hell, a living tableau of infirmity: a large, open ward packed with cots and men, everyone draped in brown blankets. The ward reeked of sickness, of blood and urine and human waste. A moaning, anguished cacophony of voices called for a medic, the same plea echoed from cot to cot. Then he comprehended his own pain, surging underneath the blanket that covered him, pulsing within his body like a fever. Pulling the blanket up to his chest, he saw that the left pants leg of his uniform had been cut away at the hip; the flesh between his left thigh and kneecap was bandaged thickly, a watermelon-size dressing sprouting tubes which coiled past the foot of the cot and disappeared. He tried wriggling his toes, but nothing moved. "Medic!" he shouted, the pain suddenly overtaking him. "Medic—" and then he was gone once more.

A hand had slapped his face and he came to, his body aching horribly. "Stay awake, private," someone was telling him. "You stay with us, all righty?" He wasn't dead; this wasn't heaven. He was being carried on a stretcher, taken up a ramp and brought inside a cargo plane, where the hold was lined with rack after rack of stretcher cases, where those who could walk—heads bandaged, arms wrapped—had to settle for benches, their shoulders pressed against one another.

"Come on, kid! Stay with us! You're doing fine!"

Someone had slapped him. There was the odor of feces.

"Oh, for Christ's sake, this one here shit hisself!"

A medic put a blanket over him. His throat was dry. Where was he then? Canvas bulkheads, dark and bloodstained—racks of injured soldiers: an ambulance bouncing along a dirt roadway, jostling its occupants while heading to an aid station. He was sweating but felt cold, and he had soiled himself. With each hard bump of the ambulance, the pain shot through him, becoming so much larger and more consuming than his wound, rushing to every single nerve. Someone screamed out for morphine. Someone groaned, lowly cursing the driver. Someone grabbed his wrist, poking a needle into a vein. As the pain subsided, a warm sensation filled his extremities, relaxing him.

"He's lost a lot of blood—"

The initial dose of morphine had worn off. He was so thirsty. Two men were transporting him on a stretcher, running across the apple orchard by the Naktong. Sunlight burned his forehead, as blinding hot as the pain which coursed in heightened, spasmodic waves. They passed a sergeant he had only spoken to a couple of times, the man's pace then quickening as he jogged alongside the stretcher for a moment, leaning a tanned, grubby face toward him, saying, "Got to hang in there, Adams. Can't go belly-up until after you get to Yokosuka. Them nurses are so damn beautiful—you'll be thanking that gook who did this to you, no kiddin'. Just hang in there—"

And so Hollis had somehow hung in there, delivered from the waking nightmare of Korea to the bright, airy confines of a U.S. Naval Hospital which hadn't yet been given an official dedication ceremony (the public works operating on twenty-four-hour shifts, remodeling and converting additional buildings, creating further ward space for a patient census which would soon triple). In time, his mind would regain its full lucidity, his memory becoming less piecemeal. The pain medication was decreased; the pain itself still flaring up when he or a corpsman or a nurse tried lifting his bad leg. But with each nurse who stopped at his bedside—same white uniform, same accommodating manner—he attempted without success to recall which one had bathed him on that first night, had wiped his body with a sponge, scrubbing places where no woman other than his own mother had ever cleaned: Nurse McGill, Nurse Hayward, Nurse Christian, Nurse—?

Subsequently, he had been washed by corpsmen or Japanese male orderlies, yet it was the invigorating touch of that particular nurse which he longed to feel. And if recollections of McCreedy's final seconds ever flashed across his mind—or the corpse of the boy he had killed beside the Naktong—Hollis banished such images by letting better thoughts of the nurse's gloved hands preoccupy him at night, his fingertips acting as her fingertips while he slid them between his legs: the breathless, viscid aftershock of orgasm producing immediate disgust and regret, a potent kind of self-loathing which lingered through the daylight hours, often turning his face red whenever any of the nurses conversed with him, causing him to avert his gaze and, too, making it impossible to simply ask who it was that had tended him upon his arrival at Yokosuka. Instead, he said very little, appearing painfully shy, and feared that his uncontrollable blushing might actually betray the embarrassing truth behind his shame.

For a while, one day at the naval hospital was much like the next, and he had only to rest and eat and heal, his needs met by the small staff of nurses, corpsmen, and doctors who busily roamed the ward—checking wounds, emptying bedpans, offering magazines and small talk. From his bottom bunk, he watched the comings and goings, aware of the new patients helped into the double- and triple-deck bunks which had previously been unused: some had slight injuries, a little shrapnel embedded in a thigh, calf, shoulder; some had shattered jaws and cheekbones, a Penrose drain inserted at their necks, their mouths wired shut; some were the worst of the worst, having bugged out at the front, escaping combat by shooting themselves in the foot or hand; some were bandaged head to toe; some didn't have arms or legs, or legs and arms. As the main military objective of the hospital was a prompt turnaround, many of the patients would be sent back to the battlefield once their wounds had mended, but those who were the most seriously injured would also leave Yokosuka, allowing extra room for incoming patients by completing their recovery at stateside naval hospitals.

Hollis belonged to the latter category, for that single shot from a Japanese-built rifle had rendered him useless, something he finally understood at Yokosuka when the bandages were changed—the gauze unfurling down the length of his left thigh, slowly displaying the extent of his injury and its repair. What he had imagined as a dime-shaped perforation was, in fact, a seventeen-inch scar after surgery was completed, with a sizable gash indenting a portion of his thigh so deeply that it looked as if the skin had collapsed into a cavernous sinkhole of discolored flesh. At some future point, he was told by a nurse, the indention would decrease, the scar would thin out. Another forecast came from a pair of young doctors—Dr. Golding and Dr. Buchman—who sat in chairs on either side of his bunk. Both similar-behaving, deadpan-voiced men leafed through files and sheets of notes while they took turns speaking, concluding a prolonged rehabilitation was in store for him, a period in which Hollis would have to use a wheelchair, then crutches, then a cane, then—if all went well—his own two feet.

"They should have you up and walking by Thanksgiving," Dr. Golding assured him, nodding at Dr. Buchman. "You'll be in good hands."

"Very good hands," Dr. Buchman concurred, nodding at Dr. Golding.

"That's right, very good hands," Dr. Golding agreed, nodding at Hollis.

"You got lucky, private."

"Very lucky."

But it was a high-strung, energetic corpsman nicknamed Sparky—a third-class petty officer, a wiry reservist, a choir director back in the States, somewhat of a dandy—who let Hollis know how lucky he had really been, lucky because he hadn't lost his leg: "Take it from me, I've seen plenty of boys brought here lacking all kinds of body parts, and they were still in better shape than you are." In fact, Sparky had taken an interest in several of the quieter patients—"the sweet ones," he called them—and managed to learn about their individual conditions in detail, doting on them even when the attention wasn't required or wanted, eventually gaining their trust with an overly generous dispensation of barbiturates and a relentless sense of humor. For the patients whose faces and eyes were bandaged, Sparky delighted in teasing them, joking about the only two older nurses on the ward—veterans of World War II, women who had seen their share of the wounded—commenting to the men whenever one of the gray-haired nurses walked by, saying things like, "Oh my goodness, too bad you can't see this knockout. She's a vision of perfection. She'd make Elizabeth Taylor feel like Eleanor Roosevelt."

It was Sparky, not the doctors or nurses, who first informed Hollis about his fate prior to arriving at Yokosuka—how his left femoral artery had been severed by the bullet and was ligated by doctors in Korea, his left foot having become cold and pale and lacking a detectable pulse, the drop of capillary circulation indicated by a delayed return of color upon a release of pressure from the skin; with edema also occurring, a couple of days had lapsed before it was decided the leg could be saved. "You came close to showing up here with just one boot, but you were probably too far gone to realize it." Sparky discreetly pressed a painkiller against his palm. "Anyway, you really must do me a favor. While you're triumphantly tap-dancing again at Carnegie Hall, please remember me, would you?"

"That pretty much goes without saying," replied Hollis, grinning.

"Good boy," said Sparky, patting him on the shoulder. "We're all so proud of you."

Hollis popped the barbiturate, chased it with a sip of water, and sank into the pillow—giving a sideways glance as Sparky about-faced on the heels of polished black shoes and flitted away, whistling happily between the rows of bunks, heading for another sweet one to comfort. Presently, while shadows crept along the floorboards and evening approached, he felt the induced fog settle across his slackened body like an ethereal weight, tiring him with ease. Hell of a way to quit smoking, was his last thought—and then he slept some more, not moving an inch, free of dreams or nightmares or any memories which bound him to such an ungaugeable present.

Later on, he was woken in darkness by a heaving cough, a throat being cleared. Overhead came a raspy voice, the Southern drawl of someone talking, mumbling from the top bunk which, hours before, hadn't been occupied. "Did you stop to think?" the voice asked, the tone languid and sluggish, medicated. "Did you stop to think to ask why it was we was fighting for? Did you stop to think to ask that? What'd it got to do with us? Did you stop and did you think?" But he hadn't heard the corpsmen bring in a new patient, hadn't sensed the rattling or shifting of the bunk as someone was made to lay above him. "Did you? Me neither. I didn't."

The voice went on and on, repeating itself with alternating degrees of volume—a faint whisper, a sudden exclamation waking others.

"Will you shut up!" somebody cried from the adjacent bunks.

"Did you?"

"We aren't supposed to ask why," somebody else responded nearby, "so shut the hell up!"

"Me neither. I didn't stop to think to ask. You didn't neither. You didn't stop to think to ask why neither. Did you?"

As the voice persisted, Hollis caught the strains of less disquieting creatures, hearing the purring of crickets just beyond the ward windows, communicating within the groupings of abundant weeds sheltering them. And if he believed it was possible to silence his noisy bedfellow with words, he might have brought up the insects and the weeds, mentioning how they never engaged in the wars of men. Perhaps, he wondered, that was why they were allowed to come back throughout the ages. People weren't afforded those kind of perfect rebirths. Individuals who died during war weren't destined to return as the exact same thing, thriving once more in the exact same place. Then he strained to perceive a vision of his own life long after his involvement in the war had ended—and, instead, saw the insects nestled inside the weeds, their shapes quivering securely among the hardy shoots, having claimed a home in an impossible world. It was a version of this sort of existence he would seek for himself, a methodical, consistent, and unburdened type of continuation—avoiding wearisome complications, unnecessary pain and, without doubt, steering clear of battles in which the outcome was uncertain or defied logic. He would take a page from the little things, from the things taken for granted and trampled underfoot. No, he wouldn't be reborn as the same old Hollis, but he would strive to be a more sensible, more prudent Hollis anyway—someone who would grow content with himself and his given surroundings, a man who believed he was done with war and pointless death.

"You do realize the war to end all wars wasn't," Lon once said, when lounging by Hollis's swimming pool one evening. "Think we're always doomed to repeat ourselves? Are we just that pitiful?"

"Probably," Hollis answered. Except, he thought, whatever comes along next won't be my war. It won't have anything to do with me. He'd paid his dues in the contextual name of freedom nearly five decades ago, and he had left Korea changed and resolved—becoming indifferent to what later loomed in Vietnam and elsewhere, having already recast the much earlier "war to end all wars" as a regrettable starting point rather than an emphatic, universally acknowledged conclusion.

"Sure, people go in circles," Lon said, sighing as he spoke. "The important lessons keep getting taught, no one learns though, I guess."

"You've got a real firm grasp on the obvious," Hollis said, scratching at his navel. "Tell me something I don't know, could you?"

Still, there had been another battle Hollis never quite anticipated facing, that most enduring of wars—as sweeping, widespread, and illogical as any which were waged in his lifetime; yet it was a taciturn offensive, routinely countered on a microscopic level, where the defending generals and corporals and lieutenants wore white coats and aqua green or light blue uniforms, and the randomly chosen, ill-prepared foot soldiers often dropped hard and irrevocably at the front lines; their deaths were now so numerous that a towering monument etched with their names would, most likely, climb beyond the moon. But this, too, wasn't to be his war, not truly; it was Debra's time at the front, it was her fight—and the best he could do was aid her, standing by as a reliable ally, fearing all the while that her defeat would also serve as his defeat.

Nonetheless, luck had always been at their side. When the 1994 Northridge earthquake jolted Los Angeles, their Arcadia house was badly shaken yet escaped any serious damage, nor were they affected by the L.A. riots of 1992—watching the neighboring violence unfold on television like a cheap action movie, remaining safe in the suburbs while police helicopters raced across the sky. They had evaded freeway accidents by milliseconds, and they had also hiked along an Eaton Canyon trail which, on the very next day, was submerged by a flash flood, the rapid waters then sweeping a Hispanic family of four to an untimely end. As a couple, they were first spared from harm in the early 1960s, somehow avoiding injury after their Chrysler got caught between club-wielding members of the American Nazi Party—who were parading through the streets of Monterey Park to demonstrate

against interracial marriage—and an angry gathering of civil-rights pro-
testers which had lined the sidewalks to confront the white-supremacist
marchers: rocks sailed back and forth above the Chrysler, vehicles in front
and behind them had windshields smashed, a bystander was struck by a
brick, and yet, as would happen again and again, they miraculously weathered the turmoil without receiving as much as a scratch. They were, as
Debra usually commented whenever tragedy had narrowly avoided them,
blessed with an abundance of good fortune.

So we will survive this, Hollis had told himself. In order to have a future together, he had needed to survive the Korean conflict, and, in turn, she
was obligated to draw out that future together by overcoming her cancer.
You have no choice, he thought. If I could survive getting shot to find you,
you must survive this to keep us from being apart. Defeat isn't an option,
even should the battle lines remain.

Although now the harsh August of his military past risked being rivaled
by the heartbreaking August of his sedate present—this last August, almost
two years since Debra was diagnosed—when the medical options had
dwindled down to the possibility of a single clinical trial, after a fourth and
final round of chemo had proven less effective than the first round. But the
end of chemo didn't crush Debra's spirit; rather, an expression of acceptance passed across her face, some small relief taken from the understanding that she would no longer have to endure the harrowing side effects of
treatment—the chemicals burning through her veins, the low white cell
blood counts and the numbness and the fatigue, the secondary ailments inherent to fighting off the disease. And there was, too, that final thread of
hope, a phase-II clinical trial aimed at inhibiting the growth of blood vessels which supply tumors with blood.

"It's what is known as an antiangiogenesis drug," Dr. Langford had
told Debra and Hollis.

"What does that mean?" Hollis asked.

Seated behind her desk, Dr. Langford moved her center of gravity forward as she calmly spoke, bringing her elbows to rest upon papers and fold-
ers, clasping her hands together: "Well, basically, antiangiogenesis agents
get in the way of the cancer, interrupting its growth. Of course, we won't

know how well it'll work until we've given it a shot—the tumors might not shrink at all, or, best case, the growths could be stopped from spreading. Who knows. The good news is you won't experience the debilitating side effects that characterize chemotherapy. However, a few risks are still involved—"

"I don't care about risks," Debra said. "Believe me, there isn't a risk I wouldn't take right now."

Hollis's hands clutched the chair arms. "What sort of risks?" he asked, sounding unusually sharp.

Blood clots leading to a stroke—Dr. Langford stated matter-of-factly, eyes fixing on Debra—or fatal bleeding in the lungs. "The fact is, there's about a twenty percent chance of this drug resulting in your death. Should clotting occur, though—and should a lethal break or rupture transpire—it'll happen quickly. You won't have much warning, and you'll feel little if any pain."

"Fair enough." Debra gave a slow but confident nod. "I can live with that," these last words producing a lingering, incongruous smirk on her face.

Then came a promise from Dr. Langford, a straightforward agreement made to the sickest of her patients: at the point the disease became unstoppable and nothing more could be done to prolong the patient's life in a meaningful manner, she would say so without hesitation. "Except we're not quite there yet," she said, lifting her chin slightly and running a hand up over her throat. "Not yet." Even so, Dr. Langford wanted Debra to begin considering end-of-life decisions, to ask herself what she wanted to do with whatever time she had left. "In other words, do you want to spend your time receiving therapies with a low rate of response but documented rates of toxicity? Or, instead, would you like to take a trip, go visit somewhere you've always wanted to see, or perhaps accomplish something special? One doesn't necessarily exclude the other, mind you. But it's important thinking along those lines—while you can."

"I understand," Debra said. "I understand," she repeated.

As for Hollis, Dr. Langford suggested he look into attending a class on caregiving at Gilda's Club, as it would likely come in handy. "It's not an easy role to play," she told him. "Also, you must take care of yourself, continue doing the activities you like—don't let yourself feel guilty for allowing yourself to enjoy life during this difficult period. It's okay, and I'm telling you it's okay. You've got absolutely every right to do some things just for yourself, and that'll give you the capacity of taking better care of Debra when and if it should come to that."

Hollis averted his eyes and sat stiffly and awkwardly. Why are you saying these things? he thought. Why are you telling us this now?

"He worries too much," he heard Debra say, her voice suddenly breaking, and felt the warmth of her hand briefly squeeze against his wrist before retracting.

"I know he does," Dr. Langford said, pushing a box of Kleenex across her desk.

His hands began shaking, his eyes started welling. Debra sniffled beside him, but he wouldn't glance up. He refused to acknowledge her tears, because she wasn't supposed to weep; she didn't do that: she was the stronger of them, he had always told himself. Nor would he recognize those other tears forming around Dr. Langford's eyes, brushed away by the doctor's fingertips as Debra both chuckled and wept, saying, "Damnit, doctors aren't supposed to cry. That's not right."

Dr. Langford chuckled too, even as the tears continued. "Oh, lord," she said, breathing deeply and then exhaling. "The day I quit crying is the day I really should stop being called a doctor."

Both women laughed, each one reaching for a Kleenex. It isn't funny, Hollis wanted to say; instead, he forced a smile, his hands shaking uncontrollably but imperceptibly, and gazed at the woven gray patterns infused throughout the industrial carpeting around his shoes—a perfectly flat, cold expanse of fabric, befitting an office where the illusion of hope was kept in check by a less ideal reality. But the faint trembling of his hands wouldn't cease—not while he wrung them together, or hugged Dr. Langford goodbye, or drove off into the desert toward Nine Springs with Debra staring out the passenger window, lost in thought as her palms slid on her jeans. His hands shook in the driveway, when opening the passenger-side door, helping Debra rise to her feet, unlocking the house; they shook inside the entryway—in the living room, in the bedroom, in the bathroom—while holding the unused vial of pain pills left over from Debra's surgery, the safety cap slipping his grasp and falling into the sink, his unsteady fingers pinching two pills and bringing them to his mouth.

As Debra watched television in the living room, Hollis stretched out for a nap, resting on their bed, staring at the yellow ceiling. He awaited the forgotten sensation to wash over him—that escape from unimaginable pain, that medicated reprieve he had relied upon so long ago—and soon his nerves settled, the trembling soothed by the medication as he began to drift. Shutting his eyes, he reached down, touching his left leg through his pants, pushing at the area where he had once been shot; but he felt nothing there which summoned his old injury, just hard bone and skin belonging to a badly scarred leg which had carried him into retirement and, for almost as far back as he could remember, had pressed against his wife every night—such an unassuming yet intimate mingling of their bodies, so comforting and, until now, so easily taken for granted.

15

Debra would not get better. "They've done all they can do for me, dear." A final clinical trial, a few more drugs, with each subsequent exam or test confirming results which her withering appearance had already telegraphed: no signs of improvement, if anything a continued decline. But, her tired voice assured Hollis, she would be fine regardless of the likely outcome, and, as well, she insisted he must be fine, too. Yet following restless, anxiety-filled nights in which even medication couldn't induce slumber, her mood was erratic and depressed, the nails on her fingers chewed down to the flesh. And that once oval face was ravaged not just by sickness but also from a lack of sleep—the hollow cheeks, the deep-set eyes, the drawn lips devoid of color.

Now alone in his garden, Hollis wonders if he hadn't done enough to save her, to find different solutions or investigate radical alternatives, making an effort to suggest other treatment options. Maybe he should've spoken up in Dr. Langford's office, pressing the doctor harder—rather than sitting passively by, unsure of what to do next, senseless from the continual bad news while Debra did most of the talking; yes, he should have pounded his fists on the doctor's table, confronting the woman: "This bullshit isn't good enough for us, and it isn't working! We need to cure my wife!" Except that kind of behavior would have only added to the stress and futility of the situation. No, he is convinced, there was reason for temperate, rational, straightforward talk: it kept them from immediately panicking when, in truth, they should have been hurling chairs at walls and cursing God at the top of their lungs.

Then last Wednesday Debra raised her head at the kitchen table and spoke almost as a whisper, so that Hollis paused and looked at her, his fork stopping midair between his open mouth and a large serving of barbecue-grilled portobello mushrooms. "Tell me about us," she'd said; but her quiet voice had reached him with the clarity of a scream, and he had, in that moment, grasped both the direct and indirect meaning of what she uttered—her hushed request underlined by an expression which, as it appeared on her face, conveyed two different states: a pensive, half-formed grin; sad, gently blinking, smiling eyes. "Will you, please, tell me about us."

"Of course," Hollis answered, setting his fork aside. It didn't matter that only a few bites of his dinner had been swallowed, or that he had bothered to prepare the meal for them, or that he was, in fact, quite hungry; none of that mattered at all, especially when Debra—sitting directly across from him, her plate untouched and the food still steaming—could no longer share with him the illusion of having an abundance of time. Instead, her mind had gone searching backward of late, retreating into the past more frequently: perhaps, Hollis worried, because her present and her future had begun to merge, narrowing in so as to become nonexistent. With whatever future remaining for her close at hand, she had nowhere else to go but back to where those left-behind years felt tangible yet distant, and, to some degree, infinite. And while Hollis wished to think otherwise, there possibly could be no next year for Debra, no welcoming of the new century, no slow amble into old age for her; this was likely her future, the last of their future together, and the past now held more hope and promise than what might soon lie ahead.

Such an eminent feeling stemmed from yet another turn in Debra's failing health which, after so many months of trying to keep despair away, cast something of a portentous shade upon the optimism they had sought to maintain; it certainly marred Hollis's faith in her chances of, eventually, overcoming the disease. For even with the antiangiogenesis clinical trial under way, she became conscious of her midsection thickening, swollen and distended and hard, a severe bloating in her abdomen which, she knew, was an indicator of tumors blocking the lymphatic system from draining fluid. "At least I know how I'd look pregnant," she half joked, staring at herself naked in the full-length bedroom mirror, her normally rapid-fire tone labored by a shortness of breath. "Better late than never, I suppose."

"I don't think that's very funny," Hollis said, moving next to her, studying her reflection as if that other version of herself was glimpsed in a fun-house mirror—the scarred stomach jutting bizarrely outward, supported in her palms where it curved downward from the navel, conjuring up the bloated, malnourished third-world children he had sometimes seen on late-night television commercials.

"I don't really think it's funny either," she snapped.

"Ascites" was what Dr. Langford called the condition, although Debra was already positive of the name before the doctor confirmed its onset (derived from the Greek word *askos*—Dr. Langford had gone on to explain—meaning bag or sac): a further sign of advanced ovarian cancer, that point when the disease had infiltrated the lymphatic system and had grown well beyond the ovary—often leading to bowel obstructions, pain and pressure, nausea and vomiting, difficulty eating, sometimes requiring a nasogastric tube or gastrostomy tube to be surgically placed through the abdomen and into the stomach. But until the clinical trial was finished, any kind of surgery was to be avoided, and, instead, the excess fluid was removed like gasoline siphoned out of a car, temporarily alleviating the pressure while also robbing her body of much-needed protein and nutrients.

Within five weeks, Debra's stomach had been drained three times at an outpatient clinic, a thin cannula tube depositing between two to three liters of fluid inside a plastic drainage bag. Each of the paracentesis sessions brought on an increased loss of muscle mass—a visible physical depletion, sagging skin and pronounced bone structure—which caused her to look more haggard than ever before, more wasted away and enfeebled; the quick transformation bowed her body, making her stooped, somehow smaller, seemingly fragile and years older than Hollis. Her walk had become a hunched shuffle, her movements sluggish and wavering. She required assistance when going from the house to the Suburban, the Suburban to the clinics, the clinics to Dr. Langford's office. She couldn't grocery shop anymore, or run errands on her own—the frustration of which was sometimes expressed with tears, the occasional throwing of a drinking cup or a pen or a paperback. And as Halloween approached, she lamented the lack of children in Nine Springs, what would be the complete absence of trick-or-treaters on their street, because—as she noted—her appearance wasn't too far from the Wicked Witch of the West. "I bet I'd scare the living daylights out of them," she'd commented. "Wouldn't even need a costume or any makeup. I'm just plain spooky."

But last Wednesday morning was when Hollis realized their continually reduced optimism had already evaporated into thin air, coming shortly after Debra had finished the third paracentesis session and was informed by a young outpatient-clinic physician—not by Dr. Langford, not by anyone she had dealt with much during her cancer—that the ascites couldn't be managed any longer without causing serious problems. She would, naturally, collect fluid again in her abdomen yet receive no relief (to treat it further would only make her sicker faster, not to treat it would only make her sicker). Moreover, the clinical trial hadn't produced a single encouraging result, although it was an ongoing effort. All things being normal, they might have experienced a feeling of profound grief, of unfathomable fear, as if a kind of sword of Damocles had been hung above her head. Except they were accustomed to repeated setbacks, having forgotten what it was like to expect a breakthrough. "Oh well," she had said at the clinic, shrugging indifferently. "It is what it is. That's life—at least what's left of mine anyway."

"Stop that," Hollis reproached her. "You're still here."

"True enough," she said.

Even so, the moment of Debra's defeat was now unquestionable, expressed symbolically that afternoon in front of their house when Hollis helped her step gradually down from the Suburban to the driveway. But rather than slip her arm through his arm, allowing herself to be guided forward like an invalid, she shook free of him, a look of simmering anger upon

her face—eyebrows bunched, lips contracted—and mustering a brief re-
bound of vigor, she ambled quickly behind the Suburban, as Hollis followed, saying, "What is it? What's wrong?"

And there beneath such a blue, cloudless sky—the sun blazing across
rock gardens, tile rooftop shingles, glinting off parked vehicles—Debra
peeled a ribbon-shaped, teal-colored Ovarian Cancer Awareness sticker
from the Suburban's tailgate. Muttering furiously under her breath, inhaling and exhaling in punctuated gasps, she pushed around Hollis, shuffling
up the driveway, as he watched bewildered: lifting her hand, she slapped the
sticker hard against the garage door, affixing it crookedly, before taking herself on into the house. Still, Hollis remained by the Suburban, his eyes flit-
ting from the garage door to the ground to the house, and, unable yet to
move, he felt himself grow cold in the sunshine. Afterward, he found her
seated at the kitchen table, holding a paperback mystery, reading with the
same furious look on her face. Nothing, then, would be spoken, nothing
said for over an hour—nothing mentioned at all until, raising her head a
while later at the table, she spoke to him almost in a whisper, so that he
paused and looked at her, his fork stopping midair between his open mouth
and a large serving of barbecue-grilled portobello mushrooms.

Tell me about us.

"Well, now, let's see, what can I tell you about us." Without fully standing upright, Hollis changed chairs at the table, seating himself beside
Debra—near enough to stroke her shoulder, to gaze at her gaunt, hawklike
profile while she slid her plate away, then folded her hands upon the table-
top, then glanced at him intently and nodded once, letting him know she
was ready for him to proceed. "Where should I start?" he asked, searching
his memory, sifting through their life together, glimpsing random scenes
which sprang out of nowhere—lighting fireworks on his sister-in-law's
lawn, skinny-dipping among cattle at a West Texas watering hole, buying
snow cones somewhere in Nebraska or Kansas when hauling their few possessions to California—as if he were flipping the pages of an old photo album. "It's odd thinking about it, but I'd sort of seen you before we actually
met," he told her with a calm, steady voice. "I'd caught sight of you from
another side of the globe, during Korea, over in a country you hadn't even

been to—and I didn't know we were destined for each other, didn't have a notion we'd meet one day like we did." He wiped sweat from his forehead while speaking. Two flies buzzed against the kitchen window; the ceiling fan whirred high above a platter of veggie kabobs which had been brought to the table from the outside grill; the yellow Hawaiian shirt and tan Bermuda shorts he wore were stained and damp in places with perspiration. In four days there would be snow on the ground. "But I guess you were like a ghost to me until we became aquatinted." He hesitated, frowning at his choice of words. Debra, however, was grinning, appearing duly interested, somewhat pleased. "I mean, I'd first seen you, except I hadn't really seen you, if that makes any sense." Everything was suddenly dim around him, the kitchen engulfed by shadows which covered the floor like black, stagnant water, and, just then, he realized it was getting dark a little too early. "So, what can I tell you about us?" he said, rubbing and patting her shoulder as dusk set in, aware more than ever of how good it had always been to simply touch her.

From Hollis's perspective, their story had begun prior to its true beginning, the wheels already set into motion elsewhere upon his return stateside: those remaining few months of 1950—late September through late October—at the U.S. Naval Hospital in Oakland, California, where he recuperated on an orthopedic bed which was equipped with traction gear, weights, and trapeze bars. The bed frame had been welded down, and his mornings were spent, much to his own initial amusement, with his ass literally in a sling, his body gyrating about while he grasped the overhead bars, methodically exercising his chest, arms, legs. The ward he recovered in was long, sanitary, like a high-end barracks. Windows were propped open for fresh air on nicer days, and at night there was central heating. His wound was redressed at sunrise, medication prepared and distributed between 7 a.m. and 8 a.m., followed by sick call (the checking of temperature, pulse, respiration, blood pressure—the vital-sign log updated for the doctor's rounds). The linen was changed regularly, the floors mopped with a heavy disinfectant which saturated everything with an unrelenting medicinal smell. Morning meals were served twice (7:15 a.m., 11:30 a.m.). At exactly 1 p.m. the ward was darkened for a rest hour—no talking, no exercising, just rest. He was washed daily, lightly scrubbed from head to toe, and never in his life had he felt so clean and yet, at the same time, so defective.

But Hollis didn't become dispirited, for in that spit-and-polished ward were forty other injured soldiers like him—only a couple of which he had seen or met beforehand in Japan—each with an orthopedic bed like his and a hanging chart displaying a name, a status, a condition. He saw these men, and, in their faces, he saw himself—straining as they reached for their own trapeze bars, necks tightening to show veins, struggling while lifting their bodies upright, like a patch of similarly designed but unsynchronized oil-well pumps, rising and falling at different intervals. They laughed at their ineptness, their weakness, or groaned profanities, darting aloof, self-conscious glances around even when no one was paying attention. Sometimes, after lights-out at night, the nurses let them listen to the radio on low volume. Or if a radio wasn't allowed, they whispered in the darkness, talking to one another for hours. And all the while nurses came and went, bringing cups of water whenever corpsmen weren't available, frequently dispensing pain pills upon gaining permission to do so from a doctor.

Sooner than was expected, though, Hollis's rehabilitation took him from the bed during afternoons, assisted at first by a corpsman or a nurse, so that he could limp along hallways, transported by crutches, his wounded leg responding a little at a time to the process of building up strength and mobility again. Holding clipboards and meal trays, often carting medical equipment and gurneys, hospital staff hurried about in deliberate fashion—alone, or in pairs, or in groups—moving assuredly through the hallways as if the world was theirs; they exited and entered private rooms, leaving the doors ajar and transistor radios playing inside. Within the hallways it was still possible to glimpse the most damaged of the men beyond those half-open doors, covered in their beds, appendages missing, heads bandaged yet showing black holes where mouths and nostrils existed, plastic cups of milk or orange juice at their bedsides. And urging himself forward—keeping close to the walls, taking step by agonizing step and sometimes navigating around stalled wheelchairs—was Hollis. He proceeded slowly but purposefully, as well he might: for every step brought him closer to home, every small, aching effort hastened his release—the bad leg successfully raised and placed ahead of the better leg meant his days as a soldier were almost over. In the near future, the moment would arrive when he could limp briskly off the hospital grounds, putting the military and the war behind without as much as a wave goodbye; that, more than anything, kept him on his feet whenever the pain felt too great for standing.

Then how unanticipated it was, Hollis realized, that the hometown he had previously decided wasn't worth revisiting should now feel so missed. Already letters were delivered to him from Critchfield, sent mostly by people whom he couldn't immediately recall—the woman who ran the local florist shop, a bar owner, a high-school student whose older brother had once bullied him for a nickel—all wishing a speedy recovery, explaining how incredibly proud they were of him. Never before in his life had an outpouring of random kindness come his way, nor had he ever received letters from much of anyone, let alone letters of praise. In less than a year, it seemed, he had shaken loose the skin of an awkward town loner to become Critchfield's current war hero, achieving the distinction without fully understanding that he was, indeed, perceived as such.

Only later would Hollis learn of the photograph which had appeared in *The Critchfield Gazette*, taken by the day-nurse supervisor while he rested in his orthopedic bed, mildly narcotized and not yet capable of standing on his own; rugged, large, pale hands decorously laid a Purple Heart upon his blanket-covered stomach as if the medal were a tiny wreath—and he stared up at the tall, imposing figure of Captain Z. L. Trendon, his pupils completely dilated below an immaculately uniformed, silver-haired man who, looming above him like one accustomed to the pulpit, spoke with a deep, tremulous voice: "In the name of the President of the United States and as authorized by reference A of your citation, you—PFC Hollis J. Adams—are hereby awarded the Purple Heart Medal for wounds received in action against the enemy on the eleventh of August 1950 in the Korean theater of operations."

"Hold it a sec," the nurse supervisor said, hoisting the camera. "Oh, yes, right there, that's it—"

The captain became suddenly inanimate, gazing down at Hollis with an unflinching, benevolent expression, staying perfectly frozen while the camera took aim, clicking and flashing twice. "Good job, son," the captain said, springing back into motion and firmly clutching Hollis's pliable right fingers; afterward, the man promptly about-faced, striding out into the middle of the ward—where he stopped for a moment, surveying the injured in their beds, saying loudly so everyone in the ward could hear, "God bless every single one of you." With that, the captain flexed his shoulders and sauntered toward the far doors, clasping his hands behind his back—the nurse supervisor jogging ahead of him to hold the doors open, the camera dangling at her side.

But the photograph wasn't intended as a personal memento; it was, in fact, destined for the offices of the local Critchfield newspaper, along with a copy of the Purple Heart citation and a short press release specifying his bravery at the Naktong River. Had Hollis's mother and stepfather not been officially informed of his wounded status early on—or had he not seen fit to have his medal sent home for safekeeping with a brief note attached (*I'm okay, Don't worry. I'll be home soon. H.A.*)—they would have first heard of his overseas military service and injury when one of them stooped to retrieve the *Gazette* from the porch steps, a front-page headline proclaiming: LOCAL BOY AWARDED PURPLE HEART, ACT OF HEROISM UNDER FIRE QUELLS ENEMY SNIPER.

Then, in turn, it would be Hollis's mother, Eden, who was slow to respond, eventually sending him a clipping of the newspaper article with a brief note, simply stating: *Glad you're doing okay and you're safe. Keep me informed. Your bedroom is ready whenever you are. Love, Mom.* Thereafter, she began sending weekly notes—each missive a little longer than the previous one—with the notes soon evolving into full-blown letters, often accompanied by a package containing homemade chocolate chip cookies, or sand tarts, or shelled pecans. Eden wouldn't, however, travel to see him at the hospital, nor did he ever ask her to visit. He suspected she was waiting for him to come to her, staying put as a silent protest against the son who had run off, departing angrily from her life, joining the army without making any effort to inform her of where he had gone. But she continued writing

every week, and he was always quick with his replies. Their letters grew
less stilted—the sentences becoming more demonstrative, the general tone
warmer—yet were careful to avoid the hurt feelings or irritations both harbored; in this manner they overlooked whatever resentment lingered between them, an indirect healing which would be repeated again and again
throughout the years, reconciling their relationship via long distance while
never actually speaking their minds.

When Eden's first note finally reached him, Hollis was already maneuvering on his feet, albeit with a single crutch; he had, by then, received half
a dozen letters from Critchfield citizens, and, over the course of several
evenings, he had responded to them all, thanking each person for their kind
thoughts, concern, and encouraging words. But it wasn't until he studied
the newspaper article—the black-and-white photograph, the three columns
of journalistic hyperbole—that he realized something was amiss, that somehow the truth had been altered without really being changed. The written
account explained the event correctly—a sniper had killed a fellow soldier,
and Hollis had, after also being shot, killed the sniper on the banks of the
Naktong while in hot pursuit. Aside from a number of false adjectives
(eagle-eyed, valiant, stouthearted), nothing else in the article had been totally distorted. Although the hours and minutes leading up to the shootings,
or the actual deaths themselves, were lacking from the story; instead, the
moment was reshaped with surface details which conveyed a cinematic
sweep—close-range gunfire, beads of sweat, grim determination—rather
than the eerie stillness of that fateful morning, the mutual dislike fostered
between two Garryowens, a stolen pack of cigarettes, and a fallen Korean
boy with a Japanese rifle.

Nonetheless, Hollis wouldn't explain otherwise, nor would he do much
to downplay his role as a minor war hero of sorts; for he had killed a communist sniper, he had been wounded, he had possibly prevented other soldiers from being shot at that morning—it made no difference to the
townfolk of Critchfield if he was or wasn't highly decorated for his actions.
To those who wrote him, his role was subconsciously envisioned in Tech-
nicolor, befitting the likes of Audie Murphy. Ultimately, his mind adjusted
itself to accommodate how he was now regarded. Compared to the surreal,

entangled facts of Korea, the superficial yet grand revisions were much easier to adopt and live with, and, as it happened, the revisions then functioned like a glowing portal which had appeared in front of him, shining white light across its threshold, beckoning him to pass through to find something better for himself. These assumed three-quarter truths, he would tell himself, weren't exactly lies.

16

On Halloween Day 1950, Hollis was given a brand-new regulation uniform to wear, cab fare for the Greyhound bus depot in downtown Oakland, and, as a parting gift bestowed upon him by the nursing staff, a mahogany cane to use on his trip home. With whatever few possessions he had acquired shipped on ahead, he clutched only at the cane, limping out of the hospital before dawn, moving toward a waiting Yellow Cab. Seconds later, the naval hospital slid from view, and he found himself emerging into another world—a land of dim urban streets, of brick buildings and unlit storefronts. In the gaps between the buildings he stole glimpses of a waning, reddish moon which sank for the horizon line; its faint glow was in contrast to the opalescence which had started washing over the streets and parked cars. These Bay Area mornings, it had seemed to him, always arrived quickly, as if a curtain were being lifted. So dawn had already begun, heralded by the warbling of birds greeting him when he climbed slowly from the cab; the darkness which had, minutes earlier, engulfed him at the hospital was being eaten away by the sun.

Even as Hollis loitered by the front entrance of the Greyhound depot the sidewalk was beginning to brighten around him. On the other side of the street an angle of golden light suddenly sliced against a brownstone and voided the blinking green neon of a motel sign. Down the sidewalk ahead of him the shapes of taller buildings loomed in places where just moments before black space had been visible. But there were no other people to be seen, although he had unconsciously expected the downtown section of Oakland to be active. Nonetheless, a blue sky would soon awaken the city, and, as well, he didn't feel inclined to sit alone inside the depot for two hours until his bus departed. Yet he was unfamiliar with the downtown, unsure of how exactly to kill the meantime; however, his restless state of mind wouldn't let him stand there for too long. He scanned the buildings across the street for somewhere to go, but now that he was at last a free man nothing readily presented itself to him; the stores were still closed, the sidewalks remained deserted.

Then for the first time in months, Hollis began walking without direction or purpose, the cane tapping beside him as he limped on. All at once two trucks and a cab and a bus came rumbling past on the street, but along the sidewalk—where the darkness was rising inch by inch—no one else moved except himself. His shoes were glossy with a coat of polish and in the quiet morning he could hear his soles squeaking against the pavement. He kept walking—crossing a street, turning a corner, crossing another street—as if attempting to escape the sound of his own footsteps, and at one point a vivid sensation of having previously wandered those downtown Oakland sidewalks came to him: not as a memory of a similar experience, but, rather, it was that very same moment in time being somehow revisited by him now. Naturally, he understood that he had never before walked there; yet, for a while, the heightened paramnesia pressed at his consciousness, and he found himself recalling that morning with a kind of hindsight even as it was still unfolding around him.

But only with the actual hindsight of forty-nine years would Hollis decide it was pure chance and not a form of pre-destiny which had sent him in the right direction—taking him several blocks away from the Greyhound depot, off the main thoroughfare and into a narrow alley-like avenue, bringing him to the massive driftwood-made entry of the Zombie Cantina. Even at that early hour an OPEN FOR BUSINESS placard had been hung crookedly on the cantina's door near a large wooden effigy of an Easter Island deity; ukulele music could be heard playing inside, enticing him to step gingerly beyond the entrance—and then standing just inside the murky doorway, letting his eyes adjust before limping forward, he saw a tropical oasis faded in through the opaqueness. Exotic orchids covered the ceiling rafters, drooping directly above a red-carpeted path lined on either side by small palm trees, marantas, calatheas, and dozens of colorful anthuriums.

Drawn toward the music, Hollis followed the winding red carpet, passing themed dining sections—Malayan, South Seas, African—and yet encountered no one until reaching the grog bar at the end of the path. A Seeburg jukebox pulsated against a wall of bamboo, and stacking glasses behind a bar decorated with miniature Japanese fishing boats, carved wooden tribal masks, native spears and shields was a tall, thin elderly man sporting a gray handlebar mustache, wearing a Panama hat and a white duck suit, looking more befitting to a yacht than a cocktail lounge; his nimble fingers were in constant motion—straightening various bottles of rum so that the labels showed, wiping the counter at the same time—seemingly oblivious to the only patron in the establishment, but finally speaking when Hollis took a seat at the bar, saying with his back turned, "Can't serve you anything good until six, unless you're wanting java or a cup of water. If it's something stronger, you'll have to wait about ten minutes. So what'll it be then?"

"Not sure," Hollis said, setting the cane on an adjacent stool. "What do you recommend?"

The old man dropped from sight, stooping below the bar. "I'll tell you in ten minutes," he said, his voice mingling with the clanking of silverware. "Sit tight."

At six o'clock sharp the cocktails began to materialize as if borne of liquid alchemy, strange and beautiful concoctions Hollis had never previously tasted, one coming right after the other—measured, shaken, poured, and conjured by the cordial barkeeper—landing in front of him in tiki-shaped glasses, garnished with tiny blue or orange Japanese parasols, presented to him with names as unique as the drinks themselves: Pagan Love, South Sea Cooler, Planter's Punch, Dead Man's Delight. Once the alcohol had kicked in, making Hollis more effusive than he had been in ages, it was another name which rolled proudly out of the old man's mouth, revealing himself to be Skipper Ken, the Zombie Cantina's owner, explaining, too, that he was also a foremost authority on rum drinks and had visited practically all the islands of the West Indies. Everything which adorned the bar, he told Hollis, had been collected on his many travels—except, of course, the jukebox and much of the furniture.

"It's a pleasure to meet you, Skipper Ken," Hollis said, reaching over the bar to grasp the old man's hand.

"The pleasure is mine, son. Now, what should you try next?" Skipper Ken pivoted, facing the shelves of backlit bottles, hands placed on hips while contemplating the next selection. "Let's see—"

One day, Hollis thought, I'll have me a joint like this—make my own little private cantina somewhere, won't leave it for a minute. One day I'll be Captain Hollis, old and dignified and happy, sailing my very own land-locked ship.

"I'm figuring a Hunchback's Nipple might do the trick. Or maybe a Rusty Hook is what you're needing."

And soon the final round was poured, and, shortly thereafter, Hollis managed to find his way back to the depot, pouring himself onto a Greyhound bus bound for Minnesota. But he wouldn't remember exiting the Zombie Cantina that morning—forgetting the cane at the bar, staggering along sidewalks which had gained foot traffic since dawn—nor would he recall buying a ticket or taking up two seats as he slumbered for hours on a Silversides coach. Well before noon he was snoring gently with the vibrations of the bus, consumed by a liberating sleep which carried him from the West Coast and far across the desert. Outside the flat midday light dimmed to darker hues, and in the distance storm clouds canvassed mesas, producing sheets of black rain which appeared like vertical streaks of lead rubbed upon paper.

Debra sat in silence, keeping perfectly still while Hollis talked. It was the first she had heard of the Zombie Cantina, although the story didn't surprise her. In the past, he had mentioned his intense need to get drunk after being discharged, yet he mostly avoided the specifics, hardly addressing the consequences of his brief drinking spree even when she had asked him to elaborate. He had, in fact, always shrugged off the alcohol abuse as simply a transitional bump on the return road to civilian life, a fleeting misstep of his youth which wasn't worth dissection. But sitting there beside her at the kitchen table, his voice trembled as he spoke of those days, recounting what she already knew while, without actually elaborating, also shedding some light on the confusion and lack of understanding he maintained for the actions of his younger incarnation; then that which he had always told her was trivial or no longer relevant began, instead, hinting at a man who couldn't help but look back on his life with apprehension, often discovering a stranger occupying the pockets of his memory where fragments of his previous self should have resided.

"That Halloween," Hollis said, staring at the table, "pretty much set me on a course for a five-week bender, as you well know. The odd thing is, I'd barely touched a drop prior to then, but when I got started I didn't want to stop. Can't say why for sure, I just can't. I guess I was having a difficult readjustment, or likely it was an ill-conceived attempt to stabilize my frazzled nervous system. Don't know why, I don't. I mean, it's sort of like I fell asleep on that bus home and didn't wake up for a month or more. So you can imagine very little is clear in my head about those weeks—very little really, almost nothing at all—until the moment I met you. That's when I woke up, that's how I think of it."

Hollis paused for a moment, thoughtfully biting at his bottom lip, tugging the skin with his front teeth. The moon shined through the kitchen windows, illuminating the countertops and the no-wax vinyl flooring. Debra shut her eyes, breathing deeply. Then he, too, inhaled deeply, exhaling like a prolonged sigh before continuing. Everything was like a dream, he went on to explain. The minute he carefully maneuvered down the steps of the Greyhound bus—having arrived in Critchfield three days later, bringing himself to the asphalt of his hometown on a cold, overcast November morning—everything felt unreal to him. "I suppose I didn't realize I was big news in ol' Critchfield, probably only because nothing much of note happened there anyway." But the trombone-heavy C.S.D. high-school marching band and a crowd of about fifty locals had come to greet him with applause and cheers, at first encircling him with a cacophony of music and hard slaps to his shoulders, then fanning out to give him enough space in which to limp self-consciously toward the weeping, hand-wringing figure of his mother—while a discordant, halting version of "When the Saints Go Marching In" accompanied his lurching, Frankenstein-like gait.

"She had on a pale print dress," Hollis said, when thinking of his mother, "and her hair had been done up nice, and she was crying. I'd never seen that woman cry for anyone—Eden wasn't a crier—but there she was, crying at the sight of me. She wore face powder and dry rouge, except the tears were making a mess of it. Next thing I know she's hugging me in those big arms of hers, and she's holding me so close I could feel her corset pressing against my uniform. And after that—well, you know—they paraded me straight home, I guess. I got properly paraded after that. That's what they decided to do, for some idiotic reason."

Led by the town's single fire engine, the mayor of Critchfield drove a chariot-red Olds 98 convertible along the downtown stretch of Ripley Avenue, chauffeuring Hollis and Eden at a top speed of ten miles per hour. "Local hero Hollis," the mayor shouted, repeatedly honking the horn. From the convertible's backseat, a bewildered Hollis smiled uncomfortably next to his beaming mother, responding in kind to the enthusiastic waves of the people who had braved the chilly weather to stand outside to welcome him—an array of pale, flushed faces he had seen throughout his life but who hadn't much acknowledged him until that morning. Even so, his contentious, tactless stepfather, Rich, was nowhere to be seen—nowhere among the townsfolk who had greeted his bus, nor glimpsed with those who were waving at the passing convertible. But soon enough the well-wishers thinned into empty sidewalks, and then, as if transporting him back in time, the convertible accelerated, parting ways with the fire engine when turning onto a residential street—speeding past Hollis's elementary school, and the First Methodist Church he had attended since childhood, and the familiar yards and brick homes which had always been there—rolling to a complete stop in front of the two-story Craftsman-style house he had previously vowed never to revisit, the property looking no different than the day he had left it, or, indeed, than the day he was born: front window boxes filled with withered flowers, mature trees providing a canopy over the shed-roof dormer.

There was no question, he now told Debra, that his memory had become unreliable over the years, and as a result certain events likely didn't occur in the same manner in which he was relating them to her. Although he recalled with some clarity the oppressive atmosphere which consumed him when he entered the house right behind his mother, seeping into him from all sides within the foyer; and like the swift drumming of a hammer against a nail, whatever fleeting happiness and relief he had felt was immediately leveled, supplanted by an interminable weight in his gut which made him want to twist around and quickly hobble to somewhere else, anywhere else.

"Who knows for sure what I was expecting. I mean, as long as I wasn't fighting North Koreans, I should've been fine and dandy. As long as I was alive and standing on my own two feet and wasn't in the hospital anymore, nothing on earth should've gotten under my skin, especially anything inside that old house, and especially a petty, mean-spirited little guy like Rich. I suppose in my head I'd thought I was going to be someone else when I got back there, a full-grown man and not just a kid anymore, and so I'd react to things maybe differently—except it wasn't quite like that, unfortunately."

His stepfather—jowly and overweight, a short man with a smattering of gray hair combed neatly on his balding scalp—emerged from the living room folding a newspaper, dressed in his normal attire of black suspenders, black slacks, and a pale blue button-up shirt. Staring at Hollis while avoiding eye contact, Rich spoke in his customary curt way, saying, "Isn't that something, you actually made it in one whole piece. Wouldn't have bet my money on it. But let's not worry your mother sick like that anymore, all right?" There was to be no welcome back, no glad you survived, nor the simple courtesy of a handshake—just the subtle resumption of what had always been a one-sided pissing match.

His mother stiffened. "Now, now," Eden said, forcing a smile. "Now, now—"

Then Hollis knew, without a doubt, that he was home again—although an opportunity to say anything wasn't given, for already Rich had shifted his attention to Eden, asking her before she had had a chance to set her purse aside, "What are you cooking me for lunch?"

"Oh, I hadn't thought about it yet," she answered, glancing nervously at Hollis, then at her husband, fidgeting all the while with her purse strap.

"Well, start thinking about it," replied Rich, chuckling and grinning smugly.

At that moment Hollis had the urge to slap his stepfather, to strike him hard on the cheek, shutting his mouth. He considered grabbing Rich by the suspenders, peering at him coolly, making it clear that better men than him have had their bodies blown apart and scattered like hay across hillsides. While you were waiting for her to serve you sandwiches—he wanted to tell him—good men were dying near me, and I'm sure I killed much kinder men than you, and I was almost killed, too, and why don't you cook your own damn lunch today. But, instead, he expressed only fatigue, politely excusing himself in order that he might catch a nap, requesting to be awakened later so he could join them for the midday meal Eden was bound to prepare.

As he moved unsteadily along the creaking floorboards of the shadowy main hallway—going past the open doorways of the downstairs bathroom and the unlit domain of Eden and Rich's bedroom—the interior of the house seemed imposing to Hollis. Various framed photographs were displayed on the walls—his deceased father in healthier days, his mother and her four sisters as farm children, a younger but still chubby Rich on a fishing trip, a number of departed or distant relatives whose names had been mostly forgotten by him. The odor of mothballs was as potent as ever. While heading up the worn-down staircase, he became aware of a sudden chill in spots, air pushing from hairline cracks on the wooden stairs, a momentary coldness sensed like the unseen presence of a spirit as he crossed through it; yet that, like everything else there, was nothing new.

How disconcerting it was, then, for Hollis to feel as if he had never been anywhere but at home; the weeks and months serving overseas in Japan and Korea, the violence and murder which was at once epic and tragically intimate—all of that unfolding around him on a broad scale, altering him forever, while day in and day out the rooms, smells, and aura of the Critchfield house had endured. Aside from the shoebox-shaped package which had arrived ahead of him and now waited on his bedroom floor (shipped by the naval hospital, packed with a set of six ceramic Japanese teacups, a parcel of letters, a few articles of clothing), he found himself entering the room where his belongings felt frozen in time: the plaid comforter folded at the foot of the bed, a stack of *National Geographic* magazines on a writing desk beside a bay window, the white-and-silver-striped wallpaper interrupted here and there by tacked-up pencil drawings of imaginatively rendered spaceships or airplanes of his own design, the Coca-Cola bottle on the night table which contained a small amount of the beverage he had neglected to finish. Then as if the passing of months hadn't transpired, not even a single day or hour or minute, those familiar belongings seemed to be telling him, "Everything has remained as it was—nothing here has changed for you."

There was, however, the slight discomfort in his leg as Hollis stretched across the mattress, the uniform covering his body, and the memory of distant terrain and people he wished to dismiss from his mind (not wanting to dwell on anything—where he'd been, where he was now). The white ceiling above his bed remained stained with brownish spots, the result of water damage from two springs earlier in which rain had dripped through the attic and wetted his forehead while he slept. "You're home," he said tiredly, moving his gaze away from the ceiling, focusing on the gray clouds filling the bay window, as though avoiding something, some internal quandary he hadn't expected would arise. And later he thought, his stare returning to the stains on the ceiling: What on earth am I going to do?

Shutting his eyes, Hollis attempted to push aside the emptiness he was feeling within, to banish the dread he associated with the war and, also, with his own hometown; yet now every single thought suddenly involved one or the other, and as those competing ruminations came and went, the urge to fall asleep and never stir again increased. But shortly before sleep took him, another memory rescued his thoughts, presenting itself like a shimmering oasis in the middle of a hopeless landscape—a pleasant ideality of bamboo walls, miniature Japanese fishing boats, wooden tribal masks, tiki idols, and a multitude of colorful drinks served with tiny parasols; such an assuring, comforting vision it proved to be, lingering there when he stirred from his nap, staying with him during lunch, and, as evening loomed, encouraging him to venture outside so that he might find somewhere which could roughly approximate its hospitable imprint.

Debra smiled at the kitchen table—grinning from side to side, momentarily amused at the idea of him searching for a tropical hideout in Minnesota—while Hollis rubbed at his temple with an index finger, saying, "And so it seemed the obvious answer was to drink, and to keep drinking, from the hour I woke up till I couldn't climb off a barstool or walk myself home at night. Obviously, there wasn't a Zombie Cantina, but we had us the Shelter, and the Rattlesnake Inn, and the Tap Room, and lord knows what else. There wasn't any Rusty Hook or Hunchback's Nipple either, I can tell you that, but there was plenty of other stuff I hadn't tried before. My main beverage of choice became the Mickey Slim, probably because it took me somewhere beyond the ether, sent me higher than a kite and as far from myself and Critchfield as any drink could. Getting drunk like that I didn't think or feel anything, at least anything I'd be able to recall the next morning. There's nothing, I guess, like gin and a splash of DDT to zap you into the stratosphere. Also, my injury didn't flare up or bother me when I was hammered, and the only reminder of the war was my uniform—which I wore for as long as possible, because that way no bartender asked if I was of legal drinking age or not. The uniform alone meant I'd earned the right to throw a few back, and it also was my passport to free drinks. There were always those people who wanted to buy me a round or two whenever I had it on. So I suppose it became my drinking uniform, as it were, and it stayed on my body for weeks, except it didn't ever get washed, and it started to get ratty, smelled pretty ripe, stained by everything I'd spilled on it, not just beer or cocktails but also my own vomit and piss, you name it. Except at some point the uniform got to be too much for even me to tolerate, and so I stripped it off and rolled it up into a ball and set it on fire in the backyard trash barrel one bone-cold afternoon—almost buck naked except for a skivvy, poking at the flaming pile with a stick, and wondering if I'd still be getting free drinks without it. And sure enough, a lot of folks were still kind enough to do me the honor. I mean, for a while there I got a lot of mileage out of being the local war hero, I'm sure a lot more than most other guys got back in their hometowns."

Hollis fell silent, staring at the untouched platter of veggie kabobs at the center of the table. Suddenly at a loss for words, he reached forward, grabbing his glass of beer, and then he leaned back in the chair while taking several thoughtful sips. Debra remained with her eyes closed—although the grin had now shifted into a thin line of cracked, dry lips. Above them, the ceiling fan droned on, its blades vibrating.

"Naturally, the alcohol melted my reserve, made me glare a bit harder at people, made my mouth move faster than my brain," Hollis said, resuming in a somber tone as if this realization hadn't previously crossed his mind. "You can imagine the problems it caused between me and Rich, and Rich and my mother. I just wasn't a nice drunk, probably because I was too young and wasn't equipped to handle what the stuff did to me, and I didn't know how to stop once I got going, so the idea of moderation wasn't something I'd understood yet. One or two drinks, I was fine. More than two— and there was always more than two—all bets were off. It's probably a good thing I can't remember everything I said and did, because I'm sure I did and said some awful things. I do know Rich got scared of me, and I know he'd told my mother he didn't want me in the house anymore. But he never wanted me there to begin with. Anyway, he told her it was either him or me. To her credit, though, she stuck by me, ignoring his fake ultimatums. I mean, it was her house and her son after all, and I suppose one of the good things was him staying out of my way most of the time, for whatever the reasons. I guess I had him pretty spooked. To be honest, I think I had me spooked, too. But on those nights when I was passed out somewhere—on the floor of some tavern, or on a bench, places like that—my mother managed to get me home and into my bed, and she never, and I mean never, said a word to me about what I was doing to myself. It's sort of like she understood it, or in the very least she didn't fault me for it. Or maybe she just knew I'd eventually come around, and her patience would help bring me to my senses. Who knows for sure."

Hollis hesitated—nodding to himself while finishing the last of his beer—knowing that what must be imparted now should be carefully weighed before being articulated; there are the facts of the matter, he thought, and then there is the gist of the truth. "The turning point came early that December," he said, placing the cup in front of him and clasping it, absently rotating it between his palms. "Maybe it's what they call a moment of clarity, I don't know. Or a breakthrough, right? Because after a hard night of drinking, I woke up in my bedroom feeling like death froze over, and as crappy as I felt it dawned on me I didn't want to feel that way anymore. Plus, I really desired a future for myself, some kind of life outside of Critchfield, and I wanted to fall in love, find that woman of my dreams. I didn't want to be the drunk soldier anymore, or the local hero basking like a wild man in the attention—I just wanted to be Hollis again, except I wasn't at all sure who Hollis really was yet. But there was no way I was going to find myself or escape that town if I got loaded all the time. If I'd kept on like I'd been doing, I knew I wasn't going anywhere but to the nuthouse. It's as simple as that. And the really odd thing was, on that day I decided to turn myself around and clean my act up, I realized my leg didn't hurt anymore, my limp had all but gone away. My mother thought it was a miracle, and I suppose I did, too. It was like I'd walked on water, or something amazing like that. I mean, overnight I was a new man. Even ol' Ilich didn't know what to think, especially since he'd been telling Mother it was just a matter of time before I got arrested. He seemed sort of disappointed things didn't end up worse for me. So for a while there it was church every Wednesday evening and Sunday morning, and I avoided the bars, and started reading more and contemplating a steady job, considered aiming for the university—and when I prayed, I always prayed for something to come along and guide me forward, some kind of sign to give me an answer and direct me to where I needed to be heading with my life."

Yet Hollis had no intention of discussing what was, in reality, the actual turning point—that December morning in which he stirred awake, bloodshot and hungover, and momentarily glimpsed the ghost of his own image: a duplicate Hollis standing at the end of his bed, arms hung rigidly at its sides, mirroring him in almost every way, with the same faded blue jeans, tan leisure shoes with rubber soles, bright blue Windbreaker, white T-shirt. No, he couldn't bring himself to tell Debra at last about the recurring specter now known as Max, how it frightened him away from binge drinking and continued to materialize in front of him throughout the years—at grocery stores, on city streets, among golf course greens—eventually growing older and more decrepit than its tangible counterpart, disappearing for prolonged periods only to reappear when least expected, as if to remind him who he was really meant to be: a figment cut adrift into the world without a person or a purpose to ground him.

Nevertheless, anything seemed probable once Hollis had become accustomed to the disquieting presence of his other self, little else would strike him as too fantastic or implausible from then on. A blizzard of frogs was no more unexpected than a lightning storm. A plague of flesh-eating locusts could have swept across Critchfield, devouring the entire town in minutes, and he wouldn't have blinked an eye. The next-door neighbor's Labrador retriever could have started whispering to him with Jack Benny's voice, the lengthy branches of sinister oak trees could have snatched unsuspecting children into the air as they were walking to school, gusts of wind could have tightened around the necks of Lions Club members like invisible nooses—and none of it would have fazed or startled him all that much; the mundane and the illogical, he had decided, were composed of identical properties.

But it wasn't important for Debra to learn that part of the story, especially now. Instead, Hollis spoke of a more relevant curiosity, mentioning another unforeseen entity which had made its way into Critchfield, seeking him out after his sobriety began: transported hundreds of miles— coming from the Panhandle of Texas to his home in Minnesota—ultimately landing inside the foyer on a snowy afternoon and staying there until, a short while later, he fetched it casually off the floor. What was lifted by his fingers instantly produced the kind of confusion and trepidation he felt when first encountering his doppelgänger. He held a brown postcard-size envelope addressed to Mr. Hollis Adams and forwarded to him from the naval hospital in Oakland, with a handwritten return address reading: Bill McCreedy, County Road 14, Claude, Texas.

How can this be? Hollis thought, the envelope shaking in his hand. No, no, it isn't possible. Because he knew Creed was truly gone; he had witnessed those various facets of death—all possessing a distinct aura of completeness, each an unquestionable moment of terrible truth—and in less than the passing of a second, he had seen Creed eradicated with his own eyes, an image which was indelibly carved into his memory, something which couldn't be altered. Then he wondered if there might not be a second Creed revealing himself, just as there was now a second Hollis appearing before him from time to time—a creature or spook bearing similar characteristics yet seemingly inhuman. Much to his relief that didn't prove to be the case, although it was a second Bill McCreedy who had found him—or, rather, the original Bill McCreedy, as he quickly realized upon tearing open the envelope—one who had pre-dated the man he had met in the army, and, as it happened, who was also partly responsible for the creation of that Creed he had known and so disliked.

Within the envelope was a Christmas card depicting the black silhouettes of the Three Wise Men riding camels under a starry sky; inside the card was the printed sentiment of MAY THE LORD BE WITH YOU DURING HIS BLESSED SEASON—along with a folded piece of yellow paper containing a dollar and a short letter:

Dear Son,

The McCreedy Family hopes this finds you in improved health & doing well, and that you're enjoying the holidays in the comfort of your kin.

We apologize for not writing you any sooner, but we weren't sure how to reach you until last week. As I'm sure you can understand, things have been difficult here. The service for our beloved son & brother Bill went very nice, and our faith & community has done much to tend to our grief. We draw great strength in knowing Billy's serving with the Lord, but not a day goes by that doesn't keep him square in our thoughts & prayers. We miss him so badly. Needless to say, you're in all our thoughts & prayers, too. Billy always spoke highly of you in his letters home. The sacrifice you made in trying to protect him means more to us than you can imagine.

Please know that should you find yourself passing our way, you're always welcome to stay a spell with us. We'd enjoy getting to meet you, so consider it an open invite. Until then, if you catch a moment drop us a line and tell us how you're holding up. We'd appreciate hearing from you.

Yours, in the Lord,

Bill Sr., Florence, and Edgar McCreedy

P.S. The one buck isn't much, but we thought you might like a little walking around money for the holidays.

For every Bill Jr.—Hollis found himself thinking after finishing the letter—there's a Bill Sr. He returned the card and letter to the envelope, slipping both it and the dollar into a back pocket. Already the surprise of receiving such a letter had vanished, replaced by the appeasing notion of at last having a connection outside of Critchfield. It didn't matter if it was McCreedy's family or not, just so long as Creed wasn't involved. It didn't matter if everyone regarded his war wound as a heroic sacrifice or a badge of honor. What did matter, though, was that now he had somewhere else to go, someplace new where he'd be welcomed by strangers as a friend. Prayers don't always get answered, he realized, but occasionally they do; and if the Lord was inclined to move in mysterious ways—so, too, would he.

17

The turning of the year was to mark a brand-new beginning. As Hollis told Debra, 1951 was to be a time for serious change, a time for him to make a clean go of things, disregarding much of what had previously shaped his life. That fresh start began early on the morning of January 2, when he rose in bed, brushing sleep off his eyelids, having become awake to what he thought was the sound of somebody crossing by the foot of his bed, walking quickly from the room and shutting the door behind. Sitting there, he listened for movement in the hall, but instead heard only birds just beyond the bay window. After a while he climbed to his feet and navigated the semidarkness, presently dressing himself in front of the window where the pale outside light illuminated the curtains. Prior to sleeping he had washed, slicking and patting his hair, and he had also laid out the clothing he intended to wear the following morning—clean socks and underwear, a white cotton undershirt, gabardine slacks, a lightweight lumber jacket, and a green sweater he now pulled over his head. Then it was him crossing by the foot of his bed, holding the small brown suitcase he had packed the night before, walking resolutely from the room and quietly shutting the door behind.

Moments later, Hollis went gingerly through the almost silent down-stairs, going past the doorway of his mother and stepfather's bedroom, catching their mismatched but equally voluminous snores coming from within, as the floorboards creaked beneath him despite efforts to step lightly. In the living room he noticed the Zenith radio had been left on—humming faintly with electricity, its orange light glowing—and an unfinished news-paper remained on the seat of Rich's black leather armchair (the same arm-chair where his stepfather would soon suffer a stroke, dying alone while listening to a broadcast of Toscanini conducting *La Traviata*, a newspaper across the man's lap like a blanket). When he pulled open the front door, sunlight poured into the foyer; ahead of him, in the yard, clumps of snow mingled with fallen leaves and the stems of dry grass. Whistling to himself, he bustled forward, hurrying down the porch steps, forgetting to lock the door before he went.

The train station was six blocks away—six blocks on a freezing Janu-ary morning, lugging the suitcase at his side, now ambling down residential streets that were, except for the birds above and his own tuneless whistling, as hushed and inactive as the house Hollis had just left. But he hadn't de-parted angrily or without an explanation about where he was headed; rather, he'd made his intentions known to his mother: he would pay his re-spects at Bill McCreedy's grave in Claude, Texas, visiting with his fallen comrade's family at their invitation, and, in roughly a week, he planned on returning home; this much his mother understood, this, she felt, was a good enough reason for him to leave. So he could have something to eat during the train ride, Eden filled a brown paper bag with saltine crackers, three hard-boiled eggs, three peanut butter sandwiches, and two thick slices of pound cake. In his wallet was the twenty dollars she had given him for the trip, along with the cash he had saved by doing odd jobs for the First Methodist Church (sweeping snow, clearing ice from gutters, sorting through clothing donations, organizing cardboard boxes in the cluttered basement). The money could get him there and back, providing he didn't overstay, yet already he was hoping the week in Claude might stretch into two weeks or more; for also inside his wallet was another letter sent from Texas, an answer sent by Florence McCreedy in reply to his request to pay a visit, telling him the McCreedy family would be sure to meet his train and, of course, he could stay with them for as long as he wished.

However, Hollis didn't realize his trip would last indefinitely—a life-long journey impelling him from Minnesota to Texas to Pennsylvania to California to the Arizona desert—nor did he foresee returning briefly to Critchfield some eight months later, summoned home again by his mother so that he could stand beside her in August and watch Rich's casket get lowered into the ground. On that morning, though, Critchfield was already well behind him—relegated to the past, each footstep he took pushing it further back in time—even before he entered the warmth of the local train station and hurried to buy a one-way ticket. While he stood at the ticket counter, a hand reaching for his wallet, his stomach fluttered with anticipation when he uttered where he was headed. The bespectacled woman manning the counter cocked a drawn-on eyebrow after he spoke, repeating the destination as if it wasn't meant to be taken seriously. "That's right," he said. "That's the place," and the future, it then seemed to him, bore the name of Claude.

Inside his assigned coach, only a few of the seats were occupied, taken up by people who, like Hollis, appeared to be traveling without company—a sleeping black soldier, an elderly woman whose stunted legs didn't quite reach the floor, a fat man with a cane sandwiched between his thighs, a platinum-haired young lady resting her head against pulled window curtains. The passenger car was unusually quiet, and everyone was spread apart, keeping to themselves and contained in their own thoughts. But Hollis welcomed the lack of interaction, preferring instead to watch the scenery once it began shifting and unfolding. By his own estimation, the trip to Texas was to be a long one, almost a full two days, and he wouldn't arrive in Claude until late at night. As the train lurched from the station, he eased into the green plush seat, and then, like a coil relieved of a great weight, his body was suddenly unencumbered, making it possible for him to drift off.

I'm a free man, Hollis thought, and closed his eyes. He had equated his leaving Critchfield as an act of self-determination, a necessary escape—yet, just then, an acute feeling of solitude rumbled about in his mind, dropping his stomach. Is this what comes with wanting freedom? Weighing the dif-

ferences of being lonely and being alone, he decided the mastery of the latter could surely trump the former. For he was, indeed, alone—traveling by
himself, bound for an unfamiliar destination—but now as sleep tugged at
him, he refused to acknowledge the true loneliness he had always harbored;
by doing so he could maybe go anywhere he pleased, whenever he pleased,
and he might be less inclined to rely again on the static comfort of his hometown.

Sometime afterward, the sound of his own slurping awakened Hollis,
and pushing himself upright—hair slightly disheveled, his left cheek temporarily imprinted with the design of the plush seat—he noticed a trail of
drool on his sweater. Wiping his chin with the back of a hand, he leaned to
one side so that he could gaze out at the landscape racing by. The train was
winding among a wooded area, rushing near pine trees which flashed sunlight—bright, hot, and blinding—in the spaces between their shaded
trunks; the trees faded, giving way to a sloping meadow and the hulking
shapes of grazing black cows which, from his squinting vantage point,
looked like burned patches of earth scattered about the field. Throughout
the trip the same moment reoccurred: he'd fall asleep for a while, waking
every now and then to stare beyond the window—catching a transitory
glimpse of bundled figures ice fishing on a frozen lake or, at dusk, the
rugged high bluffs of what he assumed was the Mississippi River. As if the
train had entered a tunnel which had no end, the night brought little more
than complete darkness, although the distant glow of isolated homes and rural communities sometimes floated by like remote clusters of starlight.

The following dawn found Hollis eating a boiled egg while studying an
expanse of yellowish, grassy plains which met the horizon. Ten percent
earth, he thought, and ninety percent sky. The monotonous terrain was in-
termittently disrupted by dirt roads and weathered farmhouses and bare
pastures divided into curving, near-symmetrical crop rows of loamy soil.
From dawn to dusk it was those very plains displayed outside the window,
an ocean of flat earth emphasizing the sky, punctuated infrequently with the
buildings and signs of junction stops. Periodically he checked his wristwatch, wondering if the train had yet crossed the Texas border. But with
nightfall he knew the city of Claude was fast approaching; and, too, he was

relieved to see a change on the other side of the glass, even if what he stared at was pure darkness and his own transparent reflection returning his gaze.

After the porter strolled through the car announcing Claude as the next stop, Hollis began putting himself in order. Using the darkened window for a mirror, he combed fingers through his unwashed hair, becoming self-conscious, then, of the thick stubble he had let grow on his face. He smoothed wrinkles from his sweater, straightened the neckline. He readied his suitcase, placing it between his feet, and pulled his lumber jacket on. Aside from having stepped off the train to breathe fresh air somewhere in the middle of Kansas, he had rarely left his seat during the entire trip, never visiting the dining car and only going to the toilet if his bladder or bowels started hurting—and now, while the train slowed down, he moved into the aisle with his suitcase, hearing the bones of his legs pop and crackle when he stood upright, discerning a short twinge of pain where he'd been shot.

But arriving in Claude, as soon as he set foot on the empty platform, Hollis began to worry he might have come to the wrong stop. Just he and two porters departed the train while everyone else had stayed on board. There were no electric signs blinking and illuminating streets, no indication of a downtown or even a city nearby. Everything around the station was still, totally quiet save for crickets, and consumed by the night. The air was sharp and dry, not at all what he had expected the Texas weather to be like, feeling almost as chilly as Critchfield. Pivoting his head one way and then the other, he went along the length of the platform rather slowly, grasping his suitcase by the handle. He stopped at the far end of the platform, beyond which he saw nothing but could hear and feel the wind blowing. Entertaining the notion of getting back on the train, he turned around, and there ahead of him, some several feet away, three people of varying heights came filing from inside the station house: a tall middle-aged man with weathered features and hair combed straight back on his scalp, a compact middle-aged woman with a round head and black teardrop-shaped glasses with rhinestones set in the corners, a gangly teenage boy with severe acne and disproportionately long arms with large hands which hung closer to his knees than his hips—each immediately looking in his direction, all having light auburn hair and pronounced cheekbones, wearing what must have been their

Sunday-morning best on a late Wednesday night, and all unmistakably related.

"We're figurin' you're Hollis," the man drawled.

"Yes, sir."

The threesome started toward him in tandem, although no one smiled
as they moved closer, no one appeared overjoyed at the sight of him. Already they weren't the people Hollis was expecting—for he had fostered a
Texas-size illusion of a loud, gregarious family decked out in cowboy boots
and Stetson hats, patting his shoulders, hugging him like a long-lost brother
after greeting his train; he had, on an unconscious level, imagined kinder,
more agreeable versions of Creed. But when the man firmly grasped Hollis's hand, his face was austere and determined. "I'm Bill Sr.," he said, "or
Bill," correcting himself, "and this here is Florence, my wife."

"Hello," Hollis said, nodding once at Bill Sr.; he then nodded once at
Florence, whose blue eyes were busy scouring his face, as if searching for
something to fix on.

"We've heard so much about you," said Florence, her voice restrained,
whispery. She managed to stare at him without meeting his gaze, extending
a small hand, her fingers becoming lax in his palm, her skin soft and cold like
oilcloth. "We're so glad you came, Hollis, but you must be exhausted.
That's an awful while to stay cooped up on a train."

"It wasn't so bad, actually. I slept most of the way."

The boy was no older than fifteen, and he stood behind his parents like
a shadow, keeping his head lowered. "Hollis, you've probably heard some
tales on this one here," Bill Sr. said, stepping aside, making room for the
boy before pointing at him. "That's our Edgar."

"Of course," Hollis said, feigning recognition, except he wasn't familiar with Edgar, nor had he previously heard anything about him. The boy
struck him as nervous, or scared, or painfully shy—it was hard to tell. Like
Florence, Edgar couldn't quite meet his eyes; even when Hollis said, "Nice
to see you at last," the boy's lips seemed to move involuntarily, forming the
word "Hi," but hardly uttered a sound. Then Bill Sr. asked if he had any
other luggage, and Hollis raised the suitcase, replying, "Just this."

Bill Sr. took his son by the elbow, urging him forward: "Edgar, help him with his bag, will you?"

"It's okay, really," Hollis protested, but the boy had already grabbed the suitcase handle, displacing his fingers.

Gently resting a hand on Hollis's arm, Florence said, "Edgar's got it, don't worry. You've had yourself a tiring trip, and you're our guest now. So let's get you settled in, get you something in your belly. Surely you must be starving."

"Thank you," Hollis said, feeling suddenly bewildered. "Thank you," he said again.

Like a disorganized group of soldiers they marched from the platform, Bill Sr. leading the way and Florence taking up the rear directly behind Hollis. When they finally left the building—Bill Sr. pushing open a door at one end of the station so they could follow him into the blustery night—Florence's lilting voice drifted to Hollis, saying, "Welcome to Claude. We want you to feel at home here—it's important you do that for—" Her sighing tone was cut short with a swift gust of wind and, it seemed, whisked away by the breeze.

But Hollis wouldn't see much of Claude that evening; rather it was an infinite void of darkness which drew his attention, making it impossible to figure out where the land ended and the sky began. And as he was driven farther into the night on a sparsely traveled two-lane highway, away from a smattering of city lights and toward the McCreedys' farm, a faint rumbling became audible—a sound which increased with every mile, like the mass bellowing of a thousand agonized souls, a lonesome howling he would soon learn was only the West Texas wind crying through the deep, yawning Caprock canyons which lay just beyond the edge of the McCreedys' property.

With the even light of midday, Hollis was able to get a better sense of his surroundings, to put himself in some context to his new environment when standing alone on the McCreedys' rickety front porch. The isolated farmhouse was little more than a well-tended wooden shack—box-shaped yet freshly painted white, lacking a proper yard but with a fence enclosing it—dotting a vast prairie which spread out in every direction as a limitless landscape of scrub brush, wild grass, and reddish dirt. Aside from a run-down, slanted barn a few yards off and the spinning blades of a windmill rising up behind its roof like an oversize weather vane, there were no other structures or homes—or the city of Claude—anywhere in sight. But the wind remained a constant companion, if a less tumultuous presence than on the previous night. The slats creaked underfoot while he paced the length of the porch, his soles catching on nails which were slowly freeing themselves, and he peered forward, realizing that all around him, even nearby, were a million patches of earth which had never once felt the influence or weight of a single human being.

How unlikely, it struck Hollis, for him to have awakened there. How circuitous his life had become of late. Then, too, it was as if he had stranded himself on the moon with three strangers who were hard to gauge. Nevertheless, after he had slept contentedly inside their home, what had felt aloof during the first night was more forgivable in the light of the next day. For he had encountered the source of their collective reticence that morning, had caught glimpses from one side of the one-story house to the other. A walnut chifforobe sat in the middle of the living room like an altar, upon which was a folded American flag, three carefully arranged letters and envelopes, a Purple Heart which had been awarded posthumously, a handwritten copy of the Lord's Prayer, and—at the center of it all—a framed portrait of a teenaged Creed, an enlarged black-and-white high-school photograph with a sepia tint and cloudy borders: his chin lifted to accentuate the angle of his jawline, his teeth flashing white and perfect, his thick blond hair slicked back on his scalp, his skin airbrushed into an unblemished surface. Smaller versions of the photograph were scattered throughout the house (on a piano beside a large cross, on a hallway wall beside a dime-store painting of Jesus, on a telephone stand beside a King James Bible), while no photographs of Edgar, or Bill Sr., or Florence were displayed in any room—just that same image of Creed residing within inches of some representation of the Lord.

"Are you redeemed, Hollis?" Florence had asked him earlier, after Edgar had led him to the kitchen for breakfast.

"I believe so," he answered from where he leaned against the doorway, but somewhere in his mind he thought: No, not really, probably not yet.

"That's nice to hear," she said in her soft, maternal way, staring down at the stove while frying bacon. "It's getting harder anymore knowing who is or who ain't."

Crossing back and forth between his mother and Hollis, Edgar had begun arranging five plates, five napkins, five cups, five forks and spoons and butter knives around the kitchen table, of which only four of each would be used. Once everyone sat down to eat scrambled eggs, pork chops, bacon, and toast, the morning prayer was given in complete silence—four pairs of hands clasped before four faces, although only three of the four heads bowed with eyes closed, shifting their bodies toward the unused setting and empty seat where Creed should have been awaiting his breakfast. The surviving McCreedys were, after all, grappling with the loss of either a beloved son or an older brother; they were, Hollis now understood, a family still very much fettered in a state of profound mourning, something they also had expected him to share. Most surely they were people in need of answers in order to assuage the grief, just as he, for less specific reasons, was in need of meaning for his life. That was why they had wished to meet him, he reasoned, and that was why he had decided to travel so far. For them, he was an accessible link to a tragedy which couldn't yet be laid to rest—and, maybe, with him at last present to them there was offered the possibility of acceptance, however meager the detailed truth and circumstances of their son's murder might get parceled.

But if a kind of healing was wanted, perhaps the process had already begun without effort, commencing quietly within the hazy glow of dawn and signaled by the mindful gaze of a boy who, from his bed, spied the broad, snakelike scar on the inner thigh of their guest; for Hollis had slept in the narrow room Creed had occupied with his kid brother, falling asleep on the twin mattress which had previously held the more muscular form of Edgar's military-bound sibling. Now the room had clearly become Edgar's domain with his brother's departure and death, the floor littered by the boy's comic books, battling green army men, model cars, and discarded socks and crumpled overalls. In fact, the room smelled of boy, musty and earthy, like wet dirt. Other than Edgar's clutter, though, there wasn't much else in the room but the two twin beds and a bureau and a chair where Hollis had put his suitcase.

Yet lingering traces of Creed remained evident on the wall above what had been his bed—three triangle-shaped high-school football flags, blue and gold, heralding the Fighting Tigers of Claude as district and regional champs. And on the bureau—in front of which Hollis loitered soon after waking, standing there in just a T-shirt and underwear—was a handful of Indian Head pennies positioned side by side to make the pattern of a cross, along with the tattered, blurry photograph of the girlfriend Creed had claimed he was going to marry someday, and a flat, slender piece of polished metal with hanja characters meticulously carved upon it and which, he had no doubt, had belonged to the monk they had seen run down on that desolate road from Yongdong. As he absently scratched at his scar—glimpsing those few items he had either forgotten about or never imagined seeing again in a place like West Texas—it seemed, to Hollis, as if Creed had recently visited the farm, leaving the good luck charms carried in Korea on the bureau before heading elsewhere—except that wasn't quite the case.

Still, Creed had been to Claude since Hollis last saw him alive, although he arrived within a sealed coffin, never making it back to his bedroom at the farm; his possessions, however, were afforded the courtesy, the military having forwarded them ahead of the body. Then how human those things now appeared, how unrelated to Creed they felt, and what had once seemed so cruel or somehow emblematic—the pennies, a memento stolen off a dead monk, even a girl's unfocused face on the curled paper of a ragged photograph—no longer held much significance when studied in the context of a dim farmhouse bedroom, somewhere far removed from the bloated corpses floating among rice fields or piled beneath bridges. And yet, for Hollis, that was where Creed continued to reside in his memory, that was where his version of Creed belonged—roaming assuredly, furiously below Korean hillsides, a cigarette at his lips, his rifle aimed and ready. No, Hollis couldn't envision such a soldier as ever having lived a life at the remote farm—

sleeping where he'd slept, going to school and playing sports, growing up with soft-spoken family members—unless, of course, that person was someone more like himself. He pressed a finger over a penny, sliding it out of the cross pattern and along the top of the bureau. Funny, he thought, that these little things outlasted Bill McCreedy—funny that just this stuff and almost nothing else would find its way home to Texas.

When Hollis turned away from the bureau, he saw Edgar was awake and sitting upright in bed, watching him without expression, thick hair pointing wildly in a dozen directions. "Morning," Hollis said, navigating around a traffic jam of toy cars on the floor, and then he lowered himself to the edge of Creed's mattress, facing the boy whose bed was less than three feet away. "How'd you sleep? Hope I didn't keep you up by snoring."

But Edgar didn't answer, nor did he now stare directly at Hollis. Instead, the boy's gaze was fixed on the snaking scar, studying the wound with fascination. "It hurt?" he finally said, pointing casually at Hollis's left thigh.

Spreading his legs apart, Hollis glanced at the scar, rubbing a palm along it. "Not so much anymore. Sometimes it does, if I think about it, but mostly it only itches on occasion."

"Looks like it hurts."

Edgar scooted forward in the bed, sliding his bare feet out from under the sheets, bringing himself to the edge of his mattress where, as if the boy were trying to see through darkness, he bent forward to peer at the scar.

"Go ahead," Hollis said. "Feel it if you like, won't bite you."

At first Edgar looked like he had no intention of getting any closer to the wound, but presently he moved a hand toward the damaged thigh, gingerly easing fingers against Hollis's skin as if he were testing the heat of a flame. "You knew my brother," the boy said matter-of-factly, two cold fingertips slowly tracing the route of the crooked scar, producing a multitude of goose pimples on Hollis's left thigh.

"I sure did."

After a second the boy asked, "Was he your best buddy?"

Unsure of how to answer, Hollis gave an indifferent shrug of his shoulders. He then heard himself say, "Sort of, I suppose," as his body unexpectedly turned rigid from the boy's touch.

"He was my best buddy, too." Edgar drew his hand back, quickly re-tracting it to a bouncing knee covered beneath his plaid pajama bottoms. "Think a fella can have him two best buddies?"

"Don't see why not," Hollis said, giving another shrug.

"Me neither," the boy said. "Don't see why not neither." Then Edgar's mouth thinned a bit before he asked, "You miss him?"

"Yes," Hollis lied without thinking twice, "I do."

The boy grinned and then, as he had just done with his hand, quickly retracted the expression as if he wasn't permitted to smile. However, in that brief moment, Hollis spotted something familiar on Edgar's benign face, catching a glimpse of the exact same effortless grin he had seen to the point of contempt in Korea. Yet sitting before the boy, Hollis was surprised to suddenly feel a kind of indirect affection for Creed, an unexpected tender-ness and warmth he had never thought possible.

"Anyways, you wasn't snoring," Edgar said. "If you was I'd have told you to shush. Don't like hearing snoring, that's why I don't do it."

"Fair enough," Hollis said, smiling at one corner of his mouth. "I don't like hearing snoring either."

But later that morning—while Hollis stood alone on the porch, waiting for Bill Sr. to come outside and give him a tour around the property—something else was now puzzling him, something he couldn't really sort out in his head; because during breakfast Bill Sr. and Florence had spoken of how glad they were to have him there, how important it was for them to get to know the young man who had been a friend to their elder son and, as Florence told it, was highly regarded in turn. "You meant the world to our Billy," she had said, seated at the kitchen table across from him. "Most every letter he sent home had some kind of mention of you, said you were like a second brother to him, said you was someone he'd count on in the worst of it."

"He got a big cut on his leg," Edgar piped up, raising his right arm and holding it at the elbow. " 'Bout this long as this much of my arm here."

Like a jag of lightning, Bill Sr. struck his fork against Edgar's plate, ad-monishing the boy with a chewing mouthful of eggs: "Why don't you shut it and eat your breakfast." Then as Edgar and his arm slumped, Bill Sr.

swallowed hard, thrusting his fork at the center of the table to retrieve another pork chop.

"Please forgive Edgar," Florence said, shooting the boy a quick sidelong glance which was both stern and motherly. "His mouth ails him of late." Her glare melted when she shifted again to Hollis, and then she sighed: "Just for the life of me, I can't begin imagining what all you boys endure over in a place like that. Except you was blessed to have each other—you and our Billy—and I take great heart knowing that. We all do, Hollis."

"That's nearer than right," Bill Sr. agreed with a sullen voice, hunched over where he sat and poking at the food on his plate.

What was said about the letters was mystifying, although Hollis could tell Florence wasn't lying. He saw the truth expressed upon her pale white face, heard it in her gentle, mellifluous voice. She had no reason to lie to him, whereas Creed apparently had reason to lie to her and Bill Sr. and Edgar. The best Hollis could figure was that, when writing home, Creed had simply substituted him for Schubert Tang—perhaps because Schubert had been Chinese instead of white, a person who, by last name only, might have sounded more like the enemy than a friend. But even that didn't make much sense. Then after Florence's unlikely revelation came another consideration—a horrible possibility lacking any logic to it, a horrible realization squirming and growing inside his brain—calling into question his memory of Creed, as well as what he believed he had understood for certain about his days serving overseas: Maybe Creed hadn't lied. Maybe, instead, he was the one remembering everything wrong. Maybe everything had happened in slightly different ways and the reality was too awful for him to have sustained, lest he fall apart at the painful recollection of it. Maybe the facts had escaped him on the morning he and Creed were both shot, rattled from him on the banks of the Naktong, ebbing further, then, in the weeks of recuperation, medication, and alcohol. Maybe—maybe—he had been nurturing lies without realizing it, fitting them into the places where he was no longer able or willing to access the truth.

And soon enough Hollis would be asked to dig among those grievous places in his mind, surprising himself with what was lurking there and, as the words slipped easily and dispassionately past his lips, with what he then heard himself say. For Bill Sr. would take him away from the farmhouse, just the two of them jostled inside a red pickup truck, bouncing along a rutted dirt road which wound down and through a valley of craggy, barren mesquite trees. When the truck growled along a steep hill, climbing higher, the ghostly mesquites began decreasing in number until they were gone. With the trees behind them, the truck topped the hill and an expanse of open fields flooded into view. That over there, Bill Sr. went on to mutter while he drove, was for cotton; that one, too; that one up yonder, that's where oats will sprout come spring. Hollis looked to his left, to his right, up ahead, nodding all the while. Keeping his eyes toward the horizon, Bill Sr. stopped the truck in the middle of the road, turning off the engine. Hollis glanced woodenly at him, saying nothing.

For a minute, Bill Sr. continued looking beyond the mud-spattered windshield with his face set. Then wetting his lips, he lowered his head, staring only at the center of the steering wheel. "Son," he said in the gravest of tones, "I don't like askin' you this, 'cuz it's been hard on you, I know, and I ain't sayin' it ain't been—but you got to tell me something, 'cuz there's something I need knowing and it couldn't rightly get asked in front of Flo and the boy. So I promise you I won't be badgering you again on this while you're here—or ever again, I promise—but I'm needing to know how it happened that Billy got himself killed exactly. We already know when and where he got hit, we already know that. We know about that damn sumbitch sniper. We know you was there, too, and how you got hit bad in the leg and, son, that's a mighty rotten thing you had done to you—glad you got that sumbitch back, better believe it. But that's about all we got reported to us, and I can't stomach not knowing the whole story, 'cuz it was my boy who got killed and I've got me a right to know more than just two-bit information on pieces of paper. So I'm hoping you can shed a little more light for me—and I won't ask again, I promise you that—I just need knowing for my own sake, 'cuz it'd make a world of difference to me, and I'd sure sleep a ton better by knowing."

The events of five months earlier seemed like they belonged to another lifetime. Still, Hollis would oblige Bill Sr.'s request because, at that moment, it felt as if he had no other choice but to do so. He leaned forward, bringing his stare to the dashboard, saying, "I don't know." Dust coated everything—the dash, the steering wheel, the seat; unsettled motes of dust floated between and around them like minuscule constellations, as both Hollis and Bill Sr. held their respective gazes within the truck. "I don't know," he repeated, searching for the proper starting point. "It's not anything I've talked about before." But already a confident voice he didn't recognize was whispering inside his head, urging him on—some separate part making itself known, speaking to him with an increasing volume and, in due course, speaking from him in a straightforward, deliberate manner.

Then Hollis would talk of that fateful morning at the Naktong; he would relate an account which wasn't entirely familiar to him yet was plausible enough, revising and editing as he went. He and Creed had had a peaceful night at the two-man listening post. Pressing their shoulders against sandbags, they had swapped cigarettes at dusk and talked in low voices about insignificant things, the way friends tend to do—people they missed back home in the States, food they looked forward to eating again, mostly small talk Hollis couldn't now begin to recall. With darkness their conversation had drifted toward silence, both holding positions on either side of the post, monitoring the night, entranced by the purring of crickets and the steady burbling of the river. A few times they had heard rustling in the nearby wild grass and reeds, but it always proved to be nothing more than the invisible hand of nature. By first light the air had become cooler and smelled sweeter than it had throughout the uneventful night. In the calm morning the crickets grew quieter, and the hillsides were turning green and golden. It was almost time for them to leave, to return to camp on a trail which ran along the edge of an apple orchard. Beside a dying pine tree at the rear of the listening post, he and Creed had stood up to urinate, putting the trunk of the tree between themselves and the river, half shielding their bodies there. But no sooner had they unfastened their pants when Creed saw something glinting beyond Hollis, several yards away in the reeds and reflected by sunlight. Perhaps, at that moment, Creed had shouted a warning, although Hollis couldn't say for certain. However, he remembered Creed pushing him violently aside at the very instant a loud crack erupted within the reeds, and he remembered looking up from the ground as Creed staggered back into the trunk, bleeding at his neck. After that, Hollis told Bill Sr., his mind was a jumble, a mess of black spaces and frozen seconds. Of course, later on, what had then transpired was pieced together and made plain: he had pursued the sniper on the banks of the river, had chased the gook bastard and killed him—but not before also getting shot, not before feeling the same burning sting which had taken Bill McCreedy Jr. from the world.

"He saved my life," Hollis said miserably, "and I couldn't save him. Everyone said I'd been a hero, even though it's not anything I'm proud of. The real hero was your son, sir, and I can't stand how I'm here now and he isn't, doesn't seem right some way. What keeps me going is not letting myself forget I owe the rest of my days to him. So I've got a duty to keep my head above water and let my life from here on out serve as an honor to his memory—and that's what I'm intending to do, that's pretty much all I can tell you, sir."

Bill Sr. raised his head. He brought his stare to the driver window, lost in thought. After a while he said, "I appreciate it, son," sounding as if the wind had been knocked from him.

Except what was just said might as well have fallen on deaf ears; for Hollis, too, had raised his head, glancing toward the passenger window— his attention immediately caught by two indistinct figures standing far off in a sloping back field, a pair of black shapes framed with blue, loitering where the flat horizon of the field cut a line underneath the sky. With a blink of his eyes, the taller shape standing to the right vanished from sight. But the other figure remained slumped to one side as if it were on the verge of toppling, both arms outstretched like Jesus nailed to the cross. You're only a scarecrow, Hollis told himself. Only a stupid scarecrow—that's what you really are.

18

On the following Sunday, Hollis and the McCreedys had a late lunch in picnic fashion among the deceased, a newly adopted weekly ritual which the
family, especially Florence, felt was necessary. They ate outside during the
afternoon, shortly after church, and the weather was nicer than usual, warm
enough for coats to be unbuttoned once Sunday worship was behind them.
Yet the Baptist church had been different than any church Hollis had previously attended; the service wasn't conducted inside a proper building but,
rather, beside a dry riverbed at the bottom of the Caprock canyon, presented under a large revival tent–like structure lacking walls and covered by
a corrugated-metal roof which was held up with slender wooden poles; instead of pews there were rows of long weathered benches, instead of a sea-
soned, soft-spoken minister there was an agitated boyish preacher with
yellow bloodshot eyes—shaking his arms in front of the congregation, a
Bible gripped in one hand, pacing like a caged lion and wagging his tongue,
wearing a blue suit which was a size too big for him, spitting as a man possessed while he gesticulated, telling them they were no better than stray cattle! But Jesus had died a horrible death so they might be delivered from the
slaughterhouse of damnation! Jesus, the preacher screamed, was greedy for

their unworthy souls! The Lord couldn't care less about their spoiled flesh, but He would die again and again if only to redeem their wanton, sinful souls: "An eternity of Hell fire awaits you who are ripe with the taint of Satan's lure and choose not to heed His word lest you abandon the reckless pleasures of this here diseased world! Oh, heed His word! Redeem yourself, or perish!"

Redeem yourself, or perish.

Hollis's brain had begun to ache, throbbing somewhere deep within his forehead as the boy preacher shouted his wrathful message. By the time the service was finished, the pain had spread, becoming more unbearable, coursing with the pulse of his heartbeat and pounding along the cords of his sockets; it was an acute and near-blinding sensation which stayed with him while he rode in the backseat of the McCreedys' Ford automobile, sitting beside Edgar and massaging his temples with the points of his thumbs. Florence sat up front, rigidly and silently, arms cradling a wicker picnic basket which pressed down against the folded baby-blue quilt on her lap; next to her, Bill Sr. drove northward, taking them straight through Claude without stopping. Beyond the windows was mostly a clear sky marred only by the presence of a small wayward cloud which, to Hollis, resembled a question mark. Presently a white gravel road appeared on the right side of the highway and Bill Sr. turned onto it, driving toward a fenced-in property, then he bumped the car across a cattle-guard entrance and beneath an arching iron gateway which read CLAUDE CEMETERY. For a while the car continued on the gravel avenue—winding amid tombstones and empty plots—traveling farther into a cemetery which was flat and barren save for patches of brittle grass. The surrounding fields were no less desolate—to the east was a wide-open pasture of nothing but dark brown soil and to the west, just past the highway, was identical terrain with the questioning cloud now floating over it.

Soon they were walking above the dead—Bill Sr., as always, leading the way, Edgar trailing his father closely with the blue quilt sandwiched underneath an arm, Hollis following the boy and squinting from the pain inside his skull, Florence at the rear carrying the picnic basket—crossing a trodden path which cut directly between family plots where the unseen heads of the buried lined the trail on one side, the entombed feet of the deceased bordered the other. All at once Hollis felt shaky, felt his hands tremble, could feel the color draining out of his face—and the inexplicable pain was expanding, reaching into his chest, his gut. "About there," Bill Sr. said, staring forward but, Hollis understood, addressing him. "Had us a pretty nice gravemarker done, 'cept that fool engraver got the name spelled wrong—so we had him come and fetch it last week to put it right."

"Oh, there he is," Florence said in a pleased manner which sounded no different than had she greeted Creed at the train station. "There's my boy."

As if the path had been designed only to lead them there, they approached a mound of bulging dirt at the place where the trail ended, set apart from the rest of the graves and obviously a recent addition to the cemetery—for the dirt was not yet level with the earth, nor had any grass been planted upon it; although a few dark green weeds were sprouting on the unmarked rectangular grave, immediately getting yanked by the hands of Bill Sr. and flung aside. With the weeds discarded, all that adorned the dirt was a bouquet of fresh pink carnations, left there by someone who had dug a hole at the top of the mound so the flowers could splay upright as in a vase. Then while Edgar readied the quilt on the nearby ground, and Florence began unpacking the basket, Hollis and Bill Sr. stood at the foot of Creed's grave, looking down and, for Hollis, peering through the compressed layers of dirt to discern what lay below inside a simple black coffin—but seeing just a void of blackness instead.

Without a tombstone, Hollis found himself thinking the grave could be anyone's grave. It could, the now paralyzing pain in his body suggested, be his own grave. With that, he suddenly doubled over, clasping his stomach. "Son?" Bill Sr. said, except Hollis's ears were deafened by a ringing sound. Hunched in front of the mound, gaze still fixed on the dirt, he opened his mouth to speak, but the pain was too great. "You all right?" Bill Sr.'s hand was at his back, patting the spine of his jacket. "Son?" An unintelligible noise spluttered past Hollis's lips, escaping like a final heaving of breath. He tried to scream; he tried to bellow for the whole of humanity. However, the pain wouldn't release his voice; it shot around within him like a pinball, silencing his cry. The chasm of blackness he had glimpsed far beneath the dirt began bubbling up and poured like water through the soles of his shoes, consuming him as he collapsed headfirst against the mound, eyes rolling back into his skull.

When Hollis regained consciousness, he was being handled by Bill Sr. and Florence, both of whom were tugging at him from behind, their arms wrapped about his waist and chest. Dirt, mixed with spittle on his lips, had filled his gapped mouth. "Bless your soul," Florence was telling him, whispering over his shoulder. "This is a lamentable place, it's true—a lamentable place for us all." As Hollis was pulled to his feet, a thick clump of dirt fell out of his mouth like dung; he coughed a bit, clearing his throat, tasting grit on his tongue while catching his breath—then it felt like he had been exhumed from the grave, somehow resurrected. After Bill Sr. and Florence managed to turn him in their direction, they started brushing dirt off his face and clothing, both of them resting a hand on his right shoulder, neither looking straight at him but saying, "Let's get you something to eat, son," and "Lordy, figured I'd lost you for good," as if they had brought Creed back to life in time for lunch.

"I'm sorry," Hollis said, realizing the pain had completely vanished, leaving him weak and light-headed. "Please forgive me, don't know what got into me." His hands weren't shaking anymore, but the blood hadn't yet returned to his face.

"Shouldn't fret on it," Florence said, tidying his hair with her fingertips. "These things have a way of creeping up on us."

"I got 'im," Bill Sr. said, maneuvering next to Hollis; he pressed a palm across Hollis's neck and began guiding him forward, walking a short distance to the quilt—"Easy does it"—where he then helped him sit down near the bewildered stare of Edgar.

"Hey, you okay?" the boy asked, rubbing Hollis's knee.

"I'm okay," Hollis mumbled, scanning the quilt, taking in an array of foil-covered plates and napkins and a clear-plastic pitcher of tea. He glanced at Edgar, who was smiling with a concerned expression, and, mussing the boy's hair, he returned the smile.

"C'mon, let's eat," Bill Sr. said, clapping his hands together while lowering himself on the quilt.

But Florence loitered at the grave, stooping to touch the carnations. "Looks like that girl was here," she said, carefully rearranging the flowers, fanning the stems farther apart.

"Don't matter no more," Bill Sr. said, crossing his legs, grasping the ankles of his boots.

"No, I suppose it don't," she said, drawing her hand from the flowers before standing upright. "Poor child, that girl's got to live with herself, there's punishment enough I imagine."

As Florence turned, moving toward the quilt, the pink flowers shimmered upon the earthen mound, infused with sunlight and swayed by a gentle afternoon breeze; and, for a moment, Hollis sat transfixed at the sight of the carnations fluttering there, his body feeling as weightless as the cloud which had hung alongside the highway—the cloud which now, from his vantage point, had dissipated into almost nothing, forming a faint squiggly line in the sky beyond Creed's burial plot.

That girl.

From then on, at the Sunday picnic and in the days to come, Hollis would ponder the girl, contemplating what she might actually look like while never settling upon anything specific; for she remained only as when he had originally glimpsed her on a slightly bent black-and-white photograph, first shown to him within the bowels of a transport ship during that turbulent crossing of the Sea of Japan: a nameless, indistinct dark-haired girl posing in the blurry foreground, arms hanging at her sides, her features difficult to perceive; by contrast, the background of the photograph—a wide-open field of tall wild grass—was plainly visible. "That's my girl," Creed had explained, the animated clip of his voice becoming solemn. "She's waiting back home in Claude, missing me like tomorrow ain't ever coming." Months later and thousands of miles away at the McCreedys' farm, the photograph was studied once again by Hollis, and from time to time he paused before Creed's bedroom bureau, examining the remote image of the girl yet resisted touching the now-worn photograph with his hands. But he didn't feel comfortable asking the McCreedys about her, nor did it seem appropriate to do so, for Hollis sensed the family's disapproval; more specifically, he sensed Florence's disapproval, as she occasionally made derisive reference to *that girl* when talking with Bill Sr. at supper: "Passed that girl's mother in town today, carrying on like she owned the place," or "Heard tell from Alma Branches that that girl was up at the cemetery last week, can you imagine? Too little too late, I say. Can't understand what Billy ever had for her to begin with."

"Don't matter no more," was Bill Sr.'s weary stock response. "It just don't matter."

Then toward the latter part of his visit, with sunlight filtering through the shut drapes, Hollis dressed in front of the bureau early one morning, buttoning up his shirt while looking down at the photograph. As if from nowhere, Edgar appeared beside him, wearing pajamas and not yet fully awake, tapping a middle finger against the edge of the photograph. "Scrunchy," the boy said, yawning afterward.

"Scrunchy?" Hollis asked, glancing to Edgar with a somewhat amused, puzzled expression.

"Scrunchy," Edgar repeated while turning around. "That's what my brother called her."

"Why?"

Edgar plodded back toward his bed like a sleepwalker, shrugging as he went. "Don't know," the boy said. "Guess he liked how it sounded."

Hollis watched Edgar climb beneath the sheets, promptly vanishing under the pillow so a little extra rest could be had before getting ready for school. "Scrunchy," Hollis said slowly, savoring the word, trying to comprehend its flavor; his stare moved from the boy, and at last he lifted the photograph off the bureau, bringing her image closer. "Hello, Scrunchy," he heard himself say, peering into the indecipherable gray-and-black grain of her.

Except, of course, her name wasn't really Scrunchy—and she wasn't just *that girl*. Rather, for Hollis, she was destined to become *the girl*. But other than his own mild curiosity about a face he couldn't quite distinguish, there was nothing in the fuzzy photograph which hinted at the role she was meant to play throughout his life. Still, the curiosity was finally enough for him to probe further, to draw information from the boy he had previously been uncomfortable to seek. Subsequently, during the late afternoons, he accompanied Edgar around the farm when the boy did chores—learning how to milk cows, helping feed livestock—anticipating the right moment in which he might interject some question concerning Scrunchy.

What Edgar would then tell him, what was imparted as the boy's hands squeezed along teats or scattered hay upon the ground, cast a small amount of light on the girl, yet, at the same time, did much to explain Florence's disapproval of her; for while she had been Creed's sweetheart, a younger high-school student he had dated and planned on marrying someday, Scrunchy hadn't attended her boyfriend's funeral service. And although the girl lived nearby, less than a mile off at her family's large ranch house, she hadn't offered a single word of condolence, nor did she even sign the sympathy card her own mother had left inside the McCreedy mailbox. In fact, the girl had kept mostly to herself since Creed died, rarely spotted anywhere other than the halls of the high school. Edgar had caught sight of her every so often, usually at dusk while he was roaming the farm property or the adjacent fields. He once spotted her riding a Tennessee walking horse along the fringe of the canyon, and twice he spied on her from afar, tracking her like an Indian scout when she strolled alone within an isolated grove of mesquite trees—her body moving slowly among those gray arthritic branches, arms folded across her chest as if to embrace herself.

Nevertheless, the girl hadn't totally avoided contacting the McCreedys. Several weeks following the funeral, she came by the house on a Saturday, showing up when Florence and Bill Sr. happened to be in town. It was Edgar who opened the front door, taken aback to find her standing there, her lips tightening as she blinked nervously. "This is for your mom and dad, and you, too," was what she said with a sort of wince in her eyes, handing him a freshly baked peach cobbler, and she didn't say much else except goodbye. However, the cobbler was an empty gesture where Florence was concerned; she wouldn't touch it, didn't want it in her kitchen—even after Edgar and Bill Sr. both sampled a piece, each agreeing it was pretty darn good. But Florence didn't care how delicious the cobbler tasted: that girl wasn't worth the effort it'd take to chew a bite of the stupid thing—and she had never been worthy of Creed; she hadn't truly felt for him as he, apparently, had felt for her. No, she wasn't really her deceased son's special

Scrunchy, not by a long shot. She was, instead, a selfish, thoughtless Debra, that's all.

Now fully permeating the consuming shadows of the Nine Springs kitchen, their past swirled about in the darkness around them, the blades of the ceiling fan stirring it like windblown leaves. "It's tough faulting old Florence," Hollis told Debra, "because she needed someone tangible to blame, otherwise she'd have been sunk. Her grief was just too great for her to recognize your own level of grief, that you were too heartsick and distraught to see them bury the boy you loved, or that facing her and Bill Sr. and Edgar simply underscored Bill being gone. She couldn't understand it. How could she? Plus, I think anger is a lot easier to live with than sadness—I'm sure of it. I mean, she couldn't attach any meaning to the loss of her son, so you became a bit of a scapegoat for that pain, I suppose. I'm not saying it's right, but sometimes that's what people do. We do it more than we probably realize."

Sitting at the table, with Hollis by her side, the rest of the story was as clear to Debra as it was to him. But the perspective she had always wanted was his perspective, his version of how they met—that timely encounter when, as dusk concluded, she had wandered from What Rocks to the Mc-Creedy farm and sought him out because she had learned he was staying there: the soldier who had been shot with Creed, the one who had survived and could, hopefully, make her understand why her boyfriend had died. And so he obliged her now as he had done back then; he spoke of that other night long ago, after the chores were done and supper was finished and the McCreedys were all shut inside their bedrooms, and he sat by himself on the porch steps, in the cool winter night, gazing upward at a sky which glimmered brilliantly with more stars—blue, red, white, yellow—than he had recalled seeing before or since.

As Debra had approached the farmhouse—trudging up the dirt drive, unclasping the gate of the front yard—Hollis didn't notice her until sensing something below his line of vision, something or someone emerging toward him in the night. Lowering his head, bringing his stare from the heavens to the earth, he saw a fluttering of white up ahead, a slight billowing of fabric, and then on the concrete walkway he recognized her—for she was the same as in Creed's photograph, indistinct and impossible to define, a girlish representation made alluring by lingering just beyond his perception. But with every step she took, the aperture of his mind brought her into clearer focus, honing her shape and features and outward manner. She wore a heavy beige-colored wool coat, blue jeans, and sneakers, with a white chiffon scarf which was knotted at her neck but rippled out across a shoulder like a wind sock. As she drew closer, he spotted a cheap paperback clutched in one of her hands, the kind found on the revolving racks of dime stores, and he imagined she had cradled the book in her palms, thumbs holding the pages open while she navigated around scrub brush and prickly pears, reading during those last fading minutes of the day.

He raised an arm off his knee, casually waving to her once. "Hi," was what he then heard himself say, when she had stopped in front of him, standing some three feet from where he sat on the steps. With her face as colorless as the scarf she had on and the dark glossy locks of her hair bathed in the glow of the yellow porch light, she seemed to be frowning at him, her brown eyes assessing him suspiciously. Behind her, in the pitch surrounding the yard, the night loomed as her ally and gave bearing to her diminutive figure.

"You Hollis?" she said in a flat, direct way, asked with a gruff tone which sounded older than her years—one her body would, gradually, see fit to match over time.

"That's right," he replied.

"You was in that mess over there with Billy?"

"I was. Yes."

His answers seemed to lessen the frown, although her expression remained determined and willful, unflinching while she loitered on the walkway, staring down at him with the frays of her black hair made iridescent by the casting of soft yellow light. Her stare narrowed as the breeze howled swiftly through the yard for a moment—lifting the scarf, and, like unseen fingers, sweeping her hair from her forehead. Once the breeze had passed, that curious frown was there again, that reserve and somberness, staying put when she introduced herself. "I'm Billy's girl," she continued, as if Creed were still among the living and waiting for her inside the house. But she didn't intend to bother him long. She merely wanted a few minutes of his evening, just whatever it would take for him to accurately make plain the circumstances of her boyfriend's death; the specifics of which had been mostly hearsay, elaborated about town in hushed, piecemeal fashion and exaggerated like gossip—forming an incomplete picture in her head and heart, puzzling her more than any of the mystery novels she read every week.

"Of course," Hollis said, a solemn note creeping into his voice. "I understand." And there and then, he was struck by the girl, captivated for reasons he couldn't quite sort out. It wasn't as though she was a perfect beauty—her cheekbones were too high and broad for the small, round shape of her head, her eyes were too far apart—not nearly as beautiful as what the photograph had repeatedly allowed him to conjure. Yet the force of something inevitable seemed to pound at his gut, prodding him with a need for her while, too, filling him with apprehension as she stood above him. He hadn't, until that evening, bought into the idea of a definitive love which could blossom between two people in an instant. However, if such a love were real, he regarded it as an awful thing, a destructive thing, because with it also came the possibility of real loss, of complete and utter desolation in its absence—a bitter outcome he had no wish to experience.

As his voice initially wavered with his thoughts, Hollis began imparting the only full account of Creed's final minutes Debra would ever hear, a version of the event which, from that point on, she accepted as being true. But during the telling, his voice grew steadily more confident, more vivid; and what was then described about that morning at the Naktong wasn't so different from the tale he had given Bill Sr., save for one dramatic shift: it became Hollis, not Creed, who had seen something reflected by sunlight as they shielded themselves behind the dying pine tree, something glinting among the reeds and hidden several yards away; in a split second, Hollis had jumped toward Creed, attempting to push him down at the very instant a loud crack erupted within the reeds—except, of course, he couldn't have moved fast enough. The resulting moments, he went on to explain, brought no appeasing resolution; no degree of satisfaction was had by single-handedly avenging Creed's murder—pursuing and killing the sniper, also getting badly wounded before it was finished—because he would be forever haunted by the knowledge of having failed to protect his friend.

"Everyone called me a hero," Hollis said miserably, "though it isn't anything I'm proud of. I mean, a real hero would've reacted a second earlier, he'd have caught that first bullet and kept his pal from being shot—that's why I'm hardly a hero. And now I can't stand that I'm here and he isn't, doesn't seem right somehow. So I remind myself I've got a duty to keep my head above water and let my life from here on out serve as an honor to his memory—and that's what I'm intending to do, and that's pretty much it."

Once Hollis was done talking, Debra appeared poised to speak, but then seemed to prevent herself. Instead, she looked at him, withholding a single trace of emotion, and for a while neither of them spoke. Yet he was completely drawn to the impassiveness of her expression, warmed thoroughly in her strong presence—as though she was absorbing the chilly air between them, heating it inside her delicate body, releasing some of it for him to feel.

"See, you aren't alone," Hollis finally said. "I'm like you. I lost him, too. We both did."

"Ain't nearly the same thing," she said, reversing herself, stepping back. "Anyway, all of us are alone."

Hollis then felt as if he had not said anything right, not expressed himself well enough to comfort her. After she turned without another word and headed across the yard, he sprang off the steps, unwilling to let her recede from view. "Scrunchy," he blurted. "You'll always be his Scrunchy." When she pivoted around to him, suddenly, her pale face—peering forward, hair tousled by the breeze—was like one which had encountered a phantom; and yet she stared at him, there in the night, with acceptance, with vague recognition, and while he extended a hand to her, she smiled discreetly and cautiously, as if benignly accepting an unexpected but desired gift. Then, too, he sensed there was a kind of strange magic in himself, an unrealized ability to heal without speech or considerable effort; he had but to touch her, to press his palm against her palm, and her troubles would subside; in this he would find his meaning, his real salvation.

"I'm Hollis Adams."

"I know who you are."

"I know. I know that."

Again and again, Hollis was destined to reach for her—in the yard, during the nights and days, on long walks among the mesquites—and with every movement of his arms, his hands, his fingers, time began accelerating, whirling effortlessly about them. Soon enough their clothing was cast aside at least once within each of the forgotten, empty bedrooms of the old What Rocks house, their entwined bodies exposed by the dusty rays of light which angled downward through the murky windowpanes and illumed the barren floorboards. But prior to any of those furtive couplings—as their self-imposed states of isolation gave way to a greater want for togetherness— the pieces of the picture had begun taking shape, falling smoothly into place: the Saturdays in Claude, the two of them strolling leisurely on down-town sidewalks or sitting side by side at a Dairy Mart booth—paying little mind to the glancing, disapproving onlookers likely whispering, "The very gall of them two," and "Poor McCreedy boy ain't even cold in the earth and see how she's going on thata way."

For a while, the covert animosity was hard for Debra to tolerate, al-though she didn't harbor regrets about being seen with Hollis—nor did she believe Creed would have resented them. Better, she figured, that Billy's best girl and best army friend were joined at the hip than either one relying on a complete stranger for comfort; in some regard, she told herself, they were adhering to Creed's memory by consoling each other's grief, by also resuming and furthering the kind of relationship he had enjoyed with her but could no longer take part in. Then the passing of judgment she felt around town—the whispers, the snide remarks insinuated within earshot— seemed petty, unwarranted, as if the people of Claude just craved some-thing, anything, to stir their indignant and self-righteous natures. When she went to buy some fabric patterns at Christian Dry Goods, the fat girl be-hind the counter, a former classmate of Creed's, told her in a hushed, well-intending voice, "You and that fella ought shouldn't be flaunting yourselfs like you do, it don't favor you, dear." Debra smiled politely, thinking all the while: Trudy, I ain't the one who's six feet under—and I'm nobody's widow yet.

By then the rumors concerning them had spread beyond quiet gossip, and already Hollis had been asked to leave the McCreedy farm. At the supper table one evening, Florence fumed in silence, behaving like he wasn't even there—serving everyone except him, never letting her gaze travel to where he sat—frowning with dismay while Bill Sr. forthrightly said it was probably time for Hollis to head home to Minnesota. Edgar, like his mother, was also frowning, but only because the boy had grown fond of Hollis and would miss having him at the house. "I understand," Hollis told the Mc-Creedys, rising from his chair, "and I want to thank you all for your kindness. It feels like I've gained a family here."

"You got yourself a family of your own," Florence scoffed, talking at her plate. "You belong with them, not us."

"Mother," Bill Sr. responded to his wife in a reproving tone.

"That's okay," Hollis said. "Maybe it's best if I get my things gathered."

But Hollis wouldn't ready for a trip back to Critchfield, and—after packing his suitcase, stealing the photograph of Debra off the bureau and concealing it in a jacket pocket—he wouldn't return to where the Mc-Creedys ate supper. Instead, he immediately left their house without as much as a goodbye, relying on that stealthy departure he had, of late, repeatedly used while fleeing elsewhere; he then walked a mile or so—slipping between the gaps of barbed-wire fences, wandering through grazing pastures—until arriving at the imposing residence standing out on the plains: the crumbling, half-deserted hilltop house known as What Rocks, a place which—as Debra had previously made known—afforded more than enough space for him should he find himself wanting a bedroom of his own. Still, in order to earn his keep, he would be required to work on the property, taking over the chores her alcoholic father was incapable of getting done, loading a pile of cedar posts in the bed of a pickup, mowing the lawn and tending the backyard gardens, yanking weeds and burrs, any sort of odd job; a small price to pay, he had no doubt, for sleeping under the same roof as *that girl*, a tiny penance, indeed, for what was given in return at What Rocks during the nights, or afternoons, when the door of an abandoned room would lock behind him and Debra, ushering forth a private world which, in the heat and collision of their bodies, was about as far removed from the McCreedys' sorrowful existence as anything he could hope to conceive.

So regardless of what Florence might have finally thought of him, Hollis wasn't bothered in the slightest. He didn't care if she was angry and disapproved, or felt betrayed by him and Debra. He didn't care if she would eventually shun their wedding, or, for the rest of her days, speak ill of them to anyone who would listen. He didn't care, and whatever she thought truly didn't matter in the big picture; for he had redeemed himself through love, doing so without any help from her or the Lord. As such, he and Debra, by simply finding each other, had freed themselves to create a new reality together, divining their own singular path which just they were meant to embark upon; that alone, with hindsight, provided an answer as to why it was necessary for Creed to have died before him—why Hollis, too, had found himself thrown amidst the early chaos of a divided Korea, getting wounded beside the Naktong—and, later on, it became his sole reason for ever having made the tedious journey to Claude to begin with.

"And that," Hollis said at the kitchen table, stroking Debra's liver-spotted hand, "is probably all you need to know about us."

Except now his magic was failing him, his ability to heal her and, ultimately, himself. Then it wasn't him reaching out for her in the night, but, rather, it was she who moved toward him, pressing fingers to his arm, gripping at his shoulder. She gently spoke his name, saying it as a question, and, seconds later, he was helping her to stand, assisting her; yet it was she who led, guiding him from the kitchen table—from the darkness which had facilitated the past—bringing them squarely into the light of the present. Soon they sat together again, their knees touching, their fingers interlaced, facing each other on the living-room couch.

Debra took a deep breath, appearing quite forlorn as she then said, "There isn't much time left, at least for me. So it's important I have some say on when and how my life ends."

"What do you mean?" he asked, with an uncomprehending expression.

"I'm saying cancer shouldn't get the last word, even though it's killing me."

The living-room curtains were open, and suddenly Hollis's eyes shifted to the window where he saw the black of night softened by the bright transparent reflection of the living room.

"It isn't easy for you, I know," she said. "It isn't fair either."

"No," he said, sounding irritated, "it isn't fair." Our story wasn't supposed to go like this, he thought. This isn't how I wanted it to finish. He shook his head, biting his bottom lip, and continued staring at the window.

Debra sighed tiredly, squeezing his fingers, and said, "Hollis, you need to hear me. It's important what I'm about to say, so please listen."

And now it was her turn to talk, although she wouldn't be revisiting their past; instead, she addressed the near future like an unapologetic fortune-teller prophesying the details of her own demise, revealing what she—and Hollis—could expect in the weeks ahead. Just that afternoon, while returning from the outpatient clinic in Tucson, she had decided not to pursue any more treatment, because it was obvious the disease hadn't stopped spreading even with the preventative use of chemotherapy agents or, for that matter, other experimental drugs. As such, the cancer cells would keep wrecking havoc, creating a bowel obstruction; there would be nausea and vomiting, an inability to pass gas, and her abdomen would swell in girth, surpassing the discomfort of the current ascites. At the end, whatever remained inside her would be expelled by traveling up the esophagus, moving through her throat and out between her lips as a dark greenish bile-like substance carrying the odor of feces—and her withered body, malnourished in appearance, would begin shutting down. Of course, drops of morphine would ease her through those final hours; she would exit this world within an incoherent fever dream, whispering unintelligibly and incessantly as if speaking in tongues, laboring for air while drifting to and from consciousness—until, with the transitory span of a second, she ceased breathing altogether.

Debra fell silent for a moment; her sunken face, lacking any makeup, seemed much older than it should have looked. Outside, Hollis couldn't see a thing—not the houses across the street, nor the stars above them. Then she said, without urgency, that they had to accept her death was fast approaching, but the last painful act wasn't yet a given; for a brief period remained in which she could trump the concluding onslaught of the disease. She could, with his support and permission, depart a bit prematurely, doing so on her own terms—by her own hand, in the tranquillity of their beautiful home—circumventing the indignity of what otherwise would be, for both of them, an excruciating, almost unbearable endgame.

Debra paused, hoping Hollis might now offer her something, but instead he shook his head with confusion, saying nothing. "Anyway," she went on, "it's about over for me, except I don't want to waste away any more than I already have—and I don't plan on going through the worst of it—and if you won't help me go then, please, at least give me your blessing so I can do it alone with peace of mind. I want to be aware of myself and where I am at the conclusion of my life—I deserve that, after all, and so do you."

Hollis felt a jolt deep inside himself when bringing his eyes to her. He felt a tightening in his chest. "Deb, I can't give you my blessing," he said, his voice breaking, "but I can't say I'd blame you either—because I wouldn't."

"I know you wouldn't," she said, resting a hand against his neck. "So that's good enough for me. Thank you."

His eyes began welling, and when he then tried to speak, the words he most wanted to say confounded him, becoming uttered in part through a stifling, gasping shortness of breath.

"Love you, too," she responded, pressing dry lips against his chin as he leaned forward to kiss her forehead.

Hugging each other, they both wept for a little while—and afterward, they sat back without talking, the tears dripping off their faces, shaken by the irrevocability of the moment. Then Hollis rose from the couch and went to stand at the window. When Debra finally left the living room for bed, he was still there at the window, staring into the night—as if reluctantly awaiting the snow which would soon fall, somehow already sensing that frigid morning where everything around him would become transformed.

19

And so it was to be that snow, at dawn this morning, which beckoned Hollis and Lon forward while the Suburban's hazard lights blinked near the golf course—while the whole of Nine Springs conveyed a listless existence and fireplaces had begun to tinge the air with a woodsy autumnal flavor. The pair trudged straight across the deeply buried greens as a vision of red and cobalt—Hollis in his metallic-colored duvet jacket, Lon in his scarlet parka—going away from the place where Lon had slipped, both leaving a trail of footprints through a glaring, unbroken white expanse: neither speaking now as the sun reflected off the snow and washed out their sight, neither questioning their slow progression which fractured the pure white earth below a pure blue sky, neither asking why it was that they had felt the need to venture forward on the golf course instead of returning to the temperate comfort of their respective homes. Thick, visible exhalations of breath curled up in front of their rosy-cheeked faces like hot industrial steam, preceding them beside hidden sand traps and icy man-made ponds.

Holding hands for support, walking side by side, the two men swallowed the cold and the wind, remaining mindful of each step crushing the snow, aware all the while that if one should suddenly fall the other was likely to get dragged down, too. Yet Hollis couldn't maneuver quite as deftly as Lon, for his left thigh ached somewhere below the scar while his feet had grown numb inside the leather boots. But pressing onward with an increasingly painful limp, Hollis was bolstered by a recollection he had been fortunate enough to have never experienced firsthand—those bitter winters during the Korean civil war, that subzero march southward from the Chosin, exposed skin bonding to metal and bloody palms stripped off by frozen mortar shells, frostbite blackening heels or toes. Then Hollis sensed his winter footwear was absorbing moisture; it seemed his socks were growing damp and squishing around within the boots, although the loss of feeling in his feet prevented him from knowing for sure.

It was Lon, however, who paused to catch a breath, shaking loose the snow caked on his galoshes before removing one of his black mitts. While Hollis blew into his bare hands and rubbed his palms together to generate heat, Lon held the mitt out for him, nodding once but saying nothing. Hollis accepted what was offered, working the wet mitt onto his left hand. Just then a crow's scream broke the morning calm, its harsh call echoing from where the bird circled far overhead and appeared to be monitoring them from up high. As if prompted by the ominous cawing, Lon resumed walking, seizing Hollis's bare hand in his own bare hand, tugging him along. The crow screamed a second time, its uneven circle moving and traveling with the pair.

Farther they went, past the eighteenth hole, farther still—the streets and homes now well behind them, the eastern section of the golf course having been designed to jut into undeveloped desert like an oasis—until reaching the edge of their known world, dead-ending at a chain-link fence where, ahead of them in that no-man's-land beyond Nine Springs, was a grove of orange trees, then sloping terrain, then the distant ranges of the Catalina Mountains. But what summoned them lacked reason; what drew them to the fringes was only revealed when at last beheld, and in its august presence they stood dumbstruck at the fence: a lone Hereford cow was waiting on the other side, standing several yards away beside an orange tree, as if sanctuary from the snowstorm had been sought below the branches—a

solitary brown-and-white cow which had seemingly anticipated their approach, facing them with eyes agape, glistening while long pendants of ice
dripped from its huge nostrils and underside, staying erect but releasing no
breath—lifeless there yet frozen upright in tableau.

How strange, Hollis thought, for death to leave the beast standing. But
he also understood that death—that trespasser of safe places—was often
curious in method: whether it came beneath a bridge, or by a river, or on a
golf course, or in a hospital, or beside a tree. Death, he thought, was like the
downfalling of snow last night, so quiet and so pacifying, inevitably blanketing all which might hope to remain untouched. So the pain of dying was
one thing, he told himself, whereas death itself was something entirely different, something which was benign by nature and not unkind.

"No," Lon uttered, "no, no, don't understand it, don't get it—how'd
we find ourselves here?" His hand flexed and squeezed against Hollis's
hand.

"I don't know," were the words which floated within steam from Hollis, his body shivering. "I don't know," he repeated, glad for the small bit of
warmth Lon's bare hand afforded him. At that moment the crow screamed
a warning at close range, making the pair start and glance up to where it sat
nearby. Neither had noticed the large bird's arrival, how it had glided noise-
lessly right above them as a shadow—wings fully expanded, rigid talons
slicing the air—to land atop the fence, turning itself around toward them,
and perching there now like a sentry, watching with coal-black sockets and
darting, questioning movements of its feathered head.

"We need to go," Lon said, sounding agitated. "I'm suddenly not feeling all that great. Something isn't right."

"Okay," Hollis said, meeting the crow's stare, peering into a blackened
socket but perceiving a hollowness where an eye should reflect.

"I think I overexerted myself, I think that's it. And I think Jane is probably worrying, so we really better go."

Cocking its head, the crow thrust its beak forward, bellowing furiously
as if ordering them to leave.

"Okay," Hollis repeated, hesitating long enough to cast his gaze one last time at the poor creature beneath the orange tree: while Lon—refusing to look anymore, pounding the snow with his galoshes—about-faced and tugged on his hand.

"I'm going."

Hastily they returned upon their own beaten trail, and as Lon led the way among the field of white which was quickly melting under the sun, Hollis soon discerned the figure of someone else in the distance, an inert shape pausing where Lon had fallen earlier on the ninth hole green. The trodden, slushy trail wound back from the desert and brought them closer to the residential lots of the community, the snow ebbing to a grayish muddy surface as sidewalks and asphalt thawed. But the ultraviolet rays thrown off the ice had become excruciating, and with photophobia now hampering their progress instead of the snow, he couldn't quite yet make out who it was they were fast approaching. Perhaps, he thought, it was another person entranced by the aftermath of the snowfall, or possibly an officer from the sheriff's department who had been alerted by the blinking hazard lights of the parked Suburban, or maybe even one of the many groundskeepers investigating the post-storm condition of the golf course; and if the person hadn't been so tall, he would have assumed it was Lon's wife searching for her husband when he had failed to come home.

Since Lon was leading and held a better vantage point, Hollis asked, "Who is it? Can you tell?"

"How's that?" Lon huffed, short of breath, still pulling Hollis by the hand.

"Do you see who it is?"

The figure was a few yards in front of them, marking the spot where their journey had started and, presently, would conclude.

"Who are you talking about?" Lon answered, his labored voice imparting an entire day's worth of exhaustion. "I don't understand who *who* is."

Just then Hollis realized what must be loitering on the ninth hole green. "Never mind," he said, finally recognizing that familiar likeness he had encountered throughout the years—stock-still with arms hanging at its side, expressionless yet vigilant—that time-ravaged twin who wasn't ever meant for this life: a long, unkempt gray beard flowing from its haggard, wrinkled, and stooped body, dressed as always in jeans which had grown ragged and frayed, worn-down leisure shoes, a moth-eaten T-shirt, and a soiled, once bright blue Windbreaker. "I guess I was seeing things, it's nothing." For a second Hollis wondered if he should not simply head in a different direction, but upon reaching the ninth hole green he let go of Lon's hand and continued forward. Unaware of Max's lingering proximity, Lon accelerated his pace and brushed past the spectral figure, tiredly waving a hand in the air as he proceeded downhill, almost slipping again while hurrying for the sidewalk.

With long, limping strides Hollis walked directly toward his weathered counterpart, fixing on those vacuous eyes which were, somehow, his own eyes. You'll go, he thought. You'll disappear. However, Max didn't fade from sight or vanish in a blink, and Hollis was now closer to it than he had imagined possible; one stayed put while the other charged headlong without hesitation, both on the verge of collision and unwilling to relent. You'll go, you'll disappear: Hollis winced when passing right through himself, but just beforehand he saw the movement of Max's blistered lips, emitting a parched whisper which entered his own lips and exited at the base of his skull. And then it had communicated to him; it had, in their brief merging, addressed him for the first and only time, simply uttering, "Bye."

Hollis immediately stopped, peering back over his shoulder. Max wasn't there. For a moment he thought he glimpsed a wavering of light where it had stood—then all he could see was snow and land and the crisscrossed trail. Impossible, it can't be, he said to himself and shuddered. No, he was not mistaken, it had spoken. He had heard its parting message and, too, he had felt the word reverberate inside his head. Turning around, he searched for Lon but saw instead the remaining few yards of golf course, the sidewalk beyond, his Suburban parked in the golf lane—and nothing or no one else. The city seemed abandoned, the streets were deserted, and it would have been natural for him to enjoy the solitude, but now he suddenly harbored an immense sadness for himself and everything which lived or had yet to grow beneath the sun; and with that a feeling of complete isolation

came upon him, a deep-reaching sensation of also having been abandoned
which constricted a knot of desperation in his gut. Here is the sum total of
my existence, he thought and resumed limping. This is it for me.

Then somewhere high above the grid patterns of Nine Springs the wind
raced like the currents of a river; and the invisible sheets of ether fused
within the sky were in perpetual tumult, bending westward then southward
while clouds swelled and moved accordingly. The great breaths of the
planet blew farther still along the hemisphere and the wind shifted and
shifted. Effortlessly buoyed by the rushing waves of air, itself a dark shape
gliding horizontally among the flux, a crow circled what lay far below—
that insubstantial island with square plots and tiled rooftops and one inhab-
itant climbing into a sport-utility vehicle—before changing its direction
and flying out across a limitless ocean of open desert.

After Hollis eased the Suburban into his driveway, turning the vehicle off,
he sat there for a while with the radio on, listening to the local news and
then the statewide weather report. A freak winter storm had shut down various stretches of Interstate 10, the generic-sounding broadcaster stated, but
tomorrow things would warm up, the skies would be clear from Tucson to
Flagstaff. Upon hearing that, he pulled the keys out of the ignition—and if
anybody inside the neighboring homes had been looking through windows,
they might have spied his bulky form exiting the Suburban, half limping in
muddy leather boots and made even bigger by the padded jacket, perhaps
wondering where it was he had traveled to on such an unreceptive morning.
Yet no one would catch a glimpse of the dread he was harboring within himself—as he shuffled, carefully, over icy patches on the concrete and moved
toward the house.

Once beyond the front door, Hollis entered what seemed to be a time-
less but vacuous domain, a place in which past or future concerns were no
longer permitted, and where the present was now forever sustained like the
drone of an unending chord. He didn't, though, remove the boots, or the
jacket, or the mitt on his hand; instead, he went forward, pausing for a time
at the gap between the dining and living rooms—like someone contemplat-

ing directions when stepping into a maze—with his head pivoting from left to right, right to left, his gaze alternately framing those two dimly cast, static rooms: each fractured by refined beams of angled sunlight, where the rays only brightened either the middle of the dining table or the three canvas-printed orchid photographs hung above the couch, as they would a bowl of fruit in a still life. Among the shadows of the living room were the brown-oak bookcases, the television cabinet, a black steel-coated wall clock, the tempered glass-top coffee table covered with library books—and in the dining room, also shaded, were the glass chandelier-like pendant lamp, the antique clear-lacquered pine chairs, the buffet with top cabinets which held white plates and bowls and cups and pitchers. But in the slow aquatic tumbling of radiant dust motes, everything felt submerged to him, peacefully settled somewhere beneath water; and he was there, too, among wreckage which had, surely, sunk so calmly as to leave so much intact.

Don't forget to breathe.

Before proceeding farther, Hollis exacted his stare, holding it on the living-room clock. He waited until the second hand had cycled the full duration of a minute; at which point he walked directly through the house— tracking dirt across the carpet, the kitchen's vinyl flooring—and headed out the back door to tend his snowbound gardens: calculating and recalculating the hours, the approximate minutes, since he had comforted Debra in his arms, kissing the side of her face as she breathed heavily against him, kissing her when her breathing had grown shallower and, like a subtle, gradual transition into the stillest of sleeps, eventually became unapparent. Ten hours, he estimated. Ten hours and twenty-two minutes, give or take a minute.

At the end, by the time Debra was ready to go—to take the mystery ride, as she had begun saying—there had been almost nothing asked or required of Hollis; she had, using what little remained of her failing health, done all the preparations on her own, researching the best methods available, going about it with the same fixity of purpose which had driven her while making interior-design choices for their home. In businesslike fashion, she determined a mixture of two barbiturate drugs—Seconal (4.5 grams) and Nembutal (3.0 grams)—would not only do the trick but would

double the lethal dose; as such, Hollis would be spared the last task of placing a plastic bag over her head once she had fallen asleep—something she
felt certain he couldn't actually bring himself to do, something she didn't
much like the idea of anyway. Then in accordance with Debra's wishes, a
sympathetic Dr. Langford agreed to prescribe the drugs; and, too, the doctor would, when everything was finished, handle the postmortem details—
signing the death certificate herself, stating that Debra had died due to
complications resulting from ovarian cancer.

The grocery shopping and errands, however, became Hollis's main re-
sponsibility, his mission. Without voicing protest, he picked up the prescrip-
tions for her at Walgreens; he also bought what she had listed on a Post-it
note—chocolate pudding mix, a bottle of Glenfiddich, Dramamine—items
which seemed better suited for a holiday than, as Debra had called it, a self-
deliverance. There were other instructions for him as well, another list she
had written on a legal pad, several after-life issues they would discuss beforehand: the letter she had recently composed to her younger sister was
folded inside the P. D. James hardback on the living-room coffee table—it
should be addressed in an envelope and sent via Priority Mail within a week
of her passing—while the P. D. James novel should be returned to the library by month's end; her credit cards should be canceled; her clothing and
shoes should be donated to Goodwill, her wigs given to Gilda's Club; she
didn't want a funeral, or a memorial service, or an obit of any sort placed in
a newspaper; most important, her body must be cremated. "That way I can
once and for all rid myself of these cancer cells," she explained. "I want my
body purified," and then Debra wanted the circle of her life completed, asking that her ashes and bits of bone be scattered on the property of the old
What Rocks house where she had been born—the closing of a larger circle
in which a smaller circle would have already been sealed; for, they both
knew without saying it, a death had brought them together and, in turn, it
was somehow fitting that a death would draw them apart. The pursuit of
happiness, he had begun to understand, didn't come without a heavy price.

And so, last evening, Hollis dutifully heeded the final directive of his
mission while snow cascaded outside the kitchen windows. On a serving
tray, he gathered and organized those things Debra had needed—a bowl of

chocolate pudding, a mug filled with Glenfiddich, one Dramamine pill in a spoon, the plastic vials of Seconal and Nembutal, a cup of green tea, a slice of toasted whole wheat bread—feeling no desire to hurry, running his eyes diligently over the items once everything was in place. When he finally brought the tray to their room—pushing the aromatherapy bottles aside so he could set it on a corner of the bedside table—Debra was propped up in the bed, the orthopedic pillow behind her neck and the comforter bunched about her, seemingly pleased by how well he had put the contents of the tray together. This was the night of her departing, the dwindling minutes of her existence, but she didn't look unhappy. As he sat down on the edge of the mattress, she told him she felt blessed. She was, regardless of the disease, content with herself—and him—and the life they had built. Beneath the comforter and the sheets the lower half of her body was hidden, naked, like a bride nervously anticipating the beginning passion of a honeymoon; where she was going, she had joked, it didn't matter whether she wore clothing or not, and he was inclined to agree with her.

"I guess it's that time," she said, eventually.

Hollis bowed his head, saying, "I don't think I can do this."

"It'll be all right," she said, squeezing his wrist. "We'll both be all right." Then she added, with the trace of a smile: "We'll survive this one, too."

For several seconds they stared at each other awkwardly; yet her thin face conveyed no obvious emotion, even as his expression trembled—his mouth curving downward, his eyes wide and scared; his face stayed like that as she ate the toast, and drank the tea, and swallowed the Dramamine pill in order to ward off nausea. She took her meal slowly, silently; afterward, they talked for about an hour, and the severity of his expression lessened as they discussed the unusual weather, the Discovery Channel program she had seen earlier on the Ice Age, various minor topics which steered clear of what would soon transpire. Then they hugged; her cheek was cold but her lips were warm, her breath smelled of tea and sickness.

"I'll miss this," he said, while embracing her. "I'll miss just talking to you, Deb."

"You can always talk to me, you know."

"But it won't be the same."

"No," she said, pulling back to look at him, "I guess not." They gazed at each other a few seconds more—before she nodded resolutely, insisting, "It's time, dear. I'm ready, I really am."

"Okay," Hollis said, suddenly numbed. "All right then," he uttered, rising from the mattress while realizing, in that instant, there was nothing left for them to discuss, nothing left to be said which might alter the outcome of that night. He opened the vials on the tray, shaking out some of the capsules—and then glanced at Debra, very seriously, as she extended a hand to accept the drugs; but he didn't hesitate, nor did she: One at a time the capsules were slipped past her lips, each chased with a swig of Glenfiddich, until there was nothing more to swallow or drink. He promptly gave her the pudding, in which the rest of the dosage had been mixed as a powder, and she ate it quickly, licking chocolate from her lips when finished.

Once the contents of the tray had been mostly consumed, Hollis helped Debra ease down from where she had sat upright, tucking the comforter around her, adjusting the pillow underneath her head. She turned on her side to face him, her eyelids appearing leaden, languidly blinking open, staying shut at longer intervals. Within a couple of minutes, she had already fallen asleep, becoming inactive. But right before sleep fully subdued her, she had said she loved him, and he had responded in kind—massaging her neck, holding her hand, staring directly at her and nowhere else; and when he thought her consciousness had ebbed from this world, she surprised him by speaking again with eyes closed, saying in a voice which had grown impossibly tired and hoarse, "Don't forget to breathe, okay?"

"I won't," he answered.

"Good," she mumbled, and was silent thereafter.

And while Debra approached her mystery ride, Hollis undressed completely, climbing into bed beside her, pressing himself against her body—listening as her life dissolved in his arms, as she slowly faltered and ceased. Then her passing, like so much about her, had an effortless quality. She didn't gasp, and her chest didn't heave; no long, labored breaths struggled from her throat. She just proceeded—as if she had crossed from one room to the next, as if she had stepped away for a little while. But the many tears

he had wept over the months while fearing this very moment didn't immediately come—nor was he yet shaken by expected waves of panic or over-
whelming sadness. He was, upon experiencing what he had dreaded the
most, much calmer than he thought possible, relaxed even. Must be shock,
he decided. Of course, it hasn't hit me, it hasn't settled in. Or, perhaps, it
was because she was with him, resting there; she was slightly warm, and she
was present somehow. With her eyes shut and her head on the orthopedic
pillow, she could easily have been sleeping. "Deb," he whispered, taking her
compliant right hand into one of his hands. "Deb," he repeated, awed by the
simplicity of her passing, the ease with which she went; yet her dying felt so
singular to him, so unique, as if no one else had experienced such a personal
loss—the fact that most others had or would couldn't help but amaze him.

Then how appropriate, Hollis thought, for his final act of love to conclude with a touching of hands, just as the first act had begun so long ago.
For now they had reached the end of touching, of mutual contact; they had
reached the end of shared hours and conversations and togetherness; beneath the painted bluebird on the bedroom ceiling, they had reached the
end. Still, for a while, he moved his palms along her face, her arms, her
breasts—those actual finishing touches; and with his chest pressed firmly
against her spine, he gave her body his heat even as she grew colder and
colder. Somewhere else, he imagined, she was readying to be born again.
Somewhere else on the planet, far away, a brand-new Debra was bound to
arrive at any moment. Even so, he wanted her to remain like this for now,
resting under the sheets; he wanted her to stay—a few hours longer, maybe
a day—until he was sure she had truly gone from him.

Sometime later, Hollis would take himself from their bed—leaving her
behind with the comforter pulled to her neck, the orthopedic pillow covering her head—shutting the bedroom door as if he were respectfully closing
the gates of a mausoleum. In the kitchen, he poured himself some of the
Glenfiddich—and then, in the living room, he stretched across the couch
with drink in hand, grabbing for the Tom Clancy novel he had left open on
the coffee table. But while reading he fell asleep, eventually dreaming of animals and people—that recurring procession—while snow continued raining as if the heavens had been wrung in the hands of God, spilling down

upon an unsuspecting desert. When waking from his nap—the novel resting against his chin, the half-filled cup of Glenfiddich sitting nearby on the
floor—he felt strangely at peace inside the house, comfortable there on the
couch and kept snug by a beige terry-cloth bathrobe. Lifting the novel,
he began reading where he had left off, although his attention wasn't really
held by the writing; his eyes scanned paragraphs, failing to absorb sentences, until, at last, he set the book aside, turning his gaze elsewhere as the
cup of Glenfiddich was absently retrieved, the liquor seeping warmly past
his lips.

On the other side of the living room the front curtains were drawn, revealing the picture window and what existed just beyond it: a torrent of
snowflakes wavering to the earth, some pattering at the glass like moths before dissolving into clear drops of moisture. Soon Hollis was standing there
in his bathrobe, resting a palm against the window, sensing the cold while
buffered by efficient central heating. There, too, he caught a glimpse of
himself as an obscure, diaphanous man reflected on the glass; his transposed
image was cast amongst the wide residential street—the adjacent and similarly designed homes, the xeriscaped lawns—backlit by a table lamp but
also illumed in that frozen vapor which brightened the night, that curious
downpouring which smothered the gravel-laden property and changed his
Suburban Half-Ton LS from sandalwood metallic to an almost solid white.

20

Except for the sound of water drip drip dripping from the thatched roof
made of palm leaves, it is quiet both inside and outside the tiki hut. Hollis
sits there now—in a corner, down on the floor—listening as water drips
above him to the earth, dripping, too, around the backyard and off the overhead gutters of the house. Everything is melting, he thinks. Everything
melts. An itinerant wind blows across the desert into Nine Springs, but it
doesn't stay very long and, instead, dissipates somewhere along the empty,
messy streets. Drops patter upon his jacket and seem to be absorbed immediately by the fabric, seeping through to his clothing. He stares up at the
leak-proof ceiling. His hair and face are damp but it is dry inside the hut. So
the water continues to drip elsewhere, nearby, not touching him and yet, he
believes, soaking him all the same. Presently the wind returns, this time
with more resolve—howling for a moment, rolling over Nine Springs,
shaking palm trees and dazzling the air with fast-swirling currents of fine
snow particles and moisture—and then, as if stopped by the flipping of a
switch, it isn't there anymore, the airy howl receding and the currents settling in its wake.

   Hollis lowers his head. Lon's mitt is on his left hand. His bare right hand is grubby, the fingernails brown with soil. Before going to the hut, the spade had slipped past his fingers, sailing to the ground and throwing mud at his feet. But rather than retrieve the spade, he went from his garden and stood for a while in the middle of the backyard, eventually walking to the edge of the swimming pool. Where previously the pool was covered by a thin layer of ice hidden underneath snow, it had now become a watery surface once more—interspersed with diminishing islands, miniature icebergs growing smaller and smaller and farther away from one another on a chlorine sea.

Standing by the pool, he could see into neighboring yards. He could also glimpse part of the street. Nevertheless, not a single person or vehicle was in sight. He looked at the blue-black mountain range washed out by the bright haze of winter. The arching sunlight reflected off the snow blanketing the desert and cast an intense, blinding glow which enshrouded the horizon, diminishing the view of the mountain even more. He hadn't thought of it previously, but just then he found himself wondering about the unseen forests and wilderness thriving on the other side of the mountain and felt an inexplicable desire to journey there by foot. The wind came and went, varying in intensity, sometimes seeming to roll across the desert with a rumbling like distant thunder. Suddenly he realized that the ground beneath him was shuddering, vibrating with a low intensity—a steady, perpetual energy quietly shaking the land and unnoticed by him until that moment. While subtle and unfluctuating, the vibration possessed a frightening and catastrophic power which, he imagined, originated from the planet's dying core.

All around him, the world was slowly coming unstuck. Cinder blocks and bricks were separating, plaster was cracking, carpet was being tugged toward living-room ceilings. Appliances, televisions, vehicles, animals, children, and entire families were about to be sent upward, gently at first and, then, with the violent speed of a rocket—smashing against overhead light fixtures, or ceiling fans, or skylights, or, in most cases, wafting recklessly like balloons set loose into the sky. If he looked at the garden, he would see cactus uprooting itself, soil and rocks and pebbles ascending as if by magic. The spade he had dropped was already hovering above the porch, encircled by satellites of mud. Soon the signposts of mankind would be jettisoned to the universe, the symbols of presence ejected from a tired, worn-down planet—the cities, the freeways, the airports, the schools, the burned-out and rusting cars, the unkempt pastures of bluebonnets, the high, brittle grass, the gutted houses abandoned on weedy plots, those vast number of commodities fashioned by human design. The great purging was beginning, he told himself. It had begun this morning.

But when turning to gaze at the garden and the house, Hollis saw that nothing had changed, nothing had been raised to the sky. The spade lay exactly where it had fallen. The roots of cacti and succulents were buried under sodden dirt. His feet remained firmly on the ground, the earth had not undone itself or stopped on its axis. The house was stable on the foundation, as always. The rooms were the same rooms, no different than yesterday. No, nothing much had changed—with the exception of one maddening thing: she wasn't there anymore, but yet she was there nonetheless. Something had irrevocably changed for her, and, too, the life he considered to be his own was then altered past recognition. No amount of mental preparation could have truly prepared him for this eventuality. He was, at that second, aware of a widening black space within himself—a profound loneliness he had never experienced, a complete and utter sense of being left alone without another recognizable soul at hand; he had, in the passing of a single morning, entered uncharted territory and, it was understood, the way back home was lost even as their home stood directly in front of him. So, he told himself, better to go elsewhere for a while and put off what the house entailed—his grief, his fears, the phone calls he will have to make. Better going where she rarely ever went, to where he could hide in the shade and wasn't supposed to think about anything.

Inside the tiki hut, Hollis hugs his knees to his chest and stays like that for what feels like an eternity. Later on, he lifts his head and stares again at the water dripping outside from the ends of the thatched roof, thinking: If the water stops dripping right now, she'll return to me. If the water will only stop dripping—all of it, every single drop—then Deb will walk out of the house, calling my name. He tells himself this, with eyes fixed on the droplets which keep forming and plunging, forming and plunging, while knowing in his heart it won't happen. The water continues dripping, and she never calls for him. And he wonders why it has to be, why was she just here earlier as she had always been—the movement of her limbs, the resonance of her singular voice, the warmth of her skin—and yet now she is gone from the world. How could she go?

Still, the love is here; the love they shared is here—it is more tangible than ever. He has that. Yes, I have that. Then, maybe, it is he who has gone away for good—not her—and he has vanished from the world without yet realizing it, somehow existing beyond the fade to black, as if in another reality, as if in an illusion. But where are you this very second? he asks himself, rocking back and forth. Where does someone go when finally gone? And what—he asks aloud—is the meaning in death? However, no answers materialize from his wondering, and yet that void of understanding, in its own vacant manner, provides the ultimate, all-inclusive answer to his questions. So decent people die each and every second of the day without reason, the living are required to forge ahead nonetheless, and that is simply that; the role of living is acted out on a daily basis, an individual's act of dying is a one-time affair—but everyone gets a shot at playing both parts, none are exempted, none are unique, everyone goes on and everyone goes.

Sighing miserably, Hollis presses his palms flat on either side of himself. The dream is over, he concludes. I'm awake. A heavy internal weight has consumed his limbs, mooring him to the floor and making it difficult to stand, but somehow he manages to pull himself up anyway. He staggers in the shadows, bracing himself against the hut's doorframe, the thatched roof jutting beyond him and sprinkling the ground with droplets. Sunlight illuminates the backyard, raining upon the garden beds and the swimming pool and the house. Except, to his confusion, the house appears miles away, although it summons him closer. Their bedroom also beckons—as beloved places do which cannot be experienced as they once had been enjoyed—because she is there, at least for a while. She is waiting.

"All right," he says, after taking a deep breath, and then steps from the shadows of the hut and into the light of the backyard, heading along a flagstone pathway toward the house. With the brightness stunning his vision, he stumbles on a flagstone slab, his body wobbling off the path, his boots crunching across gravel. Today the sun shines. The desert thaws, the cactus needles glisten with beads of water which mirror the heavens and seem to hold the sky. Tomorrow the temperature will soar at Nine Springs, burning through the day and onto the skin of golfers. There will be warmth, but not for him, not for Debra. "It's okay," he assures himself, finding his balance, returning to the pathway—squinting now against the sun and reaching his hands outward to grasp at air, weaving blindly ahead for no other reason than he must, pacified by the sudden understanding that all things born are fated to move toward their end.

SOURCES OF ILLUSTRATIONS

The two figurative paintings which, respectively, preface each section of *The Post-War Dream* were created by Peter I. Chang: I. *Dwellers* (gesso, charcoal, and acrylic on wood panel, 2000); II. *Safe Places to Die* (acrylic on developed photographic paper, 2000).

Both ovary illustrations—Fig. 29 and Fig. 30—were originally printed without the artist's name cited in *The Illustrated Encyclopedia of Sex*, by Dr. A. Willy, Dr. L. Vander, Dr. O. Fisher, and other authorities (New York: Cadillac Publishing Co., Inc., 1950).

A NOTE ABOUT THE AUTHOR

MITCH CULLIN is the author of eight books, including *A Slight Trick of the Mind*, *Tideland*, and *Branches*, a novel-in-verse. He divides his time between California's San Gabriel Valley and Tokyo, Japan, and in addition to writing fiction he collaborates on various projects with the artist Peter I. Chang.

A NOTE ABOUT THE TYPE

The text of *The Post-War Dream* is set in Fournier, a digitized version of the original font cut that was part of the Monotype Corporation historical typeface revivals in the 1920s.

Fournier was created by the typographer and printing historian Stanley Morison (1889–1967) and grew out of his admiration for the type cuts of Pierre Simon Fournier (1712–1768).